THE DARK HEART OF TIME

A TARZAN® NOVEL

By Philip José Farmer:

Published by The Ballantine Publishing Group

THE DARK HEART OF TIME

A TARZAN® NOVEL

Philip José Farmer

A Del Rey® Book
THE BALLANTINE PUBLISHING GROUP • NEW YORK

A Del Rey® Book
Published by The Ballantine Publishing Group
Copyright © 1999 EDGAR RICE BURROUGHS, INC.

Trademark TARZAN® owned by Edgar Rice Burroughs, Inc., and used by permission.

www.randomhouse.com/delrey/

Library of Congress Catalog Card Number: 99-94684

ISBN 0-345-42463-8

Manufactured in the United States of America

First Edition: June 1999

10 9 8 7 6 5 4 3 2 1

To Danton Burroughs for his suggestions regarding the text of this novel. Also, my heartfelt thanks to him for giving me permission to write an original Tarzan novel. Thus, I've fulfilled a seventy-year-old ambition.

To Edgar Rice Burroughs, the only begetter of Tarzan of the Apes, John Carter of Barsoom, and David Innes of Pellucidar. Without ERB, my life would have been much less rich and luminous.

My thanks also to Robert R. Barrett for his scholarly advice regarding the text of this work. Also, for his discovery of a new great-ape word—Umpa the caterpillar.

1

TARZAN DID NOT hear the hunters coming toward him through the rain forest of the African afternoon. Pand the thunder hid any noise they might have made. Also, Usha the wind was flowing in the wrong direction for him to detect their man-sweat odor.

He was still unaware of them as he sprang up from the ground and grabbed a liana growing on the side of a colossal tree.

The first spear thrown at him nicked the inside of his left ankle. Its steel head rammed into the tree trunk with a loud thunking sound.

The second spear slammed into the liana. Though the parasitical plant was thick and tough, it was severed by the keen-edged blade.

By then, the ape-man had climbed above the cut end of the liana. He had speeded up his ascent a fraction of a second after the first spear had thudded into the thick bark. His fingers gripping the sides of the great vine, his body bent and leaning out almost horizontally, his soles against the trunk, he swarmed upwards.

Manu the monkey could not have climbed much faster.

Just as the severed part of the vine struck the ground, Tarzan reached a projecting part of the trunk, a massive tumor on the side of the forest giant. Kando the ant had been biting him while he was on the liana, and they continued their attack. One foot on the tumor, his hands gripping the rough parts of the bark, he got around the tree to its opposite side.

Though he left behind the ants on the tree itself, he couldn't yet brush off those still on his limbs and body. To use even one hand to get rid of the savagely biting Kando would mean to lose his precarious hold. As it was, his fingers were starting to slip from the crevices.

But by him there was another liana growing on the tree. So Tarzan did release one hand. Even as he dropped, his free hand closed around the liana. Then, the other gripped the rough-surfaced vine. After that, he easily pulled his two-hundred-pound body up the liana to a point above and to one side of a large branch.

With all the ease of many years of experience, he swung his body over the branch and then dropped onto it.

One glance downward over the side of the branch revealed that the spear casters could not see him. They were trying to conceal themselves behind a bush. Only by a very unlikely accident would they see him through the mass of foliage growing from the tree.

He silently got rid of the insects. Kando were tiny, but their poisonous bites were painful. To almost anyone else, they would have been agonizing. But he had been bitten so often before that he had built up a partial immunity to the poison. So the bites were to him a minor annoyance.

Once the ants had been brushed off, Tarzan took a few seconds to check his immediate surroundings. Close by grew a great mass of giant black-and-scarlet-striped orchids. Their rotting-meat odor overpowered any other smells. The booming of the thunder racing toward him drowned out all other noises. Only his eyes could be used to check for any enemies up here. And the only ones he had to avoid this far up would be Sheeta the leopard and Histah the snake.

He saw nothing menacing.

Then he inspected the tiny nick made by, he assumed, a spearhead. The blood had quit flowing. Later, if he got the chance, he would rub some of the rain forest soil on the wound. Years before, when he was a child living with the Mangani the great apes, his foster mother, Kala, had taught him about its power to cleanse infections. The scientists of civilization didn't yet know about it.

Now, he took a longer look downward. He confirmed that the missiles that had been thrown at him were spears.

The trackers must have come across the remnants of his recent meal, the well-gnawed bones and the brown-and-pale-white-dappled hide of a tiny member of the family of Wappi the antelope. From there, Tarzan had walked for several miles before deciding to take to the trees. The Ndesi must have followed his footprints in the soft muddy soil. And they had caught up with him just as he had started to climb.

He could see that the two black men had left the bush behind which they had been trying to hide. Both were preparing to wrench the spears from their deep embedment in the tree trunk. But, just now, they were looking upward.

He knew the exact spot he had been on the tree when the hunters had thrown their spears. Their sharp metal heads would have hit his legs if they had struck their targets. Those targets, the bull's eyes, were supposed to be his legs.

If they had had firearms, they could have hit him easily.

He was fifty feet above them, but the uppermost canopy of the rain forest was over two hundred feet above him. The storm clouds covered the blazing face of

Kudu the sun. These made even fainter the light that filtered down through the many huge branches and the crowded leaves and lianas. Yet, he could see the patterns of white and yellow paint on the hunters' faces.

They were Ndesi, a small tribe which had once been a part of the Masai nation but was now its enemy. The Ndesi were splendid trackers. However, their territory was the savannah, the open spaces and relatively flat land of the great herds of antelope and zebra and their predators, the cheetah and the lion.

That the Ndesi were here surprised him. He was close to the eastern border of the Congo Free State and hundreds of miles deep into the rain forest. Yet, the Ndesi lived in British East Africa. Their villages were two hundred miles west of Tarzan's ranch, which had been burnt by the invading soldiers of German East Africa.

The Germans had left the charred body of a Waziri woman in the ruins of the great house. This was the body Tarzan had thought at that time was his wife's, for the Germans had put Jane's wedding ring on the finger of the slain female before they burned her. It wasn't until almost four years later that Tarzan had read the diary of a dead German officer and found he had been deceived. The diary had been written by a Captain Fritz Schneider, the officer who had played this trick on Tarzan, the trickster.

The ape-man had long ago slain the captain, though not before killing his brother, Major Bolko Schneider. Tarzan had mistaken the major for the captain. No matter. Both deserved to die. It was after reading the diary that the ape-man had set out to track Jane down, though the trail was cold, and the leads were few and far between.

Tarzan surmised that the Ndesi must have been lured away from their homeland with the promises of many trade goods, cattle, and weapons. Yet, who would do that?

It was not likely to be the Germans. This was half-way through October 1918. The British, French, Italians, Americans, and their allies seemed to be winning the Great War against Germany in the European–Middle East sectors. Elsewhere, too, including East Africa, they were pushing the Germans and their allies back.

The Germans there would have loved to have known the location of Tarzan of the Apes, also called Lord Greystoke. He had slain many of their white and black troops and even caused them to lose a large battle. But, much as they wanted to kill or capture him, they lacked the resources to send a hunting party after him.

Even if they had the resources, they could locate him only by accident.

If these two men were not native troops in the German forces, who could they be?

He did not know. Somebody unknown had to be on his trail.

The shadow of a frown scudded across his face. The Ndesi had gotten close enough to have killed him easily. There were no better spearmen in Africa. Yet, it seemed to him that they had been trying to cripple him, not to slay him. They must have orders to capture him alive. Why?

At that moment, the branch on which he was standing began to quiver. He felt dizzy. Then he had to cast himself headlong on the branch and cling to the fissures in the bark. The tremors weren't strong enough as yet to wave the huge branch up and down, as one tremor had done only the day before.

Suddenly, the violent shaking was gone. But vibrations still came up from deep beneath the tree, down in the bedrock.

This was the third day such quakes had occurred. So far, the quakes had not been alarming, but they might be forerunners of the great one to come. Then, the tree might be heaved up from the earth. Despite what the civilized world thought, the jungle soil was too thin for the roots of trees to drive deep into it. Thus, they spread out, took a horizontal instead of a vertical direction. The trees should have been easy to topple. But the upper-canopy branches of the trees were so interlaced with their neighbors' branches and vines that these often kept the uprooted tree from falling.

Now he heard, in the spaces between the crashing of the lightning bolts and the roaring of thunder, several men moving through the forest toward him. They were slow and very careful. But the ape-man had been trained since early infancy by Kala to detect and interpret the slightest noises. These men might as well have been Tantor the elephant, the great gray and long-nosed dread-naught, trumpeting at everyone to get out of her way.

He wasn't one to speculate overlong. Like Sheeta the jungle ravener, he would quickly size up the situation and act without delay. He knew that whoever was approaching was still at least fifty yards away. Plenty of time for him to strike and then get away.

He removed his bow from the clasp on his quiver. He strung the bow, then fitted an arrow to the leopard-gut string. The faces of the two Ndesi were turned up toward him. Though he couldn't hear them because Pand the thunder, the greatest of all noise makers, was at that moment bellowing, he saw their mouths moving. They seemed to be conferring. About what? Probably about whether they should stay here and wait for another opportunity to capture him, or as good sense told them, get out of this dangerous place.

The Lord of the Jungle made up their minds for them. His arrow plunged straight from above into the mouth and deep into the throat of one of the Ndesi trackers. He crumpled. The survivor froze for a second, then ran. When he saw the first men of the approaching party, he stopped, turned, and pointed in the direction from which he had fled.

By then Tarzan, traveling in the middle terrace of the forest, had reached a position directly above the others. They were now gathered closely together. He lay flat on the top of an immense branch and looked at those below.

Ah, how many times he had done this during his almost thirty years of life! He had always felt snug and safe, even though he knew that danger had always been his companion, more intimate that even a wife could be. Yet, danger was always ready to divorce him, to throw him to that uninvited and always hungry being, The Hideous Hunter, The Eater of All Things, including Space and Matter.

There were four blacks and four whites down there. Doubtless, there were many more men than that at their camp. There had to be bearers carrying supplies of food, tents, medicines, and ammunition. Unlike Tarzan, these men could not live off the land in the rain forest. Though life flourished around them, they would starve.

Suddenly, the storm swept over the jungle roof just above the watcher and the watched. The strong breeze strengthened to a leaf-shaking and branch-waving wind. The pale light became almost as black as midnight. Ara the lightning flashed; Pand the thunder crashed louder with each second. Even the massive branch supporting Tarzan lifted and fell violently. He clung to the indentations in the thick bark while the limb creaked and groaned. Usha the wind was indeed angry. Usha usually was during the rainy season storms. And this day marked the beginning of the season. From now on until its end, the rain would smash into the forest canopy at least once each day without fail.

However, normally, the rain fell just before sunset. Just now, the sun had been still reasonably high in the sky. And this storm was a giant among storms.

Before the deluge came, Tarzan had removed the string from his bow and put it in his quiver. From this, he had pulled out and unfolded a sack of soft, well-worked, and cunningly sewn leopard intestines. He had covered the quiver and the sharp flint arrow tips therein with the rainproof sack, tied its open end, and returned to watching the humans. By now, he could see only when an incandescent bolt from above savaged the area nearby.

The men, instead of going to the slain Ndesi, went back toward wherever they had come from. Heads down, shoulders hunched, streaming with water, feet slipping now and then on the slimy rotting vegetation on the forest floor, stopping when the lightning came too close, they staggered on. Leaves and fronds fell around them and on them.

2

THE USUALLY PROTECTIVE rain forest upper canopy had failed to soften the fury above it. Tarzan felt uneasy about this storm. It seemed intent on wrecking the jungle. Its ravaging certainly far exceeded any storm he had so far experienced. And it seemed to him that it might be a voice trumpeting of worse things to come.

Tarzan did not, as was his usual practice, stay where he was until the storm passed on. Despite the vast uproar and the shaking and quivering of the foliage and the driving rain, he rose to his feet. Then he passed through the middle level of the forest, moving from tree to tree.

He didn't, however, go swiftly or surely. Sometimes, he stopped because the lightning had blazed directly in front of him, blinding him. Twice, it struck a nearby tree.

The jaws of the storm were even more savage than the jaws of Numa the lion when he was hungry. Tarzan could fight a lion, but he could not do battle with this tempest. Discretion told him to take refuge now. Now! But, having determined that he would follow the men to their camp, Tarzan did just that.

After what seemed a long time, the men below him came to four large canvas tents, pitched around the base of a gigantic tree. Electric torches shone through the barely opened flaps of the entrances. Except for the eight men entering the camp, not a person was in sight. The

9

bearers, Tarzan reasoned, must be crowded in two of the tents.

The four whites went into one of the tents. The four trackers raised the front flap of another tent to enter it. By the light of lamps inside it, Tarzan glimpsed part of its interior. It was crowded with natives. He assumed that two of the other tents held more bearers and soldiers. The soldiers were often called askari, a Swahili word.

Boxes, chests, and trunks, all holding supplies, were stacked near the tents.

He came down slowly from a tree close to the tents. The cold rainwater that covered him head to toe would have made any other man shiver.

After reaching the ground, he walked crouching to the back of the tent which housed the white men. His hunting knife, once his father's, was in his right hand.

As Tarzan had expected, eavesdropping wasn't easy. The wind screaming through the branches, the breaking of tree limbs, the flapping of the tent, the water striking against it, and the artillery fire of the lightning made it possible to hear only snatches of conversation.

". . . Greystoke can't be . . . Pindell! What the . . . If it comes to him or me . . . Homeshon . . . As soon as dawn comes, we . . . check out . . . Aboma's body first . . . how to contact . . ."

Tarzan decided he was wasting his time. However, one of the whites had mentioned the ape-man's British title, Lord Greystoke. Thus, Tarzan was sure it was no accident that the men were here. He was equally sure that the spears had been thrown at his legs to pin him alive to the trunk. They had tried to do that instead of killing him for some reason he did not know. But he intended to find out that reason, quickly.

The storm began to diminish, so he went back up the tree before anyone could emerge from shelter. Most of the fury and the lightning had already passed on, and the clouds were beginning to disappear. No surprise. They often vanished quickly after a tropical storm.

He headed back to where the dead man lay. When he got close to the corpse, he came down to the ground. Now that the storm had ended, the leopards would be out and about on their quest for meat. But the body was as yet untouched, and he saw no sign of predators large or small.

He easily hoisted the slain tracker's body to his shoulder. Then he trotted back along the three miles of forest trail to a tree near the camp. Still carrying the corpse, Tarzan ascended the tree to a big branch directly above the tent that contained the white men. From there he dropped the body headfirst, the arrow sticking out of its throat. It crashed into the middle of the tent roof with the force of 150 pounds falling from 150 feet.

The tent collapsed.

The trapped men began yelling and shouting. The black men poured out from their tents. Shortly thereafter, they lifted up the front of the tent long enough for the four whites to crawl out. Then they all started jabbering. Tarzan smiled grimly at the uproar and chaos he had caused. But he didn't stay on the tree branch very long. Within two minutes, he was on the ground and watching from behind another tree.

The leader, a big white with a heavy black moustache, organized the rest. Darkness had begun to fall, and under the light of native torches and bull's-eye lanterns, the Ndesi's body was removed and examined. That caused more jabbering, but the leader, addressed as Helmson by two whites, quieted everyone down. The tent was erected again, and several guards were posted. Helmson ordered them to direct the beams of their lanterns up into the trees while on their rounds.

The native leader of the bearers was addressed as Tambi. He interpreted for the white man. Like the bearers, his hairstyle and huge spiral earrings identified him as a Wamabo tribesman. But when an askari spoke, Tarzan knew that he was a Serba, from a tribe which lived on the western edge of British East Africa.

This expedition was composed of four different elements. The very small minority were white men—Tarmangani. The Wamabo porters were the majority. The Serba soldiers were the third largest group, and the Ndesi trackers were the smallest group of native members of the safari.

Tarzan had the feeling that each man had been individually chosen for excellence. Only the best would be good enough to go after him, but Tarzan was not flattered. He regarded them as a nuisance. A major nuisance, true, which could become a danger. Therefore, he would have to make sure that they ceased to be a threat of any kind.

First, he would have to capture a Tarmangani. A Tarmangani likely would know more about the true goal of this safari than would a Gomangani, a black.

But, just now, the whites had gone into their tent and were out of Tarzan's reach. So he satisfied himself by grabbing an askari who was standing at the back of the mob. The startled soldier felt a hand clamp over his mouth, and then he was unconscious.

When he awoke, the askari was lying on his back. His wrists were tied behind him, and his ankles were bound together. He was not, however, gagged. The light of the full moon shone through a gap in the tree. Its beams illuminated him and his captor, standing near him. That man was a white man, tall and well muscled. He wore a leopard-skin loincloth and a leopard-skin belt supporting a dark leather sheath which held a large knife. When the man turned somewhat to one side, the askari could see the dark leather shoulder strap and part of the quiver and the arrows.

Though the forest illumination was rather dim, the Serba also noted his captor's wide shoulders and narrow waist. His physique was rangy, more a leopard's than a lion's. But a leopard could easily carry its prey, an antelope weighing three times more than the cat, up a tree to a fork to deposit it. It was said that, muscle for muscle, the leopard was the strongest of all beasts.

The Serba also noted his captor's craggy yet handsome face, the strong nose, the short upper lip, the square chin, the big scar across his forehead and the many other scars on his body, the long black hair, and the eyes, dark in this pale light, though the Serba knew from descriptions that those eyes were deep gray when seen in the daylight.

This was the fabled forest phantom, the storied jungle god. Though he often looked just like a white man, he could take many shapes, few of them comforting. Thinking of this, the soldier began trembling. He did not fear any man, white or black. But the things that came out of the land of the dead and demons . . . ?

Tarzan spoke in not-quite correct but serviceable Serba. "What is your name?"

"Tenga."

"Tenga, I won't kill you if you tell me the truth. But if you refuse to answer my questions or lie to me, you will be meat for whatever animal first finds you. Also, you are far from the camp. So don't try screaming. That will only anger me."

"I am paid to protect the bearers and the white men," the askari said softly. "But I do not wish to die for the Wamabo or the Ndesi, my hereditary enemies. Nor do I wish to die for the whites. I can't promise I can answer all your questions. What I don't know, I don't know."

"Do you know who I am?"

"Who doesn't? You are Tarzan the Ape-man, the brother of the hairy men of the trees, begotten on a female great ape by a white-skinned devil with horns and a long tail. You are also John Clayton, Lord Greystoke, and the chief of the Waziri, who are enemies of the Serba though not as great enemies as the Masai and the Kikuyu. Great enough, though."

"Why are these white men after me?"

"Truly, I do not know."

"Are the white men trying to kill me?"

Tenga was silent for several seconds, then spoke.

"Our orders are to catch you alive. However, if you are cornered but might escape if we don't use violence, we may knock you out or break a leg or arm or even put a spear through a leg or arm. The man who succeeds in capturing you will get a great reward. But the white leader, Helmson, told us that, if you were accidentally killed, the person responsible would be shot on the spot."

"Is there anything else you can tell me that I should know?" Tarzan said.

"Do you really intend to let me go if I tell you all I know?"

"I gave my word. Perhaps you have heard enough about me to know that I never break my promise."

Tenga hesitated. Then he said, "The white men talked much among themselves in English. I don't understand English, which sounds to me like the hissing of snakes. But Tambi, the chief of the bearers, does. He also speaks Serba and Ndesi. He told some of us askari that he himself has not been told why the whites want so desperately to capture you.

"But, before we set out from the base camp, the one near my village, a white man whom Helmson called Homeshon was talking to him. Tambi could not hear what they were saying. But it was evident that Home-shon was giving orders to Helmson. Tambi did overhear Homeshon say something to Helmson about Helmson's and Homeshon's master. But Tambi did not hear the master's name mentioned."

"How did you find me?" Tarzan said.

"I do not know. Each morning, Helmson gave orders for that day's march, which direction we would go and how far. The Ndesi trackers would go ahead of us. However, there was one curious thing. We went out of our way, north of the straight line we should have marched toward the Ituri jungle. We stopped near a small village of the Asheki. While we camped there, Helmson went off by himself. After several hours, he returned. He did not say what he had been doing in the jungle. He gave orders to resume the march, but we then turned south-ward. Soon afterwards, we headed into the jungle. And then . . ."

"And then?" Tarzan said.

"After that, Helmson seemed sure that he was on your track. But none of us could see anything to make him think that this was so. It was a mystery we talked about among ourselves. No one asked Helmson, of course."

There are many mysteries to clear up, many questions to be answered, Tarzan thought.

He rolled Tenga over on his face and cut the bonds around his wrists. Tenga closed his eyes. The word of a white man was no more to be trusted than a black man's. But, perhaps, what was said about this Tarzan was true. That is, that though he looked like a white man, he had the soul of a great ape.

But could a great ape be trusted?

Then Tenga thought, *If Tarzan is going to kill me, he would not have cut my bonds.*

Tenga opened his eyes, rolled over on his back, and sat

up. The ape-man was gone. A leopard screamed from somewhere not far away. As Tenga untied the leather strands around his ankles, he hoped that he could find the camp before the leopard found him.

Tenga had wondered if Tarzan had the soul of a great ape. Tarzan himself did not deal in such vague concepts as the soul.

However, from the age of one to twenty years, he had lived among the great apes, the Mangani. The only language he could speak then was the Mangani's. Hence, he had thought as a Mangani thought. But, as he grew older, he had acquired thoughts and concepts that were beyond the great apes' comprehension. For instance, the term *Wa-usha* was the Mangani's poetic name for the leaf or leaves. It meant "green wind." To the Mangani, Usha the wind did not make the leaf move. On the contrary, the movement of the leaves generated the wind. Nor did the tree bend under the impact of the wind. The tree bent and thrashed back and forth to make the wind. Tarzan had believed this to be true.

The Mangani word for rain was *Meeta*. The Mangani associated the rain with clouds, which they called *Meeta-whuff*, that is, "rain-smoke." But they did not know—or care—where rain came from. So Tarzan, far more curious and creative than they, had formed the theory that the stars, the moon, and the sun had bladders. When these were full, Kudu, Goro, and Hul passed their water from above.

Then there was the enigma of time. Tarzan learned that humans had a keen sense of time, though they could not satisfactorily explain its nature, origin, or end. The Mangani had a very limited sense of time. Tarzan had a human brain, and so he built his mental nests in the tree called Future. But he had to make up his own words for the future and for time itself.

The Mangani had no concept of God. But Tarzan had conceived a Creator, and he thought of a fearsomely polysyllabic and elegant word, with intimations of thunder, for God—*BULAMUTUMUMO*. Though he attributed all good things to Bulamutumumo, he could not believe that God would create such evil things as Histah the snake. Thus, he was at the doorstep of one aspect of what the human philosophers called Manichaeism, the belief in two creators, one good, one evil.

The young ape-man had no idea that the brain was the seat of thought and action. He did not know at all what the function of that organ was except as food. But now and then in an ecstasy, a kind of bliss of the knife, the young Tarzan had cut open the chest of a still-living prey, and he had seen the Thub, the heart, still beating. To him, the Thub was the "red thing that breathes." It was the controlling organ of life.

But his fingers "knew" when they touched something. His eyes "knew" what they saw. His ears "knew" the sounds he heard. His nose "knew" what it smelled. These organs had a sort of immaculate perception, and they "thought." And his throat, his skin, and the hairs on his head were where the powerful emotions originated.

To Tarzan, Kudu the sun and Goro the moon were living and thinking entities, very powerful beings. They could see and hear Tarzan, especially when, in fits of youthful exuberance, drunk with life itself, he had boasted that he could defeat them in a fight. Also, the trees and the grasses were living, and, when the grass rustled, the blades were talking to each other.

Life was a running brook of joy. Death, though not a fun occasion, was a part of life.

When Tarzan was ten, humans had moved into the jungle near his tribe's territory. And one of these black natives had killed his foster mother, Kala. Tarzan got revenge for that awful deed, and he never became friends with the tribe, nor did he learn their language. Until he was twenty, he did not encounter white people.

Since then, he had lived off and on in the cities, though mostly off. He thought of them as stifling and wicked, polluted streams. But he was introduced to history and the various sciences. That had been a shock. However, the adaptable ape-man came to believe that much of what he then learned was true even if it contradicted his Mangani beliefs.

Nevertheless, when in the jungle, Tarzan reverted to his old beliefs and reactions. Then, he was truly a Mangani. However, he still had the superior intellect of the human, and he had an intelligence which raised him high among humans. Of those people who were aware of him, some had said that his infrahuman rearing had combined with his superb *Homo sapiens* brain to make him more than human.

Some, less inclined to hyperbole, said that he was a unique and remarkable phenomenon. Of all the many millions of various forms that life had produced during millions of years, it had produced only one Tarzan.

He was a species by himself.

3

When Tarzan found his wife, Jane, he would also find her abductors. These would be Lieutenant Obergatz of the German East African Army and his native soldiers. If the British Intelligence reports were correct, Jane and Obergatz were somewhere in or near the Ituri forest. But the area was immense; its human inhabitants, few. Finding her there would be like locating one particular tree among millions.

Nevertheless, Tarzan was determined to find her, and no one was more dogged than Tarzan.

But Helmson and his men were stopping Tarzan from his quest. They had to be removed one way or the other before he could go on. And there was a question Tarzan needed to have answered. Just how had these men tracked him down? Their problem had been like his. They, too, had to locate a specific individual in the midst of a roadless and thinly populated wilderness.

It was true that, if he so chose, he could now speed ahead of the party and try to lose them. But, if he were to believe Tenga's story, they still would probably have the knowledge or the device of whatever it was that had enabled them to find him. So, thinking himself far far away from them, he might suddenly find himself trapped by them.

There were two other things he could do.

One, he could capture a white and extract from him the secret of their success in locating him.

Or, two, he could kill all the whites. That would bring the expedition to a halt. The blacks would go back to their home villages. And he, Tarzan, could again look for his wife.

But he was very curious about why the whites were after him. He could not rest until he knew *why*.

Tarzan was angry at himself for his inability to overcome his curiosity. He was also angry at those who had made him curious. He did not wish to devote even a moment to anything except his quest for his wife. But he had to do so. Therefore, he would do so.

As for choosing between killing all the whites or questioning one of them, he did not hesitate. Being logical, efficient, and economical, Tarzan chose first to carry off a white man, preferably Helmson, and question him. If that didn't work, then he'd kill all of them.

Tarzan followed Tenga on the ground until the Serba got back to the camp. Then he climbed to the middle terrace. Tenga roused the camp, and he went into the white men's tent. Tarzan abandoned his plan to sneak down a tree to listen at the rear of the tent. Helmson had placed a guard on each side of the tent. The conference lasted for half an hour, and several times Helmson shouted angrily. Tarzan believed that the anger was directed at Tenga. Then the Serba left that tent for the askari's tent.

Tarzan found a comfortable place at the junction of a big bough and the trunk of the tree, and he slept.

When the safari started to march an hour after dawn, it was shadowed by the ape-man. Sometimes, he was on the branches above them. Sometimes, he was on the ground alongside them or behind them. Near noon, he saw his opportunity, and he plucked it.

The plucking was literal. So it was that the Tarmangani, the white man, who had stepped behind a tree was interrupted while emptying his bladder. Two hands from behind him closed on his throat.

Tarzan, smiling grimly, hoisted the man by his neck.

His victim flailed his arms and kicked his legs, though not for long. As soon as the man quit struggling, he was eased to the ground. Tarzan turned the limp body over and looked at the blue face. After making sure the man was still breathing, Tarzan removed his victim's automatic pistol from its holster and placed it on the ground. Then, he lifted the man up onto his shoulder. Running swiftly but as silently as possible, Tarzan carried his captive far away from the rest of the party.

By the time the man had been carried to a giant branch in the middle terrace, he started to awake. He sat up, his eyes wide. Immediately after, he began coughing and choking. But he did not cry out. The knife held to his jugular vein and the sight of the man squatting by him convinced him that doing that wouldn't be wise.

He was for a while red in the face. Then, he was as pale as the ghost of a ghost.

Meanwhile, he became acutely aware of the rough bark pressing painfully against his back. Though the temperature was probably close to seventy-five degrees Fahrenheit in the relatively cool rain forest, he felt cold. Tiny flies were buzzing around and crawling on his face. One entered his nose and caused him to sneeze. That small explosion caused a shrieking and hooting and cawing among the creatures of the upper terrace.

A few minutes later, the loud cacophony sank into silence. He twitched, and he had to hold himself back from slapping at the flies. Obviously, he didn't want to startle his abductor. One slash of that knife edge across his jugular, and his blood would be spurting into the abyss below the branch.

Tenga had described his abductor, so he had to know that this man was Tarzan, Lord Greystoke.

Tarzan studied his captive while he waited silently for a full knowledge and a fear of his situation to seize the man. He knew from his eavesdropping during the day that the man's name was Mitchell. He looked as if he were thirty years old. He was about five feet and eight inches tall and weighed about 160 pounds. He was clean shaven, and he had brown hair and light-blue eyes.

Finally, the man regained his normal color, and he stopped quivering. Then Tarzan spoke in an even tone. But his face and eyes showed that he would be as merciless as a leopard if he had to be.

"Mitchell, I won't kill you if you don't lie to me. If you do, you'll die. If you tell the truth, you'll go free and unharmed."

Mitchell swallowed, then said, "I can only tell you what I know, and that's not much."

His speech revealed that he had been born and raised in Cumberland, that county in the northwest corner of England and on the southern border of Scotland. The ape-man owned a mansion in Cumberland and had spent some time there.

Tarzan's voice was harsher.

"Tell it!"

Mitchell glanced around before replying. Whatever he was looking for, it was obvious he didn't see it. Without moving a muscle in face or body, he seemed to shrug. Tarzan thought that the man was prepared to tell the truth—as he knew it.

"I am a professional hunter and collector of animals for zoos and circuses. I'm also a guide and safari organizer for rich big-game hunters. But the war has ruined that business for me, and so . . ."

"Don't talk me to death," the ape-man said. "Give me what's relevant."

Mitchell continued. He had been in Mozambique, Portuguese East Africa, on business that did not concern his being here. *Undoubtedly illegal business,* Tarzan thought, but he did not care. Then an American named Robert Pindell, another white hunter, had sent a message via a runner that he had a proposition for him. The letter added that it would be worth a lot of money. Enough for him to retire and live well.

Mitchell journeyed to the place indicated by Pindell. There Pindell had introduced him to the leader of the project, Jelke Helmson. He was an American citizen and a well-known hunter. Helmson told Mitchell that he couldn't reveal his boss's name, but his employer was a very very rich man who, for some reason, wished to capture the man known as John Clayton, Lord Greystoke, Tarzan the Ape-man.

Helmson had stressed that Greystoke must be taken alive.

Mitchell had asked what would happen to Greystoke after he was caught.

Helmson had said that it was none of Mitchell's business.

Thus, Mitchell had known that it was useless to ask why the unknown man wanted to capture Tarzan.

Mitchell had agreed to help in the hunt. First, Mitchell had to swear not to reveal to anyone outside the project anything about its true objective.

"But you are telling me that true objective," Tarzan said. "And I didn't even have to threaten you with torture to get you to talk. No more than I had to threaten Tenga."

"Would you have tortured me?" Mitchell said.

"Yes."

"I thought so. Helmson described your character. He said that you were, really, not quite human. You were basically a great ape, what do you call them . . . ?"

"Mangani."

"But you were also human. You weren't needlessly cruel. But in our case, well, the chances were high that some or all of us might die trying to capture you. Helmson wasn't the least bit backward about telling us that. And you'd . . ."

"I know," Tarzan said. "But how did Helmson locate me?"

"Helmson knew where you had last been seen and that you were on the trail of your wife and her abductors. The British Intelligence knew that. A certain officer, Major Capell of the Second Rhodesians, had told you where your wife was, in what area. So, we hired some Ndesi as trackers. They knew you because you had questioned some of them about your wife and the German soldiers with her.

"Also, we hired some Serba askari because you had questioned two Serba villages. And we hired some Wamabo because they are reputed to be the strongest and most enduring porters in all Africa. Now, I think that Helmson must have had information from his employer, and the employer had somehow gotten information from the German secret service about the general direction that your wife's abductors had taken."

"The rich American would have to be very powerful to have gotten that information from the German secret service," Tarzan said. "After all, the United States is waging war against Germany."

"Money can accomplish almost anything."

Tarzan grimaced with disgust.

Then, he said, "But how did you manage to pick up my trail? Surely, not by accident."

"You did question some pygmies about your wife. And Helmson questioned them about your wife and about you. But I think . . ."

Tarzan waited a few seconds while Mitchell's mind followed the spoor of a thought. It had been two weeks ago that he had last talked to pygmies. There was no way Helmson could have found him except by accident. And Tarzan did not believe that Helmson could just have stumbled on his often-traceless trail.

On the other hand . . .

Tarzan said, "Tenga told me that the safari did not go on

the shortest route to the Ituri. It went northward and stopped near an Asheki village. Helmson disappeared for a while and then returned. What do you know about that?"

Mitchell said, "Nothing, absolutely nothing. I swear to it!"

Tarzan spoke harshly again.

"You started to say that you think . . . then you stopped. What were you going to say?"

Mitchell said, "That Helmson has something . . . I don't know . . . some method, some device . . . I don't see how it could be . . . yet it must be. Something that can pick up your scent or see your trail, your passage, as it were."

"I'll find out from Helmson," Tarzan said.

Seeing the grim features and hearing the grim voice, Mitchell did not doubt that Tarzan meant what he said.

Tarzan stood up suddenly. Mitchell was relieved when the knife was withdrawn from his jugular vein, but he knew that he was still very much in danger.

He said, "I've told you . . ."

He stopped. Tarzan had held up a hand to indicate silence. His head was turned somewhat away from Mitchell.

It was then that Mitchell smelled a strange and powerful odor. It wasn't a human stench. He got to his feet, whirled around, screamed, spun around again, and ran toward the trunk, the same direction Tarzan had taken. But the ape-man was gone.

"He who runs away from Death sometimes runs into Death." So goes a Waziri saying.

Mitchell stumbled and fell off the branch. Screaming, he spun. He saw the upper canopy above him, the sides of the great trees above him, and the ground above him.

He had no time to ponder on why what should be below him or beside him was above him.

He struck the jungle floor. Lightning ran through his bones. Then, all things bright or dim faded to nothing.

4

TARZAN SMELLED THE unfamiliar odor. At once, the short hairs on his neck seemed to bristle. His body was charged with alarm. Ancestral voices shouted within him, urging him to flee and find a refuge from which he could observe the unknown danger.

Thus, instead of standing his ground and confronting the origin of the stench, he took the discreet course. It was what any animal that wished to survive would have done.

If Mitchell had been a friend, Tarzan would have stayed to defend him no matter what his instincts ordered him to do. But Mitchell was an enemy, and keeping him alive wasn't necessary. Mitchell didn't know enough about the motives of the man or men who gave the orders to Helmson.

Nevertheless, when Tarzan, now hidden in a mass of creepers and scarlet flowers forty feet above the branch where Mitchell had been, heard the death cry, he felt a twinge of remorse. That feeling was the result of the ethical education he'd gotten from his human acquaintances. His French and English friends and his American-born wife had managed to "civilize" him. Thus, it was regret, not guilt, that he felt.

That was brief and mild. In most of his reactions, especially when in the jungle, he was a Mangani, a great ape. His human reactions were superimposed on his ape heritage. *Not always for the better,* he thought.

Somebody, probably Helmson, shouted. Tarzan was too far away to hear the words clearly, but they sounded as if they were commands.

Tarzan had expected a volley of gunfire directed at the branch on which had been the thing that had attacked Mitchell. But not one firearm was discharged.

That surprised him. More and more, puzzling things were happening.

He had an almost clear view of the branch. Mitchell's killer was gone. Though Tarzan scanned the trees around him and didn't neglect the foliage just above and just below him, he saw nothing unusual. Nor was he now able to detect even a whiff of that heavy beast smell.

While he looked, his mind was leafing through its memories of odors. Suddenly, he knew where he had smelled that thing before, or, rather, something like it. It wasn't quite what he'd once encountered, at a zoo in London and a forest in Wisconsin. But it was close.

Very much like a black bear's, he thought, and also like a grizzly bear's.

One more puzzle.

He had read that the only bears in Africa were confined to the Atlas mountain range. This was in the extreme northwest part of the Dark Continent, the desert region thousands of miles from the lush and wet rain forest. But to attack thus, unseen, the creature would have been far too swift and too graceful to have been a bear. Its agility and deftness in the tree were more like the skills of an ape. Tarzan had not even glimpsed the thing.

Had the assailant thrown Mitchell from the branch because Mitchell was in his way? Was the beast's prey not Mitchell, but Tarzan himself? If so, why?

Tarzan squatted for a long time in a fork in the trunk of the tree. He was hidden there from the view of anybody above or below him. While thinking about the new element in this puzzle, he plucked insects that wandered within his reach and popped them into his mouth. Some thumb-sized and glossy blue beetles were especially delicious. They crunched between his teeth as he chewed, and he swallowed their squishy flesh and broken pieces of chitin.

The finest restaurants in Paris offered nothing tastier.

He was thinking back, realizing that the jungle had fallen unusually silent just before the creature had appeared. The normal noise of the upper terrace of the rain forest, the monkeys chattering and screaming, the many varied raucous bird cries, had stopped. But, after a while, the calls and the challenges had begun to chase away the breathless silence in this area. That meant that the strange beast wasn't near here.

Meanwhile, the men below had also vanished. But they, unlike the beast, would be easy to find again.

He would have to be more careful about coming near them. He must also make sure that he would be well concealed and well shielded. One of the white men was armed with a machine carbine, the Italian-made Villar Perona. This double-barreled rapid-fire weapon could empty its magazine in two seconds. Thus, it could spray a twenty-five-foot-wide area with a hail of bullets before its magazine had to be changed. Even if the shooter couldn't see his target in the foliage, he might hit it.

Tarzan now knew that these strangers were ordered not to kill him. But he didn't know when that order might be canceled or if he might be hit when the Villar Perona was being fired at something else.

Tarzan decided to follow the party back to its camp. When he got there, he would take whatever action seemed best suited to the circumstances. He wouldn't take long to catch up with them. They were on the ground. He was moving in that interlocking mass of branches, lianas, creepers, and other plants that looked so dense and impenetrable from the ground. Yet, to him, it was a wide-open avenue.

When he got to a point above the men, he slowed down. Thereafter, he traveled closely above and behind the party. Two blacks were carrying Mitchell's body between them. A thick cloud of flies hovered over the corpse. By the time the hunting party got to base camp, the porters had folded the tents and packed everything for the march.

Before the safari set out, Mitchell had to be buried. After a simple stick cross was driven into one end of the grave, Helmson made all the men take off their headgear. Then he loudly intoned a short and hurried prayer for the deceased.

After this, the bearers lifted their loads to the top of their heads, and the long-delayed party proceeded into the jungle. Leading it were a white man and two black men with rifles. Behind them were the trackers and the armed askari, who spread out on the flanks. Helmson and his gun bearer were in the middle.

The rear of the long file was guarded by two askari and the white man with the machine carbine.

All this while, though Tarzan was watching the party, he was also casting glances all around him. He didn't think the strange creature would try sneaking up on him, not now, when the thing knew Tarzan was on guard and it was daylight. What the thing didn't know was that Tarzan could smell it. At least, he hoped it didn't know. He could not take that for granted. In the jungle, you assumed only that something about to pounce on you was behind the next tree or on the branch above you.

After trailing the party for a little while, Tarzan suddenly speeded up his pace. Soon, he was far ahead of the men. He was hungry, and he must kill. On the way, he plucked from the bark and vines the insects he knew were tasty and nonpoisonous.

Once, he startled Pamba the rat. It ran for a hiding place, but Tarzan, as quick as Histah the snake, seized it with one hand. He bit off its head, peeled the skin off, bit the body in two, and crunched away until he'd swallowed both pieces. They didn't fill his belly. But the warm blood and delicate flesh were to him like fine wine and caviar to a Parisian aristocrat.

Some time later, Tarzan smelled a rotting body. His nose told him that the carcass was that of a young elephant that had died not more than a day ago. He followed the smell trail until he looked down on the body lying beside a small stream. It was one of the rare pygmy elephants, even smaller than the forest elephant, which was smaller than the behemoths of the savannah. Kando the ant, Nene the beetle, and Busso the fly swarmed over it. They formed a heaving mass as of a single organism, a giant amoeba.

But now six Horta the boar were trotting toward the elephant. These were bright orange and bore white plumes and had tasseled ears. They would eat everything, the elephant flesh and the insects on and in the flesh. And close to them was Ungo the jackal, eager to snatch bites of meat.

Many years ago, Tarzan had eaten rotten elephant and then had experienced such nightmares that he'd sworn never to eat that beast again. However, several times since, when he had been forced to eat elephant or starve, he'd suffered no ill effects.

Yet, devouring Tantor was for him too close to cannibalism. He knew how to interpret the language of the proboscideans. And he could simulate its sounds so that, in a sense, he "talked" to great gray Tantor.

However, hunger overrode any uneasiness he felt about eating an elephant he had not personally known.

He looked around and sniffed. He could neither see nor smell large predators such as Sheeta the leopard or

Histah the python. He dropped down lightly onto the thin vegetation mat of the jungle floor. The Horta and the Ungo stopped. They watched him while he cut off two flank steaks. As soon as he went back up the tree with the meat, they advanced again toward the carcass.

After devouring the steaks and scores of ants that swarmed on the steaks, he descended to a small pool of water. There he washed his hands and face and then drank deeply. After this, he kept on traveling into the interior. He went perhaps ten miles before a rainstorm began. He found a rather dry place on a branch halfway up a tree wider than an English cottage. A mass of intertwining plants on the branch above him deflected most of the rainfall. Though the downpour, thunder, and lightning would have kept most people and animals awake, he intended to take a long nap. He had to get as much sleep during the daylight as he could. Tonight, he wouldn't get any sleep. He'd be too intent on watching for the beast that smelled like a bear.

Like most Mangani or humans, Tarzan had to give a name to anything or anybody newly met. He'd decided to call the thing a Ben-go-utor. This was a great ape word for something horrible and undescribable. Ben-go-utor was as close to an abstract concept as the Mangani could come.

Like an animal, Tarzan could fall asleep as soon as he closed his eyes. But he also had the animal's faculty of somehow being alert enough to wake instantly while in an apparently deep sleep. Thus, he could spring into alertness, ready to jump up and fight or flee, as the situation demanded.

Now, though, the storm passed. Ara the lightning, Pand the thunder, and Meeta the rain were gone.

He could see a part of Kudu the sun, the flaming giant, through a break in the dense and green ceiling. Kudu was about ten degrees past his zenith. Tarzan stood up and looked around. He could not see, hear, or smell anything interesting or alarming. But the whooping, crying, shrieking, trumpeting, and booming of arboreal life should have resumed after the storm. There was a silence that he must have heard through his sleeping. Something troubling or alien was nearby.

He smelled nothing except the normal odors, damp rotting leaves and fallen fruit, rotting trees, some still held upright by the living ones, a small animal decaying somewhere near, a monkey.

Nor could he hear anything moving through the tree branches or on the ground. But that didn't mean that there weren't beasts or men hiding close to him.

After a minute or so, Tarzan saw something move near the bottom of a giant tree. It was about two hundred feet from the tree on which he stood. He saw it just long enough to know that it was black. Though it stood on two feet, it wasn't human. It seemed to be furred, but Tarzan could not be sure.

The thing—he was certain that it was the Ben-go-utor—had stepped out from behind the tree trunk, then had stepped back behind it. Tarzan waited for it to come nearer. Depending on which direction he saw it go, Tarzan would attack it or follow it. Meanwhile, he wasn't sure that the thing had tracked him down. Perhaps it had no idea that it was so close to its prey.

Just now, there wasn't the slightest breeze in this area. It would have to get near to Tarzan to smell him.

Slowly, the ape-man fitted an arrow to his bowstring. A shaft through its leg would both cripple it and perhaps paralyze it with shock. Taking it captive would then be easy.

Suddenly, he saw the second reason why the jungle life had fallen silent.

Something with a long sinuous body and a long tail was stalking the Ben-go-utor. Though still in shadow, it was unmistakably a leopard. Sheeta was the most dreaded killer of the rain forest, and with good reason. A white hunter had once told Tarzan that he thought that the leopard was the craftiest feline of all. Tarzan had agreed with him.

The big cat opened its mouth in a silent snarl. Its fangs shone dully in the shade. By now, the Ben-go-utor was trotting along, bent over, looking at the ground. It was certain, if it kept on a straight line, to see Tarzan's footprints or at least what remained of them after the heavy rain.

The creature stopped. It looked behind, as anyone should in the rain forest, but did not see the leopard. That had also stopped and had crouched down close to the jungle floor. Then the Ben-go-utor looked upward. It did not see Tarzan, but the ape-man saw it. Saw him, rather. Despite the long black fur covering his body, he was obviously a male.

His legs were short but resembled a man's. His feet were big and manlike. His arms were shorter relative to his torso than a human's arms. But his face . . . it was not as flat as a man's nor was his forehead, and he had jaws that protruded more than a man's but less than a chimpanzee's. Halfway between man and . . . a bear? Only a scientist could know if he had evolved from an ursine creature or some other animal.

Then the leopard, growling deeply, was charging. The Ben-go-utor must have heard it because he whirled around. By then, it was too late for Tarzan to shoot at the big cat.

Actually, he wasn't sure which creature should be his target. It was the huge black bearish thing who had menaced him. Tarzan knew far better how to deal with Sheeta, a lifelong enemy, than he did with the stinking half-bear, an unknown quantity. He grimaced, and he lowered his bow. Let them fight it out. Whoever won would be Tarzan's to reap.

He did not have to wait long for the fight to end. Indeed, it was over so quickly that the ape-man was nearly frozen with amazement. The Ben-go-utor, crouching, grabbed the leopard as it came down on him. Instead of being bowled over by the cat's impact, he spun and at the same time pushed the cat away from him. He also gave a twist to the leopard so that it began turning on its side. It was propelled so far that the ape-man's eyes opened with admiration and wonder. Nevertheless, though the leopard was thrown at least thirty feet, it managed to land on all four paws.

And then the bear-man charged the leopard. Instead of turning and then rearing up to slash its attacker, the big cat began running away. The Ben-go-utor, showing good sense, did not run after it. When he saw that Sheeta had been swallowed by the shadows, he turned around. His mouth was open in what looked like a grin. Though it was self-congratulatory, it did not seem friendly.

Tarzan could not see the teeth clearly, but he got the impression that they resembled human teeth. He seemed to lack the huge, sharp canine teeth of the great ape or the baboon.

Now, the ape-man unfroze. He raised the bow and aimed. But the bear-man must have been looking up and have seen Tarzan. Or, at least, a moving shape. That was enough. Just as the bowstring hummed, the Ben-go-utor disappeared behind a titanic tree. The arrow head drove into its trunk and quivered as if it feared a reprimand from its owner for having missed the target.

Tarzan strapped the bow to the side of his quiver and got down from the tree quickly. It was the bear-man's turn to be stalked. As the ape-man trotted on the narrow path, he passed the arrow in the trunk. He didn't have time to retrieve it. It was probably ruined anyway.

He lost the barely visible trail for several minutes, then picked it up again. But the tracks soon disappeared. The last faint impression of a big humanlike foot led up to the trunk of a gigantic tree. The print was deeper than usual, and it showed Tarzan that the Ben-go-utor had sprung upward. Then, the creature had grabbed one of the numerous parasitical vines clinging to the trunk. And he had gone up the vine.

Though the ape-man also went up after the creature, he didn't find much to mark his passage. The only evidence was a tuft of long black hairs caught in a crevice in the bark. But he had no idea which way the bear-man had gone through the middle or upper terrace of the forest.

He stood without moving and listened. In all directions but one, he heard the normal noise of the forest life. That exception marked the passage of Tarzan's quarry. When Tarzan traveled in the rain forest, he usually did not disturb the chatterers and the criers of the upper regions. They knew, somehow, that he was not to be feared, even though he looked and smelled like a human.

But the reaction to the Ben-go-utor was different. He and his odor were so alien that the animals feared him. Or so Tarzan thought.

However, the hush area, as Tarzan thought of it, was so wide that he couldn't tell exactly where the creature had gone. After a while, the hush vanished, and the jungle noises closed in from all directions, as usual. The bear-man probably knew his destination, and he would speed through the trees with as much ease and swiftness as his greater weight would permit. The ape-man, who had to follow him while at the same time casting here and there to locate the center of the silence, could not go as fast.

A rumble sounded in Tarzan's chest, such as a great ape or a leopard might have made. It revealed his frustration and anger at not catching up with the bear-man. It also expressed his indecision. He was very curious about the Ben-go-utor and his origins and his intentions toward him. He could not ignore the creature. He was just too dangerous.

And then there were the white hunters. What did their chief, Helmson, want of him? Who was the chief of the chiefs, the man who wanted him for an unknown reason and had given the prime order to capture him?

Tarzan growled again. He was losing time in his quest for Jane. Though he usually paid little attention to time, he could not now ignore it. The hunters and this new intruder must be dealt with as quickly as possible.

Tarzan decided to spend one more day to rid himself of them. After that, he'd go on into the Ituri forest.

Then a thought that had been flickering in and out like a snake's tongue settled in his mind. What if the hunters weren't after him?

What if what Helmson really wanted was the metal cylinder hidden at the bottom of the quiver of arrows on Tarzan's back?

5

A<small>N OLD MAN</small> named James D. Stonecraft stood at the window of his fourteen-room apartment in Manhattan. Three floors below him was Fifth Avenue. Central Park was across the street.

He was the richest man in the world and one of the most powerful. He had given many millions of dollars to charity and to the building of magnificent edifices for public use. He had donated many more millions to the arts and sciences and to his church. His oil business, the basis of his fortune, was expanding fourfold. The Allies would soon defeat Germany, but the world market for oil would not shrink. It would become even larger.

Although seventy-eight years old, his bones did not creak. His memory seldom failed him. He usually was three under par on the links. His wife kept telling him that she loved him very much. If she lied, she was clever enough to sound convincing. His children did not mock him, at least not to his face.

Yet, he frowned at the view, and he bit his lip. Then he uttered a word that the devout avoid even thinking. He turned and strode past a huge globe representing Earth, a planet which he regarded as his personal property. He stopped at his enormous mahogany desk and flipped an intercom switch. For a few seconds, the only sound in his office was the sound he loved most to hear. The click-

click of ticker tapes as they spat out paper ribbons on which were printed the current stock market quotations.

The rich and oily yet humble voice of his secretary came from the intercommunication machine.

"Yes, sir?"

Stonecraft sat down at the desk.

"Bevan! Any word from Project Soma?"

"Yes, sir. A message is coming in just now."

Though impatient, Stonecraft said nothing. Bevan was very efficient—he'd better be, he was paid so much—and he would rush in the message from overseas as soon as it was decoded. In the few minutes intervening, Stonecraft phoned a district manager in Texas. After listening to a very succinct report, the industrialist gave the manager short, clear, and concise instructions, outlining both legal and illegal ways to ensure the takeover of a small independent oil company. His tactics involved a certain amount of intimidation, but it would be subtle.

In the old days, when Stonecraft's company was relatively small and fighting to take over other firms, it sometimes used physical violence, arson, and bribing officials: sheriffs, judges, prosecutors, even state senators, and federal congresspeople. Stonecraft did not like to think about those now, and so he seldom did. Hadn't he more than made up for whatever little sins he'd committed? Weren't the millions of dollars he'd donated to worthy causes more than enough to wipe out any small slate of perhaps shady deeds?

Bevan knocked twice on the door, his signal, and walked in. He was in his early fifties, short and chunky, double-chinned, bald, and wore a black pince-nez. He looked bland and timid. However, those who thought that he was a rabbit would find a tiger if they crossed him. The only person he feared was his boss.

He handed Stonecraft a sheet of inexpensive typewriter paper. On it was a typed transcription in English of the Morse code message that had been sent from British East Africa via a shortwave transmitter owned by Stonecraft's company. Another company transmitter on the northwest coast of Africa had then sent the message to America.

It was a setup of which the government authorities of several nations were aware. But they would not publicly admit it as long as the bribes kept coming.

Stonecraft looked through large square rimless spectacles at the paper. There was no date or time of transmission on it. Nor were there any identity letters for the sending or receiving station or any name of an agent or the receiver's name.

The message was simple and short though not clear except to the initiated: Lord Greystoke located in Belgian Congo. On the trail. Expect results soon. Helmson.

Stonecraft uttered one word, "Ah!"

He looked up at Bevan. "This Helmson man, he must really be very competent. To tell the truth, I didn't expect him to find Greystoke so soon, surely not in the jungle. I thought we'd have to wait until he returned to his ranch or to the British East Africa HQ."

Bevan cleared his throat. He said, "Sir, I understand that Helmson has something to help him locate Greystoke. He won't reveal what it is, and I just can't imagine what it could be."

"Once I have Greystoke in my hands," Stonecraft said grimly, "then I'll find out what it is that Helmson's holding out on me. If it's some sort of mechanical or electric device, it might be worth millions."

"Yes, sir," Bevan said. "But locating Greystoke, catching him, and then keeping him may not be so easy. My research indicates . . ."

"I know what it indicates!" Stonecraft said. "What concerns me more is the building of the transportable transmitter-receiver station near the Belgian Congo."

He was angry and frustrated because it took so long to get messages from Helmson to the transmitter in eastern East Africa. Helmson had to use a series of native runners to get his messages to the nearest station. The Cleft Stick Express, Bevan called it. As a result, a movable battery-powered transmitter much closer to the Ituri was being built. But the jungle was deep, and the territory was unknown. There were no roads, just paths, and sometimes not even those. Also, the native chiefs had to be bribed, and accidents and diseases, especially diseases, poisonous snakes, and warlike natives had caused many deaths. The worst obstacle was the upheaval and chaos caused by the war.

The secretary broke into Stonecraft's thoughts.

"Sir! I'd like to discuss this plan I've contrived to get Greystoke out of Africa and to here. By the time he's caught, the war'll be over, and the U-boat menace will be a thing of the past. I . . ."

Stonecraft said, "I'll listen. But, as you said about Greystoke, there's many a slip 'twixt the cup and the lip."

Bevan frowned. He hated the poor, and he didn't really like women. But what he detested the most was a cliché.

6

HELMSON HAD A worldwide reputation as an authority on equatorial Africa and as a top collector of animals for zoos and museums. He had managed enough hunting safaris for wealthy men to bank more than enough for him to retire.

But few men ever have enough money to satisfy them. Thus, when he had received a proposal to make far more in one venture than he had so far earned in his thirty-five years of life, he seriously considered it. He didn't know who was supplying the money for the project. It was going to cost so much that he suspected only one man in the world was rich enough to pay for it. That would probably be James D. Stonecraft. But it was none of Helmson's business.

What was his business was capturing the feral man known as Tarzan.

When he'd been told this by the American calling himself John Smith, Helmson had had to sit down to recover his breath. Though he was physically very impressive, six feet and three inches tall, 230 pounds, wide shouldered and narrow waisted, for a moment, he had felt as if the world heavyweight boxing champion, Jess Willard, had struck him in his solar plexus.

He had never failed in courage while facing charging lions, elephants, buffalo, and Somali spearmen. But now . . .

to go after the deadliest killer in the world, the craftiest and the most vengeful . . .

"You look doubtful," John Smith had said.

Helmson had rallied quickly.

"It's that . . . you're asking me to commit a crime."

"If you succeed, you get a million dollars," Smith had said. "If you fail, you still get fifty thousand plus expenses. You'll have a secret account in a Swiss bank. Anyway, we're not asking you to murder anyone. We want Greystoke alive and well in mind and body."

"It's still a crime."

Smith had smiled.

He had said, "Let's see. Several years ago, you were collecting rare insects near Harar, Ethiopia. You and your partner got drunk and quarreled. You hit him with your fist, and he fell and cracked his skull. He died at once. You secretly buried him, and then arranged it to seem as if a maneating lion had killed him and taken his body away. Your story was accepted by the Ethiopian authorities, after suitable bribes had been given.

"And then there was the affair in Paris with the duchess . . ."

Helmson had risen from the chair. His hands balled, he roared, "How did you find out about those?"

He glared down at Smith. Smith, however, seemed to be calm. He said, "We have our ways. Please sit down and relax, Mister Helmson. I'm not threatening you with blackmail. I am merely pointing out that you are already a criminal, though not so far detected as such by the law. So your moral outrage is inappropriate."

Helmson had sat down. There had been a silence for a minute, then Helmson had said, "Very well. I do have my price, and you've offered it. However . . . I'm being honest with you . . . capturing Greystoke won't be easy. I don't even know where he is or what he's doing."

Smith said, "Leave that up to us. He's somewhere in

German East Africa and acting as his own agent in fighting the Germans. Since the war is winding down in Africa, he'll probably turn up sometime soon and get into contact with the British authorities. We'll know when and where as soon as he does that. If the Germans should capture him, an unlikely event, we'll know at once about that, too. If that should happen, your part in this project will be over. You'll be paid off as promised, though. The minimal payment, of course."

So Smith represented people willing to deal with the Germans to get what they wanted. They were traitors! Despicable people!

Helmson felt like walking out of the place. But he didn't move.

He said, "You'll have to give me a lot of time to prepare for this ... project. Maybe more than your employer is willing to allow me."

"You have a month to organize everything."

Helmson had thought then about another project, one of his own. It would make him rich and famous, very famous. But now, he had thought, it would be better to postpone it. The world would be busy for a long time, recovering from the war. *It'll be better to wait awhile, wait until the world is ready to pay full attention to my discovery. Meantime, I can become richer sooner than I had expected.* And there would be the satisfaction of capturing the feral man, the most dangerous of beasts. *If I can do it.*

Smith had said, "What's your answer. Yes or no?"

Helmson had risen from the chair. "Yes."

That discussion had taken place six weeks earlier. Since then, Helmson had sent several coded messages via a system of relay runners. These were delivered at the railroad terminal and were carried to Smith, who was then in Nairobi. The latest message from Helmson had just been received in Manhattan.

Decoded, it read: Lord Greystoke located in Belgian Congo. Expect results soon.

But that arrived a week after the reported event. There was no telling what had happened in the meantime.

7

Tarzan caught sight of the Ben-go-utor just as the first trackers came into view. Then, as if the creature had used magic, he was gone. All that was lacking was the puff of smoke.

The ape-man was high on the branch of a tree when this happened. Unaware of both him and the Ben-go-utor, the two black men trotted below. But, as they passed the tree, they must have come across the bear-man's footprint in the mud. Exclaiming softly, they stopped to examine it. A moment later, the advance askari showed up. They also stopped and began talking to the trackers.

Tarzan could either keep on the Ben-go-utor's trail or stay here to observe the safari men. He decided that, by now, the bear-man would have gotten far ahead of him again. And he might have taken to the trees again. That would make tracking him even more difficult.

One of the askari turned and ran back into the forest. Presently, he returned with Helmson, another white man, and several askari. Helmson looked closely at the print, then straightened up and began talking to the trackers. Though their voices were carried up to him, Tarzan could not make out what they were saying. But it was evident that Helmson was angry. Tarzan guessed that he was berating the trackers for having held them up.

Oddly, the white man did not think the footprint of an unknown animal was worth delaying the party's progress.

He gave the order to resume the march. The trackers ran on ahead, and the safari continued. But the voices of the bearers were not those of happy men.

Tarzan worked his silent and cautious way downward on the tree until he could hear their words clearly. They were disturbed by the footprint, and they were telling stories about various strange and rare beasts of their native areas. All these—according to the tellers—were deadly, and so crafty they were seldom caught. Obviously, the bearers were worried that the killer stalking them was one of those beasts.

Underlying that fear was another, a fear they had felt since they had ventured into the rain forest. These were natives of the savannah and the bush. The rain forest was alien to them; it scared them. The high green canopies over them, the dimness, the bottle-green light, the stories they'd heard about the bizarre and horrible creatures and demons therein—these filled them with dread.

Only pygmies seemed at ease here, and it was said that even they avoided certain areas. One of these was the very territory they were now in.

Furthermore, the man they were seeking to capture was said to be the only individual even more at home here than the pygmies. The rain forest was his native home, and it was said that he was the embodiment of the spirit of the forest. That spirit was a truly ghastly thing. To see it, to encounter it, to make an enemy of it . . . ah, that did not bear contemplating.

Tarzan knew that these men, so courageous on their native ground, could be easily spooked here. And he suspected that the white men were as open to panic, though for somewhat different reasons.

The ape-man followed the long line into the forest. He traveled sometimes in the middle terrace and sometimes in the upper terrace. Which one he moved through depended on the obstacles he had to climb around.

After an hour, he dropped onto the ground. This time his prey was an askari who had fallen behind the others by twenty feet. Though anyone turning could have seen Tarzan behind the soldier, their gazes were directed elsewhere.

The ape-man did his work quickly. He carried the corpse up the tree, then ahead of the slowly moving party.

So it was that, after a while, the body fell from a tree onto a bearer, tumbling him and his load on the ground. It killed the bearer and came close to striking another man.

Very quickly, Tarzan was several trees away from the one from which he had dropped the dead man. He was also higher. From that vantage point, he watched the frightened men. The line halted. Helmson and the white man with the double-barreled rapid-fire carbine, the Villar Perona, arrived. Helmson shouted for order and sent everybody back to their posts in the line. He listened as the white man who'd narrowly missed being struck told Helmson what had happened.

After that, Helmson examined the corpse, quickly finding a knife wound in the man's spine. He looked upward as if he knew that the killer was watching him. He then ordered that the body be buried at once. The men who did that were of the dead man's tribe. They chanted a ceremonial song while they dug the grave, lowered the corpse into it, then filled the grave again. They would have continued the ceremony, but Helmson stopped that. Though the natives looked angry, they obeyed Helmson's orders to start marching again.

As soon as the last man in the line had moved out of sight, Tarzan went to the ground. It did not take him long to dig up the loose dirt of the grave with his bare fingers. He hoisted the porter's corpse to his shoulder and climbed back up to the middle terrace of the forest.

He soon had caught up with the slow-moving safari.

Keeping pace with the men, he observed that Helmson always made sure he was surrounded by askari. Tarzan had no chance of snatching him from the others. He would have to wait until nightfall to try that. Meanwhile, he wouldn't waste time. By the time the day was done, the safari would be completely terrorized.

It was some time before he got into the position he wanted. His aim was perfect. The body fell on the white with the Italian-made machine carbine and broke his shoulder. Though several askari at once shot into the trees, the ape-man was gone.

From his hiding place, he viewed the scene below with a grim smile. Helmson came, examined the corpse, stood up, swore loudly, and took the carbine for himself. He ordered the porters to bring out a collapsible stretcher from a box and to place the man with the broken shoulder on it. Then he gave the man an injection.

He ignored the corpse. Apparently, he was tired of burying his men, only to have them reappear.

This did not set well with the porters. But, though they muttered among themselves, they picked up their loads and took their assigned positions in the line. Two of them carried the man on the stretcher.

All this time, while observing the safari, Tarzan hadn't quit watching for the Ben-go-utor. It would be ironic if the bear-man were to stalk him while he was stalking the safari, to catch the catcher unawares. The ape-man enjoyed irony, but not just now.

Tarzan traveled several miles from the safari and descended to the forest floor. He went over the ground swiftly, searching for a particular creature which would fit in with his next move. It took him a while, perhaps, as the whites counted time, an hour and a half. Then he saw it. A few minutes later, one hand grasping the creature behind its head, he trotted back toward the safari.

Presently, something from above hit Helmson on the

top of his bush hat. It fell from the hat onto his shoulder and then slid off from there. On its way to the ground, it narrowly missed sinking its fangs into Helmson's neck. However, once it was on the forest floor, it struck out again. This time, its fangs sank into the calf of an askari.

Those nearest the stricken askari were yelling and trying to get away from the cobra. Though Helmson must have been shaken up, he had enough composure to aim his rifle and blow the reptile's head off. Just after that, Tarzan's arrow plunged deep into the right thigh of a bearer. A few minutes later, the man poisoned by the cobra breathed his painful last breath. Then the other wounded man died. Both victims died more quickly than expected. No one knew why, but sometimes sheer shock hastens a man's death.

Confusion and terror increased. Within a few seconds, the entire safari was disorganized. Bearers cast their loads to the ground and ran off. Panicked, several askari fired their rifles upward at random. One bullet came close enough to Tarzan for him to hear its passage through the air and the leaves.

He went around the tree trunk and climbed higher. He kept the trunk between him and the men below, though he was sure they could not see him. Higher and higher he went, seeking a place where he could take a nap while the panic among his victims swelled.

At last, very high up, close to a break in the upper canopy, he found a desirable spot. Here the light was brighter than on the floor, but it wasn't bright enough to keep him awake. He could lodge himself within two forks of the tree. His back against one fork and his legs drawn up, feet against the sloping side of the other branch, ignoring the distant human hullabaloo far far below and the din and uproar of the birds and monkeys nearby, he slept.

How long, he did not know. But something knocked

him out of his dreams. It also knocked him out of his perch.

Dimly aware that the impact had come from above, not from below, he fell. Confusion took hold; nothing large enough to be dangerous could have struck him from above. The higher branches were too thin to have borne a heavy weight.

Then he became painfully aware that something was digging him with sharp and searing claws. And something was screaming.

Just as a branch slammed him across the back of his shoulders, he realized that the thing sinking its talons into him was a large bird—an eagle. Its beak was striking, not at him, but at a small monkey.

Later he would fully piece together how this freak accident had come about. The eagle, cruising above the jungle canopy, had dropped through and seized a monkey. However, its prey had turned just before the eagle grabbed its back. Thus, the talons had sunk into the front of the monkey.

But the monkey, instead of being paralyzed by the shock, had fought back.

Locked together, the two had fallen on Tarzan. The monkey had torn loose for a moment. The eagle had grabbed out with its feet, but its razor-sharp talons had seized Tarzan's belly.

Tarzan gasped for air while he rotated from the branch. Again, he fell, though face forward this time. The monkey bit the eagle. The eagle seized one of the monkey's arms in its beak. It almost bit through the arm.

Then the three struck another branch, much larger than the first one they had encountered. And the monkey and the eagle were between Tarzan and the branch. All three bounced off. The ape-man still couldn't recover his wind. But the eagle was badly hurt or killed by the impact. It ceased to shriek. Only the monkey was crying out, but he seemed to be as noisy as a large pack of his fellows.

The eagle, its talons sunk into Tarzan's belly, dangled from him. Its beak had opened, though, and the monkey fell away. Fortunately, the blow from the third branch was softened for Tarzan. First the monkey, then the eagle, absorbed the impact. Still, the force was enough to knock the ape-man out.

What happened during the rest of his journey downward, he did not know.

8

TARZAN MOVED IN and out of consciousness a few times, though briefly. During each dim event, he felt a sharp pain, its location undetermined. Once, he heard voices. They sounded as if they were coming up from some deep cavern. One of them seemed not to be a human's voice. A great ape's? No. Yet something about it reminded him of the Mangani speech.

These memories rushed in just as he swam up into the light of what seemed to be full awareness. Then he realized he had not completely recovered his full range of senses. He felt sluggish. When he tried to sit up, he felt as if he was restrained. The same thing happened when he tried to lift his arm.

Though the pain was dull, it pulsed slowly in many places in his body. He was drugged, though just how much he could not gauge. His back was on something relatively soft, and his head was on a pillow.

Somewhere near, natives were chanting loudly. He distinguished words from the Ndesi language, then phrases. They were singing of victory. But whom had they conquered?

Him, of course.

He looked upward. He was in a tent, a large one. And the feeling of being bound came from the fact that he was strapped to a cot. When he looked down, he saw that his bindings were leather. His loin cover was gone. An armed askari was standing guard just inside the entrance of the tent. Nearer to Tarzan stood a big white man with a bushy black moustache.

Tarzan sniffed. Mixed with the odors of humans were the scents of strong soap, iodine, and dried blood.

For a moment, he couldn't remember the name of the man with the moustache. That slowness was perhaps owing to the pain-killing drugs injected into him. He hoped it was that and not something worse. Perhaps it came from a head wound. But, if he was bright enough to reason he probably had not injured his brain.

Nevertheless, his head ached fearfully. The last time it had hurt so much was when he had been sampling, for the first time, the delights and novelties of civilization. It was shortly after he had gone to Paris with his first human friend, Lieutenant Paul d'Arnot of the French Navy. The ape-man had drunk so much wine that, as d'Arnot so Gallicly put it, he had experienced the hangover of ten thousand devils. After that evening, though Tarzan sometimes drank wine, he did so in moderation.

Ah! Now he had it! The man's name was Helmson. And he was no friend to Tarzan.

Helmson, seeing the ape-man's eyes open, came to his bedside. The hunter smiled, and his eyes seemed to sparkle. Obviously, he was very happy. He spoke with a soft southern pronunciation. It was somewhat different from the speech of Tarzan's wife, Jane, a native of Baltimore, Maryland.

Helmson held up three fingers. He said, "How many?"

Tarzan said, "Four? Six?"

The American said, "While you were knocked out, I looked at your eyes. I'm not a doctor, but I've had a lot of medical experience. Your eyes look OK to me."

Tarzan said, "I saw what I said I saw."

"I think you're a crafty bastard and you're lying. Anyway, I don't think you have any broken bones. Let me tell you, milord, you have the biggest bones, and probably the thickest, of any man I've ever seen. Like a Cro-Magnon's. I think you'll be all right. Is there any place where you hurt more than any place else?"

"No."

"In all my many years in Africa, where the strangest things happen, I've never seen anything like it!" Helmson said.

He laughed, then continued. "Absolutely nothing! Who in the world would've thought an eagle would attack a monkey, you'd be right below them, and they'd bring you down? It was a fish eagle, and they don't even prey on monkeys! Not as far as I know. It's very strange, very strange."

He laughed again, then said, "And it's a miracle you weren't killed by the fall. One of the askaris saw the eagle attack you, and he saw you fall. You finally landed on a big branch, fell a hundred feet onto a branch about fifty feet from the ground. You broke your fall by going through many small branches. We had a hard time getting you down to the ground."

Tarzan saw no reason to comment. He didn't remember landing on the final bough.

"The gods deserted you—at first, but they had pity and saved you for me. Perhaps it was pity. I don't know what your ultimate fate will be. Anyway, that's not my business.

"You came close to ruining everything by sending my men into a panic. They would've deserted me, left me alone. But I rallied them and didn't have to shoot any of them to do it, either. Then it was as if the fates were on my side. We were almost directly beneath you when that weird attack happened. Now, you're captured, everybody's morale is sky high. We'll be getting out of this godforsaken place very soon."

This man talks too much, Tarzan thought. *But that doesn't mean he's not dangerous.*

He said, "How did you find me? You were all in a frenzy to get away, and . . ."

Helmson didn't answer that question. Instead, he said, "I think it'll be OK to move you in a few days, maybe sooner."

He leaned down close to Tarzan's face. His breath smelled of whiskey. The whites of his light-blue eyes were reddened.

"Your quiver and bow were beneath you when you landed. They helped soften the impact, though the impression the bow made on your back wasn't shallow. Your bow was broken. And the cylinder you'd put in the quiver was flattened. I pried its lid off and expanded it again, and I found the parchment map and the parchment pages on which the Spaniard had written his story."

He paused. The ape-man did not reply.

"It's in sixteenth-century Spanish, but I can still make out most of it. Fascinating. If, that is, it's true and not fever-induced ravings. The City Made by God! The Voice of The Ghost Frog! The Toucher of Time! The Uncaused Causer! What *is* all that?"

"I do not know," Tarzan said.

"But you were going to find out, weren't you?"

The ape-man was silent.

"After you found your wife, of course! And rescued her from the Germans, or avenged her death!" Helmson said.

Tarzan wondered where and how Helmson had gotten his information. It was supposed to be a military secret that Tarzan had gone into the Belgian Congo to track down Jane and her abductors.

"Well?" Helmson said. "What about it? Again, I ask you what all that means? The Eyes of The Glittering Tree? The Dark Heart of Time?"

"You know as much about that as I do," the ape-man replied.

"Really? Listen. Here are other exotic references on the map. Damned little said about them in the manuscript. Martillo evidently planned to expand it when he got back. But here are several places on the map marked with *Oro*. That's Spanish for gold.

"Fascinating. But not as intriguing as The More than Dead and the volcanic mountain called The Great Mother of Snakes. But ... The Uncaused Causer, also known as The Unwilling Giver of the Unwanted? It comes from the beasts and is itself part-beast and is guiltless? Who or what the hell could it be? Sounds ominous, doesn't it?"

"I said that I know nothing of those names."

"You must have figured out approximately where the area is," Helmson said. "The map is very rough. But Martillo described how many days' march it was from the coast. Whatever and wherever the place is, it's south of here. It's hard to say how many miles, but if you followed these rivers, then you'd come to a landmark, the mountain called The Great Mother of Snakes. South of that ... yeah, it could be done.

"After I deliver you, milord, I may follow that map even though it might turn out to be figments of a dying man's delirium. So tell me now, where did you get that cylinder?"

"It's none of your concern," Tarzan replied. But his thoughts cast back, to a time only a few weeks earlier.

Tarzan had been crossing a desert west of German East Africa. Close to dying of thirst, he had come across the skeleton of a huge man. It was still clad in the iron cuirass and iron helmet worn in the sixteenth century by Iberian soldiers. A copper cylinder near the remains contained a parchment map and a manuscript written in a language he thought was Spanish or Portuguese. He could not read it, and the map had referents unintelligible to him.

Always curious, he had replaced the parchment pages in the cylinder and then stuck that in his quiver.

Then he had gone on west to the city of Xuja, unknown to any person outside its immediate area. Its inhabitants were even more irrational than the rest of civilized people, though they would not go completely crazy, but usually recovered a sort of sanity for a while. They killed male strangers, but the ape-man had survived. During his perilous stay there, he had heard about the giant foreigner who had entered the city over three hundred years ago. That man had slain many Xujans before he had escaped into the desert. What had happened after that only Tarzan knew.

He had assumed that the map and the narrative were about Xuja. It wasn't until he got to the base camp of the Second Rhodesians that he found out he was wrong. There, an interpreter translated the story for Tarzan.

Rodrigo Esteban Martillo had been a Spanish mercenary with a Portuguese expedition seeking gold in the jungle far west of the east coast of Africa. The Portuguese men had died; he alone had survived. Martillo was, as far as he knew, the only one who had ever escaped The City Made by God and the other dangers and terrors he mentioned in his manuscript.

No doubt, Martillo had expected that, if he got to civilization, he would write out his story in great detail.

Martillo's map did not show Xuja on it. Nor did the manuscript mention that city. The Spaniard had not had time to write about it because he had been too busy fighting for his life there, and too occupied with fighting for survival in the desert.

* * *

Helmson broke in on his reverie. "You're right. It doesn't matter. I have all I need."

He picked up the cylinder and waved it in front of Tarzan's face, then put it back on a small folding table.

Helmson looked very self-satisfied. His future was carved in hard glowing-pink stone. Nothing would change it. At least, it seemed to Tarzan that Helmson was thinking this.

But Tarzan knew that all humans were deep-down insecure, uncertain, and always worrying about the future. Tarzan, like the animals, didn't worry about what was to come.

Nevertheless, he was in a bad situation. Thus, unlike the animals, he'd have to make plans to change the future.

Helmson, as if reading his captive's mind, said, "You can't escape. So don't even think about it."

"I still live," Tarzan answered.

9

STONECRAFT READ THE latest message from Africa. Decoded, it read: Lord Greystoke captured by Helmson. Greystoke hurt. Not fatally. Three days maximum. Then on way.

Stonecraft should have been very happy—and perhaps he was. But his hawk face had no more expression than the face of an ancient Egyptian mummy. The old man's face had often been compared to that great ruler of ancient Egypt, Pharaoh Rameses II. It was said that his nose was every bit as huge and as curved as Rameses'. And his eyes were as dead, though they did not quite look as decayed as the mummy's.

"It's been a week since this was sent," he said to his secretary. "Since then . . ."

"No word," Bevan said. "Sir, it takes time for the relay of runners, even though they're all going top speed, to get the messages from Helmson to Station One. But Station One is the portable radio station now on the edge of the Ituri, and it's saving many days in message transmission. Even so, there's always the possibility a runner will be eaten by a lion or bitten by a poisonous snake. God only knows what could happen. So . . ."

"I know that!" Stonecraft snapped. "Teach your grandmother to suck eggs! But anything can go wrong, *anything*! I've lived by that rule all my life, and I've always tried to consider every contingency and prepare for it. Be ready for anything. The trouble is that this business is in darkest Africa. My experience there is nil. The lines of communication are still abominably long and devilishly undependable."

He fell silent for a moment, then said, "And we're dealing with a man who's not completely human, if my sources have the right information. We have to handle this very delicately. If the truth ever got out . . . what we're doing . . ."

He shuddered.

Bevan said, "Sir, you've done what others claimed was impossible. Done it many times. You won't fail this time, no matter what the obstacles."

"Yes, but he very likely carries the greatest secret in history, the most precious thing in the world. I don't want anything to happen to him, and I won't sleep easy until he's been delivered here."

Bevan wasn't so sure that Greystoke held any secret, whatever secret Stonecraft sought. Nor did he see how Greystoke could be brought to America as quickly as his boss wanted him brought. U-boats, the German submarines, were still sinking vessels crossing the Atlantic from the Old World to the New World and vice versa.

On the other hand, the Germans seemed sure to be defeated very soon, though you never knew about them. Their fighting spirit and their resourcefulness were amazing.

Bevan said nothing about his doubts. He wanted to keep this very demanding but extremely well-paying job.

The day after his capture, Tarzan was feeling much better. Toward the evening, he was able to stand up and to walk at a fairly brisk pace back and forth in the tent.

He did this well, though he had to carry a leather bag that contained a twenty-five-pound iron ball. This was attached to a chain. The other end was connected to a manacle around Tarzan's right ankle. Between the manacle and skin was a thin cloth soaked in oil to prevent chafing. Tarzan would wear the manacle and carry the ball during the day. At night, he would be strapped down to a cot. The chain was long enough to reach from the manacled ankle to a place directly under the cot. Two askari were always in the tent with him.

Whereas he had been too sore the first day of his captivity to move without pain, he now was almost as flexible as rubber. And he didn't hurt nearly as much as he had.

He did, however, fake being somewhat dizzy, though he now correctly replied to the finger vision test. Let Helmson believe that he was improving, but still somewhat handicapped.

Helmson marveled at the ape-man's amazingly rapid recovery. But the ape-man had always had this ability—he didn't know how to explain it. Whatever the reason, he had seldom been sick. When he was ill, he quickly shot back to health.

Helmson was happy because he could take his captive back much sooner than he'd expected. And, for the initial part of the journey, Tarzan could walk instead of having to be carried on a stretcher.

"Carrying the ball in the bag won't slow you down much," Helmson said. "But you'll be handicapped, and you won't be able to take to the trees. Climbing will be hard enough, perhaps impossible, but traveling from branch to branch . . . I don't think so. You're caught! And you're going to stay caught until you're no longer in my charge!"

Tarzan never boasted unless doing so helped him attain certain goals. Thus, he didn't tell Helmson how many times he had rescued himself from seemingly escape-proof situations.

Instead, he questioned Helmson about his personal life, his parents, his childhood, his adult education, his marriage, if any. He did so because he was inherently curious and because he hoped that the man might reveal something—some character trait or flaw—that might help Tarzan get free.

Helmson, however, refused to talk about himself. That surprised the ape-man very much. Almost all humans liked to talk about themselves. To them, self was the most interesting subject in the world. It also, Tarzan had to admit, was the most fascinating to the Mangani.

Perhaps this man knew what Tarzan was up to. If so, he wasn't going to be easy to trick.

Before dawn, the safari broke camp. It was going to backtrack on the trail it had made going into the Ituri. The ape-man, carrying the iron ball, was marched along the middle of the column. Two askari armed with rifles were behind the ape-man. Two were in front of him. Nearby was an askari with a large net. The askari would cast it over Tarzan if he tried to run into the forest.

Tarzan didn't despair—though, logically, he had good reason to do so. However, he did become very angry. These men were robbing him of valuable time. They might even succeed in making his search for Jane impossible.

As he walked along, he cooled off. Fury and fantasies about revenge were not helping him in the least. He had to think of some way to escape, to consider every means he might use. If physical methods wouldn't work, perhaps psychological methods would or a combination of both.

As far as Tarzan knew, Helmson was not even aware the Ben-go-utor existed.

An hour passed, and they made good time. This was the type of rain forest relatively free of thick growth on the ground. The intertangled canopies far above the men made the forest a cool and comparatively dim place. In a way, the forest was an unending cathedral with great tree trunks for columns and the ceiling a medium-hued green. Far off, seen through the aisles formed by the trunks, the bottle-green light got darker.

Tarzan took great pleasure in this place. But the blacks were still uneasy. They kept seeing shapes in the distant darkness, where the aisles seemed to end, shapes that changed from one form to another and then to still different shapes. These always seemed menacing.

It had done no good for the whites to assure the blacks that it was all an illusion, no more substantial or dangerous than those mirages that appeared in a shimmering heat wave, the distorted reflection of far-off places and beings. The blacks remained unconvinced.

And, after some time, the whites absorbed the attitude of the blacks. Even the whites, though they thought of themselves as not superstitious, began to think that they, too, saw shapes in the darkness, far down the aisles. They, too, felt as if hostile things were concealed up in the green ceiling with its splotches of blaring colors made by huge clumps of flowers and by fungal masses coated with the sheen of brightly pigmented and poisonous bacteria.

When night came, they, too, would feel that the fearsome things might come down from above, and other horrible creatures would leave the far ends of the aisles to lurk just beyond the light of the camp's fires. It did no good when they told themselves that these things were imagined.

For the moment, Tarzan waited until the safari had been on the move for another hour. Then he spoke loudly enough for the askari ahead of and behind him to hear him clearly. Though he was not fluent in the Serba language, he could speak it well enough to be understood.

"Do you men know that a being which looks half human, half beast has been dogging this safari?" he asked. "It's bigger and much stronger than a man and is covered all over with long black hair. It stinks worse than a weasel. Its teeth are long, and it has claws like an anteater."

Some of what he said was a lie, but the ape-man intended to inspire fear. So he continued lying.

"It was not I who hurled Mitchell to death from the tree. That half-beast thing did it. I saw him pick Mitchell up as if he were a baby and throw him away as if he were a broken toy. I saw the thing that looked as if it were partly a giant black badger and partly a man. It killed Mitchell, and it was trailing you when I fell from the tree into your hands."

He paused for effect. Then he said, "It has not gone away. It's still following you. Remember the footprint you saw in the ground before I fell from the tree? That proves it exists. Now, I tell you, I saw the living creature, and it looks as fearsome as I described it. Sometimes, it's on the ground, hiding behind trees, waiting for its chance to grab you and eat you. Sometimes, it's up in the trees, hoping to reach down and kill you and eat you.

"I myself came close to being caught in its long claws and long teeth. Now, I'm safe because it is daylight and you are guarding me. But tonight . . . who will be safe?"

The askari had been chattering among themselves. Since he had started talking, they had become silent. And it was several minutes after he ceased before one of them spoke.

"That thing sounds like the monster that my mother told me, when I was a child, would eat me if I didn't behave. I heard many tales about it, but I never actually saw one. I think that you are lying about that thing. You wish to frighten us so much that we will desert the white man, Helmson. Or perhaps you think we'll release you so that you can find it and kill it. If there is such a thing, you may indeed be the only one who could slay it."

The askari paused to draw in a deep breath. Then he said, "But I don't think that that thing is here or that it threatens us. Why should it? What have we done to it?"

Tarzan stopped. He pointed with his free hand up into

the trees. "There! It's there! Quick! Before it goes! Look! It's right there!"

Up above there were only some shifting patterns of light and shade caused by sunlight in the few gaps in the canopy and by the breeze. But the natives believed in such things as the half men, half beasts. And two of them saw what seemed to be something crouching on a high branch. One wasn't quite sure. The skeptic who'd been talking to Tarzan said nothing. If he perceived a shape that should not be, he wasn't going to admit it.

Tarzan's smile was slight, but it was a knowing one. Night would convert any doubters. They would look into the deep darkness and imagine many things. They would not fall asleep easily, and nightmares would awaken them after they fell asleep.

The rain began shortly after the sun reached its apex. Helmson ordered the safari to halt for a rest and a quick lunch. A half hour or so later, he ordered the march to resume. Never mind the downpour. Get going. The bearers put their loads on their heads or grabbed the handles of various rigs carrying heavy loads. They talked among themselves, as did the trackers and the askari, but their voices were subdued. What the captive had said about the thing from the Shadow World had reached every ear. Except Helmson's, of course.

After the rains ceased and the thunder and lightning rolled away, the safari picked up its pace. Helmson came up to the ape-man. The white man was wearing Tarzan's father's hunting knife in a sheath. When the ape-man had escaped from the city of Xuja, he had been forced to leave the weapon behind. But, after being rescued by the soldiers of the Second Rhodesians, Tarzan had sneaked back into Xuja. And he had retrieved his knife and bow and quiver.

Helmson now wore it so that his captive could see it

whenever he saw Helmson. That was supposed to impress Tarzan with the hopelessness of his situation.

What it did was make Tarzan look forward to the day when he would take the knife back from Helmson and plunge it into his belly.

That night, before he went to bed on the cot, Tarzan's manacle was unlocked. His ankle was well oiled, and then the manacle was relocked around the ankle. The iron ball in the case was placed under the cot. He was strapped to the cot. Two lamps burned in the tent, giving plenty of light.

Two askari were walking around his tent outside. They were on shifts so that fresh and alert sentries would be on guard detail until dawn. Inside the tent, two askari stood watch. A rope was tied around Tarzan's unmanacled ankle. The other end of the rope was secured around an iron stake driven deep into the ground at the foot of the cot.

Tarzan pretended to go to sleep almost immediately. He heard the sentries in the tent talking in low tones about the ghost that was half beast, half human. By now, the thing had become twice as big as a man and three times as deadly as a maneating leopard. Near the tent, Tarzan knew, the fires were burning more brightly than was usual. The men around them were sleeping fitfully. Satisfied, Tarzan allowed himself to sleep.

Sometime later, he awoke. He opened his eyes just enough to see the two guards walking very slowly around his cot. They were silent, but they seemed to be listening to the forest sounds.

When Tarzan spoke abruptly, he startled the two blacks. Again he was pleased. The guards were very nervous!

"I was asleep," he said. "But I had a bad dream. I saw the hairy and huge-fanged beast-ghost. It was walking through the camp. It was looking for a man to eat. Perhaps it was looking for more than one."

He paused, then said, "What awoke me was the odor

of the beast-ghost. Though asleep, I smelled its awful odor. That was what dragged me up from the bad dream. Don't you smell it?"

He sniffed. "Your nose would have to be stuffed with hyena dung not to smell that."

The askari stopped walking and faced the flap of the tent. It was open, but mosquito netting hung over it. Through it, firelight flickered. Silence reigned in the camp, and even the night birds and night beasts were hushed.

One of the askari said, softly, voice trembling, "Yes. I smell it!"

The other said, "I don't!"

"Come over here," the first one said. "It's strong here!"

The second man went around the cot and stood by the first one. He sniffed. He said, "I don't know. Wait!" He drew in a breath noisily. Then he grabbed his companion's arm.

"Akika! I do smell it!"

Tarzan had succeeded in scaring them. But he was not lying to deceive the askari. Not this time.

The odor *had* awakened him. And, though it was now a ghost of a fragrance, it had been strong. The bear-man had been near the tent.

It was then that a thought slid into his concentration on the present danger. He remembered Helmson's questions, about Martillo's manuscript and map.

". . . The Uncaused Causer . . . It comes from the beasts and is itself part beast and is guiltless?"

Was it the least bit possible that the bear-man was the mysterious entity called The Uncaused Causer? Tarzan dismissed this speculation and returned to focusing his thoughts on the bear-man.

However, though the thought seemed irrelevant, he knew that no thought was ever irrelevant. Beneath the surface of reality, behind the shell of reality, all things were connected.

10

TARZAN WATCHED THE silhouette of one of the two guards outside the tent. He was directly between the closed entrance flap of the tent and the central campfire. The guards were always a half circle apart as they marched. Therefore, just now, the other guard would be behind the tent.

Both the inside guards were at the moment in front of the cot, their backs to him. They were talking too softly for him to hear all their words. They seemed to be watching some kind of activity around the main campfire. However, the men outside had fallen silent except for one man's voice that rose in song.

Tarzan did not know what interested the guards. Maybe it was the singer. It did not matter. If he waited to go into action, he might never have another chance.

The shadow cast by the outside guard on the tent front passed to the left side of Tarzan. The other guard would be coming around the back of the tent and beginning to walk along the side of Tarzan's right.

He had about thirty or forty seconds to start his escape plan before that guard came to the front of the tent.

Very quickly and very silently, Tarzan unbuckled the three straps that passed over his body and the two straps just below his knees. He rose to a sitting position. His right hand seized the chain attached to the ball. Then he exploded.

He brought the ball up with a jerk and propelled it forward. At the same time, he lifted his right leg. Doing that gave the chain attached to the manacle more length. The twenty-five-pound iron ball did exactly as he had planned. It smashed with a loud thunk against the back of the nearest askari's head. He dropped as his fellow, gasping, whirled around.

In two seconds, Tarzan jerked the rope attached to the iron spike. The spike flew up from the ground. Then he leapt to the other askari and gripped his throat with one hand. Though the man had opened his mouth to shout, he could not get enough air out.

The ape-man's left fist slammed into the askari's solar plexus. The guard dropped his rifle and gasped for breath. Tarzan quickly released his strangling grip on the man's throat. Speechless, his mouth wide open, the man fell onto the ground and writhed.

Tarzan picked up the man's rifle, pulled back the breech bolt, and rammed it forward. By then, the shadows of both the soldiers outside the tent were outlined by the campfire. They stood outside the entrance. Both were asking the two inside what was happening.

Their answer was two shots. The bullets pierced the entrance flap and felled both.

The men by the fires began shouting.

Tarzan raised the mosquito netting, pulled the flap aside, stuck the muzzle of the rifle out through the opening, and fired every bullet in the magazine. He aimed at the moving shapes around the fire. Some fell. The others dived to the ground or ran away.

Tarzan took a large hunting knife from the askari he had first downed. He cut the rope from around his ankle, then placed the blade between his teeth. He picked up the chain and slung the ball over his shoulder. Holding the chain with his right hand, he carried the rifle and an extra clip of ammunition in his left.

When he got to the back of the tent, he placed the ball, rifle, and ammunition magazine on the ground. He used the knife with his left hand to slit open the back of the tent. Then he put the knife back between his teeth. He went through the slit on his knees and one hand, using the other hand to pull on the chain. Once outside, he reached back through the slit. He brought out the rifle and the clip. He eased the iron ball to the ground and loaded the rifle.

A moment later, naked, the rifle in his left hand, the ball slung over his shoulder, he became one of the rain forest shadows.

Another minute passed. By then, despite all he had to carry, he was fifty feet up from the ground on a great branch. From there, he could see the campfires and the men milling around. Nobody had yet volunteered to look into the tent he had vacated.

Helmson, clad in pajamas, holding the Italian machine carbine, appeared. He yelled for silence, but it was a minute before he got it. He grabbed one of the less-flustered askari, and the man told him what he knew about the uproar.

It wasn't much, but it showed the white man that Greystoke had either escaped or was loose in the tent. That Helmson doubted the latter was evident. He ran to the tent and ducked inside. Then he returned, gestured violently, and began shouting orders. But he quickly canceled them. Even though he was in a white-hot rage, he realized that nobody had a chance to catch the Lord of the Jungle at night in his native element.

Tarzan fired the rifle at Helmson, but at the first shot the American quickly dived for the ground and rolled into the shadows. Then he was gone behind a tent. The second bullet, also intended for him, felled the white man with the broken shoulder.

Tarzan emptied the rifle into the mass of fleeing men

below. He hit at least two, but their screams showed that they were only wounded. After that, the ape-man cast the rifle spinning over the camp. It hurtled into the center of a large fire and cast pieces of burning wood from it.

Tarzan might have continued bedeviling them. They were scattered and thus open to his silent attacks from outside the perimeter of darkness. However, he was handicapped by the iron ball and chain attached to the manacle around his left ankle. He had to get rid of these. And Helmson had the key to the manacle.

As he assessed his options, he glimpsed, or he thought he glimpsed, a shape in the woods. The momentary shower of burning firewood and the leaping of flames revealed a by-now familiar figure.

Then, it was gone.

Tarzan could not yet go after the Ben-go-utor. Not until he unlocked the manacle. To an ordinary man, his situation would have seemed to be hopeless. Tarzan, however, never felt hopeless. And he did have the askari's knife.

Fortunately, the ape-man had some experience in picking locks. When he had first encountered civilization's allurements with his friend and mentor, Paul d'Arnot, he had been introduced to some members of the Parisian police. One of them had taught the ape-man how to bypass such obstacles.

At the time, Tarzan had been just amusing himself. Now, he was glad that he had learned that skill. By the flickering and dim light cast by the campfires below, Tarzan used the point of the knife to probe the manacle lock. After many failures, Tarzan heard the click.

He left the iron ball, chain, and manacle on the branch. Knife between his teeth, he came down from the tree. He paused long enough to scoop up some of the thin soil and rub it over the wounds suffered when he had fallen off the branch with the monkey and the eagle tearing at him. Once he had regained consciousness, Tarzan had refused the bandages and medicines offered by Helmson. He preferred the healing properties of the forest soil.

Having seen the bear-man go around the camp close to its edges, Tarzan did the same. During this circling, he did not find the Ben-go-utor, but he did come across a porter hiding behind the trunk of a forest giant. Tarzan passed the edge of his knife along the man's jugular vein. He removed the corpse's belt and leather knife sheath and buckled it around his waist. Then he used the porter's own knife to sever the corpse's head. A moment later, he hurled the head, the knife rammed through the bone of the skull, from the dark forest into the camp. His aim was true. The head struck an askari's head. The askari crumpled to the ground.

Tarzan was gone. His half-smile showed that he was satisfied that he had left behind him even more terror among the safari men.

The ape-man believed that the natives would give up the hunt and start for home at once. Helmson would have to go with them. He could not survive by himself whether he was in the jungle or on the plains. Anyway, what was the use of his staying here? He did not know that Tarzan would not be hanging around the safari now. He would be expecting the jungle demon to be on his trail.

Under other circumstances, the ape-man would have been hot after him. But he was determined not to lose any more time while on his search for Jane, so he decided to let Helmson go.

However, if he ever had the chance in the future to take vengeance on Helmson, he would not hesitate to do so.

Just now, he was willing to put in a few hours locating the Ben-go-utor. That effort might be worthwhile. If he failed, then he'd resume his quest for his wife. He very much hoped he could deal with the creature immediately. If not, Tarzan could not be at ease—not until he left the Ituri forest. The Ben-go-utor didn't seem to be the sort of creature that would be at home on the plains. To survive, he likely needed the thick overarching canopy of the rain forest, its many trees to hide behind and to take refuge in.

Tarzan was very curious about the bear-man's origin, and just why it was dogging him. Though he had no evidence so far that it could talk, he felt certain its actions were those of a sentient creature.

So he headed slowly west. The light of the three-quarter moon was no doubt bright above the roof of the forest. But down here, Tarzan could not see footprints. He was barely able to make out the gigantic trunks of the trees. But his nostrils were as keen as ever. He doubted that the bear-man could sneak up on him. His odor would give him away. Of course, in this still air, neither downwind nor upwind existed. Tarzan knew that he might have only a second's warning of the creature's presence.

But he was willing to take that great chance.

And then he stopped. He took the knife from between his teeth. The hairs on the back of his neck stood up. He smelled danger.

The odor, however, was not the Ben-go-utor's.

Helmson didn't dare stay in his tent, though he wanted to do so very much. To hide there and leave his men to face the ape-man alone was to allow them to think he was a coward.

So, Helmson rallied his men from their hiding places in the forest. He acted boldly, exposing himself in the lights of the campfires, walking around reassuring the bearers, trackers, and askari. He talked loudly as he strode around the camp. And he shouted threats into the darkness. He challenged the ape-man to come in and fight him hand to hand. He promised that his men would not interfere even should Tarzan kill him.

Helmson did all that just to calm his men's fears and to whip them into a belligerent mood. Not for a second did he believe that Tarzan would take him up on his invitation. Tarzan was no fool. But Helmson's challenges did help the men to regain their normal courage, which was considerable.

Nevertheless, when the porter's head flew out of the shadows and felled an askari, fear made the black men pale, and Helmson turned as white as an albino. They all recovered quickly, but not until dawn came did they cease to jump at every unexpected noise. When the darkness began paling, announcing the advent of the sun, they packed up and left. Their destinations were their native villages far to the east on the plains or in the bush.

Helmson raved and ranted. He called them children and women. He compared them to hyenas and jackals. Finally, seeing that the sullen men were still going to desert him, he promised to double their pay. They paid no attention. Helmson offered triple the amount of salt, of trinkets, of bolts of cloth, of spears, of firearms and ammunition, but in vain.

They packed as much as they cared to carry. The tents and Helmson's own possessions were left untouched. A few minutes later, they set out, the trackers in the lead. Only the head askari and Helmson's gun bearer, Rakali, stayed with the white man. Their personal honor demanded that they remain faithful to the promise they'd given Helmson, to stay with him to the end.

But they probably expected Helmson to show his good sense. Only a crazy man would insist on continuing into the forest under such conditions.

Helmson knew this. Though he was very determined,

he knew when he'd been beaten. Next time, though . . . if there were a next time.

His employer might fire him. *Should that happen,* Helmson thought, *I'll raise my own expedition and go after Greystoke.* The unnamed man who wanted Greystoke captured alive would reward whoever succeeded.

Helmson wished he had not sent that runner with the news that Tarzan had been captured. To have to announce now that the ape-man had escaped was to double his humiliation. In fact, Helmson did not send a second runner with the bad news. He wanted to put that off as long as possible.

The third day on the path back to the base camp near the edge of the Ituri, Helmson saw coming toward him two black men. He knew them at once. They were runners he had used to carry his messages to HQ. Behind them were several armed askari. And close behind them were three white men. The rest of a safari strung out behind them.

He at once recognized one of the whites, an Irishman named Fitzpagel. He had been in charge of the camp from which Helmson's expedition had departed. Yet, here he was with two white men and a hundred askari, trackers, and bearers.

The American hailed Fitzpagel. They shook hands and Fitzpagel introduced the two whites, Umbrank and Silts, two Englishmen. Then Helmson asked the Irishman the purpose of this completely unexpected safari.

Fitzpagel was a small thin man with long bright-red hair and greenish eyes. His narrow foxish face was smeared with a coat of some foul-smelling insect repellent. He wore a white pith helmet, a long-sleeved white shirt, long trousers, and knee-length leather boots. A huge six-shooter was in a holster supported by a very broad and thick leather belt. Another sheath held a large knife.

One corner of his thin-lipped mouth was wrapped around a big cigar. He spoke in a Kilkenny brogue.

"Our mysterious boss, may God bless his shriveled soul, has ordered ye be helped. From the looks of ye, I'd say ye do indeed need help."

"You mean you were supposed to find us and then help us?" Helmson said.

"It was no problem finding ye," Fitzpagel said. "The runners just backtracked their own tracks and led us right to ye, though I'm amazed to see ye so soon and without yer safari, only two men. So ... why're ye slinking home, yer tail between yer legs?"

Helmson was cautious in his reply. First, he had to find out how much Fitzpagel knew. That didn't take long. The Irishman told him that the portable radio transmitter-receiver was now only a hundred miles away. It would be coming in a few days to the very edge of the Ituri. But its heavy equipment, including a small electric generator with a large supply of petrol, could not be moved swiftly.

When it was established, it could send shortwave messages to Nairobi. Thus, the runners only would need to go through the Ituri forest to the station.

Eventually, though, the distances to be crossed would be too long to use even the runners. Unless Helmson and Fitzpagel achieved their goal very quickly, the men stationed with the radio would just have to wait until the safari brought its prize back.

"You don't know who we're after?" Helmson said.

"It's a who then, not a what? Indeed, I don't know. I was to help ye get something, whatever it was. I was to ask ye what that thing was when I caught up wi' ye. This whole thing is so secretive, so lacking in information. I come here sort of blind and deaf, ye might say. The divil knows it's a most inefficient way to conduct business. What if . . ."

Fitzpagel stopped short. Three shocks, each only a few seconds from the previous, drove through the ground. They seemed to turn the earth to jelly. None of these were strong enough to throw the men down on the ground. But the men were silent until the earth had ceased to tremble.

Then Fitzpagel spoke.

"I think old Mother Nature's working up to something big."

11

I T TOOK TARZAN less than a second to identify the odor. It came from Malskree the golden cat, a feline too small to be a danger to the ape-man. It was nearby and on the ground; this meant it was hunting various little mammals.

Tarzan continued, but found no sight or smell of the Ben-go-utor.

Though angry, he kept alert. The bear-man might attack from the darkness. Or a big cat, a leopard, might encounter him. However, since there were very few leopards who were maneaters, especially in this part of the forest, Tarzan wasn't much worried about them.

While walking through the woods, Tarzan's anger grew. This time, it was because Helmson had his father's hunting knife. That weapon had been his constant companion and his frequent savior since he had been a child. He had discovered it when he had first entered his long-dead parents' cabin in his native West African rain forest. He hadn't known then that two of the skeletons were his mother's and father's. But he had found the knife near the bones of one. He had picked it up and soon learned what its use was, though he then had no name for it.

Ever since, he had felt the blade was a part of his body.

But to go back now, to shadow the safari, and to wait until he had a chance to get the knife back would mean more delay. No matter how highly he valued the knife, he placed Jane higher than it or anything else. She was beyond valuation.

At dawn, he came across some fine fat specimens of Horta the pig. He was hungry, so he stopped long enough to stalk them. Then, with the knife he had taken from the dead askari, he surprised and slew a sow. He carried the still-bleeding body up a tree to a branch closer to the sky than to the earth. He ate choice raw parts of the carcass and found them good. For dessert, he devoured some fat and juicy Umpa the caterpillar.

Then he moved on to a tree distant from the one where he'd eaten. For two hours, he slept on a large branch. Though he had no sheets or blankets, he snoozed away quite warm and comfortable. But he had set his unconscious alarm system, a sensitivity to unusual noises or odors, to rouse him instantly if danger was nearby.

If the business of looking for Jane and the threat of the Ben-go-utor had not been vexing him, he would have been content with this kind of life for a long time. Filling his belly whenever he was hungry, and traveling swiftly when the whim seized him or just loafing and thinking his thoughts, neither quite great-ape thoughts or quite human thoughts, thoughts that could be labeled nothing but Tarzanic, was the kind of life he reveled in.

He awoke refreshed and was quickly up and about. While he progressed westward through the forest's middle terrace, he snacked on insects and fruit. Then, before the evening dusk, he snatched a tiny antelope from the jaws of a genet cat. After eating most of this, he dropped the remains from a branch. They would be gone by morning, devoured by ants, beetles, and larger predators. The scavengers kept the forest floor clean.

So far, he had no loin covering. Helmson had not replaced the torn-off leopard-skin breechclout. Probably, the American thought that a naked prisoner was one who felt more helpless without clothes. It also took dignity away from the prisoner.

Helmson did not know the history of Tarzan well enough. Until Tarzan was eighteen, he had gone naked. Then, when Kulonga, a black warrior, had slain Tarzan's foster mother, Kala the great ape, Tarzan had slain Kulonga in revenge. He had taken the dead man's weapons, a heavy spear and bow and a quiver full of arrows. Also, he had put on Kulonga's leopard-skin loin covering. One of the peculiar ideas the naive ape-man had then was that wearing clothes made you more human. He had gotten this from a picture book found in the cabin of his dead parents.

Now that he was more learned in the ways of the world, he felt no need for covering of any kind while alone and in the jungle.

The morning of the next day, he came across a river. He followed it upstream, thus moving generally northward. Along its banks the vegetation became the thick bush which most whites, he knew, pictured as rain forest, though the true rain forest was relatively open, more or less bush free, and much cooler.

This jungle was thick with both tall trees and small, though the canopy was more open. More sunlight came through, so the ground was crowded with bushes of various kinds. These scratched the skin and made it bleed and so attracted even more stinging, biting, and sucking insects. And this jungle was hotter.

The river itself was sometimes narrow, mostly only a hundred feet wide but sometimes expanding to three hundred feet across. Hippos, crocodiles, and fish both large and small abounded in it. Long sleek otters thrived here, and so did the many fish eagles, kingfishers, herons, storks, and vultures above it and alongside it. Their raucous cries and shrieks tore the air.

Tarzan knew that there would be native villages along

it. They would not be inhabited by the Ituri pygmy. Those people lived in the rain forest, where the larger natives would fear to venture.

Just before dusk, Tarzan came to a collection of twenty grass-roofed huts. He moved through the trees until he was close enough to hear the conversation of the natives. They spoke one of the Bantu languages. That was clear enough. What was not so clear were the words. He could understand only a few, and he wasn't sure that these meant what similar words in related dialects meant.

Would any of them know French or English? They had metal spearheads and factory-made cloths and some European pottery. But that meant nothing. Trade routes could extend a thousand miles and involve the passing of trade goods through many tribes. These people may never have seen a white man.

Though he didn't think that Jane and her abductors had come this way, he had to make certain. Someone who could interpret for him might be in this village. Thus, a few minutes later, he walked into the midst of the circle of huts. The women were cooking and chattering away. The children were playing. The men were drinking beer and gambling. Almost all became aware at the same time that a big naked white man . . . or perhaps they thought he was a ghost . . . was standing near them. He was smiling, and both hands were held out before him, showing that he was peaceful.

That made no difference. Shrieking, they all ran off into the bush.

Tarzan shrugged. They probably did think that he was a ghost or a demon.

He found an empty ceramic pot, undoubtedly a trade item. He put into it some of the villagers' food, fish from the river and cultivated millet and vegetables. He took it into the bush and ate the food. Afterward, he placed the empty pot close enough to a hut so it would be found easily when they returned. These people had very little, and the pot was very valuable to them.

That night, far from the river and back in the rain forest, Tarzan slept high up in the fork of a tree. Sometime, perhaps about midnight, he awoke. The sudden hush, the abrupt cessation of the jungle noises, had yanked him from an untroubled sleep. He sat up, drawing his knife from the sheath at the same time. He sniffed. There was a very slight breeze. But it was enough.

Drifting from upwind was a very thin stink. Yet, it was thick enough for him to know that the Ben-go-utor was nearby.

He stood up slowly and stretched as a cat would. The moonlight spilled through breaks in the green ceiling. It made dapples here and there. He saw nothing move across the dim light. But he knew that the creature was a darker part of the darkness. It was approaching, and it could not be doing so out of a desire to benefit him.

Why? Tarzan thought. *What have I done to him?*

He heard a very slight noise above him. It could be an animal clinging to the side of the tree and its claws scraping the bark as it moved. Or . . . it made no difference. He leapt from the fork onto a big branch, whirling in the air to face the thing above if it dropped. He did not jump far enough. Looking up, he saw something blot out the moon above him. Then the creature had fallen on him, and Tarzan struck the back of his head and his back on the branch.

That impact knocked the breath from him. It tore the knife from his hand, and the knife dropped into the dark depths. He gasped for breath.

Hands . . . not claws but hands . . . closed around his throat. The thing's stench was hard in his nostrils. It would be harder as soon as he was able to draw in air. At this moment, he could not do so. He was half-stunned.

The thing growled, sounding like the bear from which it might be descended.

For some reason, the hands quit squeezing so hard. The oxygen Tarzan so desperately needed reached his lungs. But the hands resumed their squeezing. Again, he could not breathe.

The Ben-go-utor growled once more.

Then, he spoke. One word only he uttered. It wasn't from a human mouth, but it was formed well enough for the ape-man to recognize that word.

Helmson took Fitzpagel away from the natives so that they could talk unheard. He told the Irishman of his experiences with Greystoke. But he left out parts. There were certain truths that the Irishman should not know. Not yet, anyway, and maybe never.

Fitzpagel said nothing until Helmson had completed his tale. Then he coughed, drew in more smoke from his cigar, coughed again, and said, "That is quite a saga. An epic. Now . . . this man we're after, this Greystoke. Until you told me, I didn't know we were after a man or some mythical monster or what. Apparently, I'm not trustworthy. Maybe so.

"Until now, I never really believed in the existence of this Tarzan, no more than I did in leprechauns. But . . . if what ye say is true . . . I've no reason to doubt ye . . . then I ask meself a hard question that must have a hard answer.

"I ain't a coward, and I'll kill the man who says I am. But I've heard much about this man, though I didn't believe none of it. Anyway, the question? Should I go after this half-ape African Himself and most likely end up dead and in a manner not particularly to me liking? Should I stick to me promise and go after him if he be man, divil, or beast or all three? The reward's enough for me to take it easy the rest of me life and drink only the best of whiskey. But what're me chances of collecting that reward? What you tell me about him makes me doubt the chances'd be high."

"It's up to you to go with me or go back to Nairobi," Helmson said. "You're a free agent."

"Free? I have orders to work under ye, a man whom the ape-man has so far bested. Don't free me any frees."

"I haven't got all day," the American said.

Fitzpagel frowned. Then he smiled. He said, "Here's me hand, sor. One shake of yer hand, and I'm in this up to the hilt. No turning back then. And together maybe we'll be able to do what neither could do alone."

They shook hands, each admiring the strength of the other's grip. But Helmson thought that the Irishman's brogue was rather thick. Fitzpagel was surely exaggerating his native idiom. Why? So he could make others believe that he was a clown, a stage Irishman? Thus, they'd tend to underestimate him.

Then Fitzpagel said, "One thing I don't understand. How in the divil's name can we find Greystoke in that howling green hell?"

Helmson smiled, and he said, "Leave that to me."

The ball to raise money for the war effort was being held in the Hudson River mansion of one of Stonecraft's very wealthy friends. It was close to ten in the evening, near the time for Stonecraft to leave the party for his home. Early to bed, and so on.

In a minute, the music and the dancing would be stopped by the host. Then he would introduce the man whom everybody knew very well. And the multibillionaire would announce how much money had been raised this evening. After which, he would announce that he was donating two million dollars. Before the applause had ceased, he would be on his way out of the house.

A servant quietly interrupted him while he was circled by admirers. Or, as he considered all of them, sycophants, shoe kissers. The servant extended a silver tray. Stonecraft removed the envelope from the tray and opened it. There was a brief message on the expensive paper.

Decoded, it read: Helmson and Fitzpagel united. Very bad news. Greystoke escaped. Helmson's safari deserted. Fitzpagel asks, Should he fire Helmson or continue the search with Helmson?

Stonecraft turned pale. He glared. Then he turned red. The people around him wondered if this meant bad news for the stock market. If so, would he tell them what was wrong? Would they be ruined? Or, at least, considerably poorer?

The magnate said nothing. He stood still. Something momentous was making his mind whirl. What? What?

But the great man, after bowing to them, walked off. Not a word, not a word! This must be very serious!

It was serious. But it had nothing to do with them.

Stonecraft was wondering if he should organize still another expedition. This one would be sent into the Belgian Congo after Jane Clayton, Lady Greystoke, and her abductors. It wouldn't be easy to find them, but it would be easier, far far easier, than catching Lord Greystoke.

Then, if she were captured, she could be used to get Greystoke to surrender himself and to reveal his knowledge of the secret. *The Secret.* The words burned brightly in his mind. The only thing really worth having. Once he had that, he could get everything else he desired.

12

TARZAN HAD NOT at first understood the word that the Ben-go-utor had uttered. It had sounded somewhat familiar. But it had seemed to come from far away. And, if it had been English, it certainly had been distorted in transmission.

Again, the hands around his throat relaxed their grip, but they did not go away. He could breathe easier. Though the ape-man was pressed down by the creature's great weight and its stench made his intestines seem to writhe snakelike, the roaring in his ears subsided.

The bear-man again spoke the word.

Now, the ape-man understood it.

The creature's larynx, tongue, teeth, and mouth chamber probably were not quite like those of human beings. Thus, they could only approximate some human sounds. Some, however, were very close to those human languages used. But the *t*, for instance, was a click. The *a* was long and far back in the mouth. The *r* was really a *d* or sounded as such to the ape-man.

But the word was clear enough.

"Tarzan."

The ape-man had been surprised many times before. Few had matched the astonishment he now felt.

He managed to say, though weakly, "Yes. I am Tarzan."

The hands around his throat relaxed even more. Then

the Ben-go-utor spoke rapidly. Tarzan did not understand a word.

When the bear-man ceased talking, Tarzan spoke in every language he knew: Mangani, French, English, German, the speech of Mbonga's tribe in West Africa, a dozen Bantu languages and dialects, Berber and Arabic tongues, and even in phrases he had picked up from many other languages.

The creature shook his head in a quite human gesture. Then he repeated what he had said.

Tarzan shook his head.

While he had been listening to the creature, he had decided on what action he would take. This thing might not be as hostile as he had thought. Perhaps he was proposing a truce between them, a time to get acquainted. Tarzan would have liked that. For one thing, he was very curious about how the Ben-go-utor had learned his name. Where had he heard *Tarzan*?

It seemed to the ape-man that the bear-man could only have acquired some familiarity with his name in one way. He had been shadowing Helmson's party, and he had eavesdropped enough to pick up Tarzan's name. But, if he didn't understand human languages, how could he link the name with its owner? Why would he concern himself at all with Tarzan?

Why would he be trying to make himself understood to Tarzan, if, indeed, that was what he was attempting to do?

The ape-man requested that the bear-man release him. He knew that his words would not be understood. But perhaps the creature would respond to the tone of Tarzan's voice.

The bear-man did not rise up from his position.

Then Tarzan *commanded* him to get off.

That failed to get any response except a torrent of the gibberish. Several times, however, the ape-man heard his name.

Angry, Tarzan once more commanded it to release him. Then, knowing that he was getting nowhere through words, he took action. He heaved with all his strength, bracing his back as much as possible and pushing down on the branch with his left foot. He doubted that he could dislodge or raise the creature very far. But, for the moment, he just wanted to get his left arm free.

The bear-man was lifted up a little. That was enough. Though he squeezed down on Tarzan's throat again, he gave Tarzan, however unwillingly, the space he needed.

Tarzan stabbed his index finger in the creature's right eye.

The Ben-go-utor roared and grabbed his eye. At the same time, his left hand loosed its hold on the ape-man's throat. He reared up far enough for Tarzan to stab his other eye with his right index finger.

He screamed then and raised his left hand to cover the other eye.

The ape-man slammed his left fist into the bear-man's nose. Though it wasn't the stunning blow Tarzan could have delivered if he were standing up, it did rock the creature. By the dim light, Tarzan saw dark blood flow from his nostrils. Tarzan reached up and twisted the nose. He followed this with another fist against the bear-man's receding chin.

Despite his pain, the Ben-go-utor reached out with both hands and tried to seize Tarzan's throat.

The ape-man braced his left leg against the branch and rolled. His heave had all his exceedingly great strength in it. Though the bear-man must have weighed at least a hundred pounds more than Tarzan did, he was shifted to his left. Alarmed, he stopped feeling for Tarzan's throat and tried to grab the rough bark to halt the rolling.

He failed.

Bellowing, he went over the side into the abyss.

His flailing right hand seized Tarzan's hair. And Tarzan was pulled toward the edge of the branch.

The painful yank on his long hair was something he could not resist. He was dragged over the side, and he followed the Ben-go-utor.

But the creature unclutched the ape-man's hair. Tarzan could see him only dimly because both of them were now in the shadow of the branch and the canopy. He was still bellowing, and his arms were still windmilling.

Though the ape-man fell silently, his arms, too, were flailing. Then he was crashing through huge broad leaves and small branches. Twice, his hands closed on small branches. But these broke, and he slipped on through them toward the next great branch. Again, he smashed through small branches and great leaves. But his fall had been somewhat slowed.

Then he smashed into something . . . it wasn't as hard as wood would have been . . . and he became unconscious.

When he awoke, he was lying on something that was soft in some places and hard in others. He didn't know how long he had been knocked out. There seemed to be little change in the patterns formed by the sifting of moonlight through breaks in the forest ceiling.

He felt the body underneath him. It was covered with long hair, and it stank abominably. Also, Tarzan's face was pressed against a thick coat of hair and a wetness.

Soon Tarzan regained all his wits. He was, of course, lying on the body of the creature he had dubbed the Ben-go-utor. The liquid was blood, perhaps from his nose, perhaps from his foe's nose.

He noted that the normal jungle sounds had resumed. The strident high-pitched locusts were keening. The tree frogs were booming along in chorus. The night birds were calling.

His hands felt both sides of the big body just below

him. Then they went down until they touched a flat surface of bark on one side and a vertical surface on the
other. Had they landed twelve inches to either side, both
would have been shunted on down into the abyss.

The Ben-go-utor wasn't dead, not yet, anyway. The
ape-man could feel the massive chest rise and fall, and he
could hear a bubbling in the creature's throat.

Cautiously, Tarzan slid backwards off the body. When
he was entirely on bark, he rose. There he took inventory
of his injuries. He felt deep scratches or gashes on his
face, chest, and legs and other parts of his body. Some of
them were bleeding. His nose hurt, though the blood
flow from it was now slight. His ribs felt as if they had
been fractured, but he couldn't be sure. He decided, finally, that he'd hurt much more if they really were
cracked.

Just as he quit his inspection, a ray of moonlight came
through a hole overhead. Goro the moon had moved
slightly on his westward course. His silvery beam fell on
the bear-man, revealing a stretched-out form. His mouth
was open, and his eyes were closed. Blood welled up
through the thick fur from many scratches or gashes.

Tarzan was in a quandary. He wanted to take the time
to capture the creature and learn enough of his language
to find out what he was doing. Though the ape-man
learned languages quickly, he might take many days to
understand this being well enough for his purposes. But
he had to leave very soon.

What could he do with the Ben-go-utor? The creature
might die soon unless he got medical help or, at least,
nursing from Tarzan. The thought of his death did not
particularly bother Tarzan. He had no love for him. But
the bear-man might not be hurt fatally. And, when he recovered, he might set out on Tarzan's trail again.

Though Tarzan had no knife now, he didn't need one
to kill the creature. All he had to do was to roll the un-

conscious bear-man over the side of the branch. At this point there was no branch just below this one. His foe would smash into the ground fifty feet below. That would be that.

Tarzan was never indecisive for very long. He turned away from the prone body and climbed to the ground via the parasitic vines growing on the trunk. He then prowled around the tree but could not find the knife. It might be visible when daylight came. But it might not be. He'd spent too much time occupied with the safari and the bear-man. He wouldn't use up any more.

A moment later, he was walking toward what he supposed was the west. Because of his injuries, he moved more slowly than usual. While he was moving so sluggishly, he thought of what several of his friends in England had said. "Everything happens in threes."

He'd had two bad falls in trees and been lucky enough not to kill himself or suffer broken bones. But, if there was anything to this superstition—and he didn't believe that it had any substance—he'd soon have a third bad fall. And that would probably be fatal.

Or so his less sceptical friends would say.

Pure nonsense, Tarzan thought.

Several seconds later, he stepped on dirt that caved beneath his foot. Though he tried desperately to step back onto firm ground, he was too late. The covering of earth and the thin boughs and leaves holding the earth broke beneath him. He fell headlong into the pit dug to trap unwary elephants or other large creatures.

Helmson had told Fitzpagel what had happened to cause the expedition to fail. The American had left out parts of his story, but it seemed to him it would appear to be a seamless narrative.

Nevertheless, he soon became aware that Fitzpagel was questioning the askari and trackers and some of the bearers. Apparently, Fitzpagel wasn't sure that he had gotten all the truth.

Helmson did not like to be doubted. Yet, he could do nothing to stop the Irishman's questionings. If he tried to do that, he'd make Fitzpagel even more suspicious than he now seemed to be.

After a day of thinking about this, Helmson quit worrying. Why should he be concerned about Fitzpagel finding out any of his leader's secrets? The only other person who'd known much . . . and he hadn't known a lot, really . . . was Mitchell. That possible informant was dead.

So, why not let Fitzpagel pry as much as possible. He'd learn nothing he could use against Helmson.

The American had no doubt that Fitzpagel was trying to find out just how Helmson had tracked the untrackable, the legendary Tarzan of the Apes.

In any event, Helmson was sure of several things. The man who'd originated this big hunt was ruthless and unforgiving. Especially if, as he had guessed, that man was Stonecraft. Whoever it was, he wouldn't forgive those he held responsible for the failure of the expedition. He would have fired Helmson as soon as he learned of the fiasco.

But, Helmson reassured himself, the big chief couldn't do that. Once Helmson was removed, no one was left to locate their quarry. Like it or not, his employer had to keep him on his payroll.

Helmson was smug. But underneath that feeling was one that things were not quite right. It was as if all flies, except one, had been cleared out of a huge room. The buzzing of that single fly, though it was in a far-off corner, irked him. Like that fly, one question kept coming back and buzzing in his mind. Why was his employer so desperate about capturing Greystoke? This shouldn't bother him, but it did. The reward he'd get if he was successful should make him completely satisfied with his lot. Why, then, did he care that he didn't know the answer?

The point was that he did care, and he could not rest until that question was answered.

Helmson did not know it, but Tarzan had once commented, "For every cat that curiosity has killed, it's killed a hundred monkeys. For every monkey, a thousand men."

13

SELDOM CAUGHT OFF guard, Tarzan was taken by surprise when the earth opened up beneath him. Nonetheless he was as wary and as quick to act as Sheeta the leopard. Even as he fell, he pushed with his right hand against the side of the earth wall of the pit. That slight deviation from the vertical might be enough for him to avoid being impaled.

Success depended on the setup at the bottom. Was there only one large sharp-pointed stake in the center of the pit? Or were there many stakes spread out in the bottom?

Tarzan didn't actually think all this as he hurtled into the hole. His bruised muscles did not act as quickly as usual, but they responded swiftly enough. His reflexes took over, and they, coupled with his especially quick thinking, were enough.

Knees bent, he landed on soft earth. And the fact that he had not been impaled showed that he had missed the stake or stakes.

He was in a darkness blacker than the one on the ground above him. But he could feel around the pit. His luck had held. Instead of many upward-pointing stakes, there was only one. And that was in the center of the pit.

He estimated that the pit was approximately six feet long and five feet wide. At the moment, he could not estimate its height. When he stood on tiptoe and stretched up his arm, his fingertips did not reach the edge of the opening.

The trap had been designed for any large animal, but especially for the forest elephant. This wasn't as large as its fellow Tantor of the savannah, but it was stull huge—certainly large enough to provide many meals for a band of pygmies. He was fairly certain that the diggers were the small people of the Ituri jungle.

For several minutes, the ape-man launched himself upward again and again with all his power. Once, his fingertips touched the edge of the pit. But the dirt crumbled beneath his fingers, and he fell back to the bottom.

He decided to attempt to work the pole loose.

At that instant, he smelled Sheeta the leopard.

Though only a slight breeze was blowing above the top of the pit, Tarzan detected the drifting odor. He knew that the big cat was very close. He looked upwards. There was more light there than at the bottom of the pit, just enough for him to see a very vague shape. With a little more illumination, Sheeta's eyes would have reflected some light.

Certainly, the cat's eyes could collect more light than his could. So, it saw him somewhat more clearly than he saw it. And Sheetah's nose had already told it that a human was in the hole—a very sweaty and blood-smeared human.

Tarzan heard a low growl.

Without thinking about it, Tarzan growled back.

He was tense, battle ready. The hairs on the back of his neck bristled. His heart was beating fast.

If the cat was one now too old to catch its accustomed prey, it may have become a maneater. Or the great feline might be a young one, so hungry it would overcome its natural wariness of human beings.

The leopard snarled. Tarzan snarled back. Though his

human wits were not clouded, his body was reverting to the beast state.

He had very little room to evade Sheeta, to sidestep him. And he had no weapons except his quickness, his great strength, and his teeth. These had been enough in the past, and he had no doubt that they would be so in the future. If he was wrong . . . well, he did not fear The Hideous Hunter, the one who came to all, the strong and the weak. Even that inevitable one, if he tackled Tarzan, would know he had been in a fight.

For a few seconds, Sheeta did not move. He was judging the depth of the pit as well as he could in this darkness. If he decided that he could leap completely back out of the pit, then he would launch himself. If he estimated that the pit was too deep, he would reluctantly go on his way.

Tarzan, keeping his gaze on the dark mass, saw that it suddenly became bigger. He was standing up. Then . . . smaller. He was crouching to leap down.

Tarzan had felt the stake in the center of the pit's bottom. He knew exactly where it was in relation to the sides of the pit. He moved behind the stake. As Sheeta sprang out and down, Tarzan leapt up and slightly backward with all the power of his mighty legs. The top of his back brushed against the dirt wall of the pit. His hands darted out. He couldn't see any better, but his judgment was unerring.

Each hand grabbed one of Sheeta's ears. Then, as Tarzan came down and his feet thrust into the dirt floor, he yanked hard.

The leopard had time for one squall. One of his paws raked Tarzan's shoulder. After that, he was silent.

The ape-man felt around the stake and the carcass. The sharpened end of the pole had speared through the big cat's throat and come out of his neck.

Tarzan lifted the heavy body from the stake and dumped

it on the dirt. Then, as he had done so many times, he placed a foot on the dead beast he had slain in combat. The wild victorious beast announcing that, once again, he had conquered a deadly enemy, he pounded his chest and gave vent to the victory cry of the bull great ape.

It rose up out of the pit and spread throughout the forest for at least a mile. Monkeys and birds screamed with fear. Another leopard, not very far away, growled and stood still for a moment.

Again and again the cry soared out through the jungle. Not until long after Tarzan had ceased calling did the smaller creatures settle back down to their nightly routines of hunting or sleeping.

By then, Tarzan was back in a thoroughly human state or, at least, as human as he could be. And he was working on getting out of the pit.

Since the lower part of the pole was buried deep, it resisted coming up for a long time. He finally got it free of the dirt by digging it out with his fingers and jerking the pole back and forth. When he had pulled it completely out, he felt the pole where it had been in the ground. The part coated with earth was at least six feet long. The part that had protruded above the ground, still sticky with leopard blood, was at least four feet long.

He took an even longer time pushing the pointed end of the stake level with his shoulders and horizontally into the side of the pit. He drove it in by hitting it with the palms of his hands. By the time it was in far enough, his hands, though they were thickly calloused, hurt him.

Ignoring the pain, he leapt up onto the stake. He landed on it with both feet, ending in a squatting position. No man living could have made so high a standing high jump. He was so close to the wall of the pit that his right shoulder scraped the dirt from it. The pole sagged a little. But, for the moment, at least, it held.

Slowly, he stood up, his right hand trailing along the

wall. His hand felt the edge of the pit. Quickly, before the pole could slide farther out of the wall, he leapt again.

He made a quarter turn as he came up. His elbows landed on the edge. His fingers dug into the earth. Then he worked himself forward until his body was far enough beyond the edge for him to be almost entirely on the ground.

He sat up and rested. At the same time, he listened and sniffed deeply for something to indicate that another leopard was near. He heard and smelled nothing alarming.

That, however, did not mean that Sheeta was not close to him. He rose to his feet. He would go up a tree and find a place to sleep until dawn. Then, he would have to make a knife or a short spear. That wouldn't be easy without flint or chert to fashion into a cutting blade.

Just as he began climbing up a tangle of lianas and other plants at the foot of a giant tree, he felt a vibration through the lianas. His feet, braced against the side of the tree, also felt the vibration. It was coming up from the deep, the rock base that lay beneath the thin soil. It was shaking the roots and then surging up through the trunk.

He dropped from the almost horizontal position he'd adopted while climbing via the lianas. The ends of his toes banged painfully into the bark. Then he was on the ground. Moonlight flashed down on him. He looked up.

The thick canopy was moving, creating breaks through which the light of the moon blinked on and off as if sent by a semaphore. And he could feel the vibrations through the soles of his feet. He got dizzy.

Conquering the vertigo, he ran as fast as he could on what suddenly seemed to be a half-hard and dirty jelly. He didn't know where he was going. Even in this dim light, he could see the colossal plants swaying. And, from the canopy, leaves showered down on him. Then some small animals, screaming, struck the forest floor near to him. The canopy was an uproar as the many birds, monkeys, and other beasts living in it voiced their fear.

He'd been through such tremors before. But this could get worse, and he wanted to be in a clearing before some titanic tree crashed down on him. At the same time, he realized that, probably, only long-dead and very rotten trees would fall. The canopy was so solid, thick, and wide that it held up most of the dead trees in a wide area.

He was, he quickly found out, wrong.

The ground heaved beneath him, sending him tumbling onto his face. He rose into the air as the earth swelled. Then it fell. Then it rose again. As he clung helplessly to the ground, he heard the thunder of a crashing giant. It seemed to be behind him.

No! It was in front of him.

No! It was on his left.

Then it was all around him.

The shaking was accompanied by a vast beating sound. It seemed to come up from Nature's heart itself, to beat as the heart of the creatrix of all life would beat. He thought he heard an echo of the heart, a terrible booming bouncing off the center of the earth herself.

He was stunned and deafened. His body seemed to turn to a quivering substance like the earth below him. Then he was lifted even higher and dropped even lower. A sound as of gigantic cymbals clashing drove through his deafness and thrust him even deeper into silence. But he felt the earth shaking and felt the impact of tremendous trees smashing into the thin soil and the hard rocks below the soil.

Something lashed like a whip across his right arm.

He was lifted up by water and sent racing along with it. Where had that heavy body of water come from?

As far as he knew, there was no river or lake close by.

But he ceased to speculate. He was being rolled over and over on his side, then he was spinning forward like a circus tumbler. Nothing he could do to right himself and swim to the surface availed him. He was helpless under the water, and he soon would drown. Even if he could swim, he would not know which way was up and which was down.

Something struck his back—hard. He hurt so much that he opened his mouth to gasp. On his indrawn breath, he swallowed some water. That choked him. If he had been able to think, he would have expected to die very soon. But his brain, his nerves, all his body fought to live.

Then, his face was free of the heavy and relentless fluid which had been squeezing him to death. He sucked in a deep breath. Immediately after that, he was again yanked down into the darkness and the deep. He felt several hard blows in rapid succession on his left arm, chest, and right leg.

Whirling, urged onward by the irresistible, he rode to the surface once more. That lasted long enough for him to take four breaths, during which a downpour of rain pounded him from above.

How he managed to survive the long periods submerged, the objects he struck or which struck him, his being dragged over what had to be the soil-stripped rock floor of the forest, the great demands made of his muscles to keep swimming, he did not know.

In the end, which really was another beginning, the flood carried him to a river. Or so it seemed to him. He really had no way of determining whether he was caught up in a true river. But he was surely moving swiftly. And the rain striking him when his head was above the surface did not come from the usual tropical rain storms. This water would have threatened to submerge continents and their mountains, to plunge all life to the bottom of the sea.

Having managed to pull himself onto a large uprooted tree and to cling to a branch, he floated down the burgeoning waterway. Dawn came, and with it the rain. The gray fluid hurtling from the clouds slashed him. The bodies of dead animals, snakes, and birds floated by him. There were even dead hippos and crocodiles, beasts which should have survived any flood except the most prodigious. A number of times, black men, women, and children, corpses all, bobbed up and down as his tree trunk slowed or sped up to be passed or to pass. In an hour, he saw six drowned elephants.

He managed to pull himself higher on the tree and to lie in a tangle of small branches. He no longer had to hold onto a branch to keep from slipping completely into the water. Too tired to stay awake, he nodded off many times. Then he must have slept deeply. When he awoke, the sun was almost to the zenith. A hundred yards to his left was the rain forest. The trees along the edge of the river were several feet deep in the water. They probably represented the extent of the flood on this side. Tarzan could not guess how widely the river had spread or how high the flood had risen. For all he knew, he was fifty feet above the preflood level of the river.

His body was covered with dark bruises, scratches, and gashes. Even his bones seemed to hurt, though none seemed to be broken. Every time he moved, he was stabbed with pain. Nevertheless, he was glad that he was still alive. But he was also angry that his quest had been delayed even more. The course of the still-swollen river was in a general southern direction. Every second kept him from Jane and carried him farther from the country where she was still captive.

At last, just before the cloudy sky again became completely black with night, the tree trunk he was riding on grounded against a tangled pile of trees at a swerve of the bank. He didn't try to climb over the mass to the bank or try to swim to the bank. Though somewhat cold and waking often, he slept on the trunk.

He awoke with a start in the grayness of early dawn. For a moment, he did not remember where he was. Then, after rising and stretching like a big cat, he made his slow and painful way through the hill of timber, the tangle of trunks, branches, and high-piled mats of vegetation.

Just before he began wading through the water, he found a dugout boat. It was wedged between two massive trunks in the pile, and was relatively undamaged. All Tarzan needed was a paddle. However, he'd have to work hard to withdraw the craft from between the trunks. Just now, he wasn't physically able to do that. He needed rest and food before tackling the task.

The rain had ceased, though the black clouds were still muttering. Knee-deep in water, he entered the jungle. Here the plant life was thick. A native would have had to cut his way through with a machete. But Tarzan used the highway of the upper reaches when he could and plowed through or slid by the ground plants when he had to. The number of insects that had escaped drowning was amazing. There were thousands, and every one seemed to have bitten Tarzan—or was about to.

Along the way, he combined revenge with sustenance by eating some of the insects. He also ate fallen fruit until he caught a small violet-colored rodent. This he devoured. And then he found a newly dead bird tangled in a man-made net of grass. That meant that a settlement of some kind might be not too far away. Tarzan ate Nene—the beetles that were rapidly covering the bird—defeathered the bird, and ate it raw.

After this, he set off to locate the village. There he surely could find weapons and a paddle. He would return to the dugout and get it back into the water. Then, he would go as fast as he could up the river against its strong current.

He was lucky. The village for which he was searching was only two miles from where he had walked ashore. It was set back from the edge of the flood about a quarter of a mile and was on a large hill. He walked up the hill, concealed from the sight of anyone above by the trees and bushes. At the hilltop, he climbed a tree to survey the scene.

It was a typical native village, its round huts arranged in two concentric circles around the central space. There, women were working, preparing food, or taking care of the children. Their chatter was in a language unknown to him. It didn't even sound like Bantu.

There were very few men. Most of these would be out hunting now that it was not raining. The fields of crops below the village were completely or partly under water. The future looked grim for these people.

He saw a slight movement in a tree on the other side of the village. There, sitting on a branch, partly shielded by leaves, was someone Tarzan did not expect to see.

It was the Ben-go-utor.

14

HELMSON AND FITZPAGEL were awed by how much the earthquake had savaged the land around. Where the rain forest canopy had been one almost unbroken ceiling, it now had many great holes. The plants and the beasts and birds which had seldom seen full daylight were now exposed to its full glare. The safari had to swing wide to avoid the piles of colossal trees and the huge mass of vegetation which the trees had pulled down with them. This had resulted in a trail as curving and unpredictable as the path of a demented snake.

After a day of hard progress, Helmson announced that they would all rest tomorrow. They would not march for at least another day. But he left the camp in the morning and plunged into the forest, taking with him only two men. One was a tracker, and the other was his gun bearer, Rakali. Just before he walked into the ruined jungle, he spoke to Fitzpagel.

"I may not be back for several days. On the other hand, I may be back very soon. In either event, you're in charge while I'm gone."

Fitzpagel took off his bush hat, scratched his red hair, then smiled. His greenish eyes seemed to look into Helmson's mind.

"Ye're lost, ain't ye?"

"Of course not!" Helmson said. "What makes you say that?"

"We've not been traveling as fast as we should if ye knew the way. And now . . . ye look puzzled. Like ye don't know where to go. Maybe ye don't know where Greystoke is."

"I know!" the American protested.

"Sure ye do."

But Fitzpagel's grin made it clear just what he believed.

The truth was that Helmson, once so certain of locating Greystoke, though not with pinpoint accuracy, was getting desperate. The earthquake had destroyed the trail, so far anyway.

He wondered if Tarzan had been killed by the quake. If so, he—Helmson—would get only the sum he had been promised should he fail to bring back the ape-man alive. That was considerable. But it was small compared to the wealth promised if he succeeded. It was true that Helmson had had something else to ensure his fame and a very large fortune. But the quake may have ruined that, too.

He cursed silently, but was not one to give up easily. He strode away swiftly with the look of one who literally shone with confidence. Mgonda, the tracker, was fooled. But Rakali, the gun bearer, knew his employer too well. After so many years with Helmson, Rakali could read the white man's body movements and the expressions flitting across his face. They spoke to him as if they were his native language.

Helmson was very worried. And his air of confidence was false.

Knowing that did not make Rakali happy. The look on his own face made it clear he was afraid in this vast demon-haunted forest, and so was the tracker. That made three of them filled with dread. Three people alone, three who only had each other to boost their courage and lift their morale.

Rakali reviled the day he had agreed to go with Helmson into this frightening place.

Fitzpagel watched Helmson, Rakali, and Mgonda as they left the camp. Then he turned to Swifi, his own head askari. He told him to get rations and anything needed by a tracker and an askari. These two must leave within the hour to follow the Helmson party.

"They will stay on their trail but will keep out of sight. If Helmson finds Greystoke or Greystoke's trail, one will stay to observe. The other will return here at once. But he will go swiftly so that he can get here first. I want his report before Helmson gets here."

"Banki and Dweena are good men," Swifi said. "Though they will be afraid to go into the forest without many to accompany them, they will do it, or they will die. However . . ."

Fitzpagel asked, "Yes?"

"What if Helmson sees them following him? What do they say to him then?"

"Good thinking," the white man said, "but I've already thought of that. Banki and Dweena will tell Helmson that I sent them to guard him, to protect his party if it is in danger. They should claim to be his invisible backups. Also, if Greystoke should attack Helmson, Banki and Dweena will be watching, and they will try to capture him. I will remind them that they can wound Greystoke in the arm or the leg, so he can be captured. But they must be very careful if they have to shoot."

"What if Greystoke attacks them?"

"The orders still hold. They *must* not kill him."

"They are very good men," Swifi said. "But they are only men. I fear that they might have to kill him to keep him from killing them. Then what?"

"Tell them that, if that happens, they will die anyway. And tell them that their wives and children will be killed, and their village will be burned to the ground with all their tribe in the fire."

Swifi's eyes became very wide.

"You mean that?"

"Sometimes I lie," Fitzpagel said. "But I'm not lying now."

Swifi didn't see any sense to what the white man had said. What use would it be to kill Banki's and Dweena's family and tribe if Greystoke was already dead? He could understand taking such a revenge on an enemy who had killed a member of Swifi's tribe. However, usually, a murder could be paid for in cattle. That made good sense. Everybody satisfied and no more bloodshed. Why couldn't the white man understand that?

Nonetheless he said, "They will do as ordered."

He thought, *I'll tell them to run as swiftly as they can if the white demon does attack them. Then, if they can't escape him, they must try to kill the white demon. If that could be done. If the demon is invulnerable, then it's too bad for Banki and Dweena. But if he can be killed and if my two bloodbrothers kill him, then they must kill Fitzpagel. I will help them.*

He hoped that none of this would happen. He also wondered just what the sly one, Fitzpagel, was planning for Helmson. Nothing that was good, he was sure.

15

Tarzan didn't move. Flies crawled over him, and one ventured into his left nostril. But, like all those born and raised in the jungle of equatorial Africa, the ape-man could tolerate the annoying swarms of insects, for a time at least.

As suddenly as he had appeared, the Ben-go-utor was gone. He was very quick and graceful for such a huge and clumsy-looking creature.

Tarzan moved as quickly and as smoothly. He was down from the tree and running swiftly around the village and as close to the trees as he could. He hoped to catch sight of the bear-man before he was gone. It would be easier to trail him visually than by his scent or footprints.

When he got to the path from the village, near the point where it disappeared into the flood waters, he had to wait a while. The to-and-fro traffic of the natives lasted for several minutes. When nobody was in sight, he dashed across the path to the jungle on the other side. In a short time, he was at the tree on a branch of which the Ben-go-utor had sat. There was little wind, and the strong odor still hung here. The earth was so wet that the creature had not been able to avoid making prints.

Tarzan wondered if the bear-man had seen him. Or had he just retreated from the village to a place where he could be hidden yet could continue to watch? Did he plan to come back at night to the village to steal food?

Tarzan did not have to wonder long. The footprints abruptly disappeared. Not in the least puzzled by this, Tarzan stopped and looked up along the trunk of the tree just ahead of him. There, sitting on the lowest branch and looking down at him, was the Ben-go-utor.

He said, "Tarzan!"

The ape-man said, "Yes?"

The bear-man gestured with one hand. Tarzan understood at once. He was signaling that the ape-man should come up to him.

Tarzan shook his head. He made signs that the Ben-go-utor should come down to him.

The creature looked steadily at the ape-man for a moment. He could see that Tarzan wasn't hiding any weapons. Then, he smiled. At least, it seemed that he was smiling, though the expression might well have been his threatening grimace. In any event, he came down from the tree. He landed on all fours a few feet from the ape-man. Then, slowly, he stood up.

He raised both hands, palms outward. No mistaking that. It was a peace sign.

The bear-man uttered one word. Tarzan did not understand it, though there was something familiar about it. He shook his head. Again, the word was spoken. Tarzan listened carefully. Suddenly, he understood it.

Though the pronunciation only approximated the English name, it was now recognizable.

"Helmson!"

Tarzan was staggered. That one name seemed to open up the sky. Revelation roared from the sky and threatened to sweep him away as he had been swept away by the deluge.

Tarzan asked, "Helmson?"

The creature nodded. That may not have been his native way of expressing assent. But if it wasn't, then the bear-man had learned that from the American. Tarzan was certain of that.

The bear-man said, "Helmson!" Then he said, "Yes." Or what sounded like it.

After that, he seemed to have exhausted his stock of English. He spoke what was to Tarzan just gibberish. Finally, Tarzan raised his hand to indicate that the word torrent should stop. He then made signs that he would have to learn the bear-man's language. Then, they could communicate clearly, or more or less clearly, enough for Tarzan to comprehend, anyway, if aided by sign language.

By that time, the ape-man had become used to the Ben-go-utor's stench. And he did not believe that the creature was hiding bad intentions toward him. Not now, anyway, though Tarzan had no clear idea of what had changed the creature's mind. He had no doubt that Helmson had much or everything to do with it.

He now knew the answer to the question that had been bothering him. That was, how had Helmson always been able to locate him? Helmson had used the bear-man, a creature with a sense of smell that probably was superior even to the ape-man's.

But how was Helmson able to control the Ben-go-utor? Tarzan would have to master as much of the bear-man's speech as was needed to solve that puzzle.

He pointed northward. Then he made signs to ensure that the bear-man understood that he, Tarzan, wanted to go back northward, up the river. The creature indicated that he, too, wished to return to where they had come from. At least, that was what Tarzan thought he said. Tarzan then indicated that they first go back to the area of the village. They needed a supply of food and a boat. On a boat, they could travel much faster, at least for a long while. Also, Tarzan wanted to get weapons, especially a knife.

The bear-man agreed. On the way back, Tarzan

learned his companion's personal name. Or what he thought was his name—Rahb. Tarzan also learned that the name of Rahb's people was Shong.

The aspiration just before the *b* in Rahb was very strong. Close to the *ch* in the Scots *loch*. The *a* was halfway in pronunciation between the English *a* and *o*.

Rahb! Rahb! Tarzan repeated that several times. Then he began learning the names of various types of trees, the words for leaves, earth, and the birds, beasts, and insects they glimpsed. Actually, Rahb seemed to have very few names, just for living beings and objects. Every name was embedded in a phrase, and Tarzan had to separate the name from the attached particles if he were to translate the name into English.

When they got to the village, they stole a dugout, a bow, a quiver full of arrows, plantains, yams, two steel knives, and other trade items. Then they paddled back over the flood waters through the trees. When they came to what seemed to be the river itself, they paddled northward. By the end of the fourth day, Tarzan had learned enough of Rahb's language to communicate on a somewhat more than basic level.

By now, Tarzan felt that he could query Rahb about Helmson. He would have to use many signs to fill in the gaps left by his ignorance of the language. But Tarzan was sure that he would get a somewhat better picture of Rahb's past situation than he now had.

An hour before the sun was due to plunge below the tops of the trees lining the bank, seven boats came around the bend of the still-swollen river. Four were portable and collapsible aluminum craft. The rest were dugouts. They were only a quarter of a mile ahead of Tarzan. But he could easily identify Helmson and some of the natives.

However, he did not know the three white men. Of the black men, he recognized only two faces.

Apparently, Helmson saw him at the same time. He stood up in the prow of the big lead boat, and shouted a single word, unintelligible at this distance. Then he turned and yelled at the men behind him. Instantly, the many paddlers stepped up their pace. They began chanting.

Then Rahb stood up in his dugout. He roared a single name. "Helmson!"

It was doubtful that the approaching party could hear what he said or would have understood his not quite human pronunciation.

But at sight of him, the paddlers fell silent and quit paddling. For a moment, the fleet slowed down.

Helmson, however, grinned broadly, and he whooped.

Tarzan pulled Rahb down by his long black hair and spoke harshly.

"Shimdukwalunaseka!"

In Rahb's native tongue, that loosely translated as, "Head for the left bank! Quick!" Or that was what Tarzan, also using Rahb's signs as aids, intended the sentence-phrase to mean.

They got to the shore only twenty feet ahead of the first war boat. They slipped onto the solid green wall of the jungle. A moment later, the lead boat grounded, and two trackers left it to follow them. Behind them, swinging his machete to clear away the dense tangle, came Helmson. And behind him was the first of many pursuers.

Rahb and Tarzan at once took to the trees. The trackers did not even consider taking this avenue.

The swacking sound of the machetes trailed away and then was lost. After some time, the travelers on the trees came to what the ape-man considered the true forest, his beloved high-canopied forest relatively open at the ground level. He climbed to the very top of a giant tree and stuck his head above the green roof. Squinting against the brightness of the sinking sun, he looked westward. He could see only the seemingly solid mass of the jungle extending for countless miles.

But when he turned to the south, he was startled. There was a mountain there, far away. It seemed to be the only eminence within sight. It wasn't part of a range, not as far as Tarzan could see. But he knew from Martillo's manuscript and map that it was part of a range and that the rest of the range was out of view.

If he could have been able to climb higher, he would have seen the peaks of other mountains behind the lone one.

This mountain was black or seemed to be because of its distance. A wisp of smoke drifted from it. On its northward face was a gigantic mark. It was a reddish mass forming, with the help of imagination, the profile of a snake's head. Extending from the crude image of its open mouth was a long red streak. It was a forked tongue.

Tarzan was excited, though his normally stoic face did not reveal it. This was the volcanic mountain briefly described by the long-dead Spaniard in his manuscript. On the map was the legend, in Spanish, The Great Mother of Snakes. Martillo had not lied about this. And, if the mountain was here, perhaps the other things Martillo had written about also existed.

The manuscript and the map were now in Helmson's hands. But Tarzan had a photographic memory. For the first years of his childhood and early youth, he had been unable to read or write. The great apes who raised him knew nothing of writing or printing. Thus, he had developed powers of recall that depended entirely on his mind. Now, he could visualize the map and the manuscript as if they were projected on a screen.

Behind The Great Mother of Snakes was a land strange

even for Africa, that strangest of all lands. Martillo had described some of its wonders. Others, he had just named. These were more than enough to excite the imagination. They hinted of things exotic and also dangerous.

What especially made Tarzan wonder was what Martillo referred to in his manuscript as The Toucher of Time. What or who could that be? Tarzan vowed that, once he'd rescued his wife, he would return here. And he would explore this land.

Meanwhile, he had to retrace the many miles back to where the flood had carried him off. Then he would resume his quest to find Jane.

Rahb had decided to climb up to Tarzan's side. When he saw the mountain, he gestured violently, and he spoke to Tarzan in a fierce and intent manner. But his speech was too fast for the ape-man to understand any of his phrases. He would not have comprehended more than a few of them, anyway. Though he had made great progress in the language lessons, he still had a long road to travel.

Finally, the ape-man dammed the verbal flood. He then made it plain to Rahb that he was not yet at the point at which he could understand him easily. They would have to be patient until that time came.

Meanwhile, they'd have to augment the phrases with signs.

Tarzan asked him if he wished to accompany him back to the place where they had been carried off.

The bear-man nodded vigorously. But then, partly speaking, partly making signs, Rahb indicated they should stay for a while. Tarzan asked why.

He wasn't very surprised when Rahb indicated that they must take Helmson prisoner. Helmson held Rahb's mate as a hostage, and only he could tell them exactly where Rahb's wife was. Then Rahb revealed that she was pregnant. And he added that, once Helmson had told them where Rahb's mate was, he should be killed.

Rahb feared that, if they left Helmson behind, he might survive, and he might get back to where he kept Rahb's mate. He could move Rahb's mate—her name was Hbarki—to a place so far away that Rahb would never locate her.

Then he communicated to the ape-man—it wasn't easy to do so—that Rahb, his mate, and the unborn child were the last of their kind. The very last. Though his face was not as expressive as a human face, he managed to look very sad. Tears welled in his big pale-red eyes.

The last of his kind, Tarzan thought. He was touched with an empathetic sadness. There was little chance that *Homo sapiens* would disappear. A worldwide war, though it had killed many many millions, hadn't come close to making them extinct.

But the Mangani, the great apes, those whom he thought of as his own people, were very few. He didn't think they would survive for more than a few generations, if that long. Especially if the "civilized" people discovered that the Mangani existed. Then they'd be hunted down, shot, and stuffed as zoological specimens. Or those who escaped this fate would be caged, placed in zoos. In any event, they were doomed.

Thinking of this, he could understand what the Bengo-utor was feeling.

Nevertheless, there was Jane. He communicated to Rahb that her situation still demanded that he start immediately upriver. His own mate had to be rescued first—he did not wish to waste another moment, even to try to take Helmson captive. That wouldn't be easy since the white man was always surrounded by many of his own men.

If Rahb wished to stay here, he could do so. But if he came along with Tarzan, the two of them might find

Tarzan's wife. After she was safe, Tarzan would go with Rahb to rescue Hbarki. They would make Helmson very sorry indeed that he had caused them so much trouble and pain. Perhaps Rahb did not understand all that Tarzan tried to tell him. But the ape-man was sure that Rahb got enough of it to take whatever action he would wish to take.

Rahb did not reply at once.

Before he could speak, a firearm exploded, a rifle by its sound. A bullet whistled through leaves not six feet from Tarzan.

Tarzan launched himself away from the branch on which he'd been standing. He fell, and he grabbed the branch ten feet below him. Then he was hidden by a huge mass of purplish fungi.

He couldn't see Rahb. But, looking downward, he could see the men gathered near the base of the tree. All were black, and all were different from any he had ever seen before.

Then, several of them fired their rifles. A bullet struck the trunk only an inch from his head, though he was sure he had not been sighted.

Up to now, his pursuers had not been trying to kill him. But the situation had changed. These strangers were trying to shoot him dead.

He did not know why. He would find out.

16

SEVERAL MINUTES PASSED. By then, Tarzan understood that the strangers weren't shooting on purpose at him or at Rahb. The newcomers probably did not see him or Rahb.

Tarzan discovered their intended target. He was in a tree next to the one on which Tarzan hid. He was a black man and was lying face down on top of a huge branch. His hands were gripping the rough bark as if he feared he'd slide off from it. But he could not be seen from below. The newcomers were just firing at random into the foliage, hoping to flush the man out.

Tarzan could see at least twenty of the strangers. There might be more behind the trunks of nearby trees. All were blue-black, short, and husky. Their faces and bodies were painted with green, white, and red symbols. Affixed to their snakeskin headbands were green, white, and red plumes from a bird unknown to Tarzan. Apparently, the one who wore the most feathers, seven in all, was their chief.

Six men had rifles. Tarzan could not tell what their make or year was. But they were single shot and bolt action. They could be trade weapons of mid-nineteenth-century origin.

The rest of the warriors were armed with spears, machetes, and bows and arrows.

The man they hunted wore no headband or feathers.

The symbols painted on his back and legs were different from those of his hunters. He wore only a hyena-hide loincloth and a leather belt holding a sheath which held a huge iron knife.

Beside him lay an object that intrigued the ape-man. It was about two and a half feet long, two feet high, and six inches wide. It had an irregular shape. It seemed to be made of hippopotamus hide and was attached to a leather strap worn on the man's left shoulder.

Tarzan didn't have much time to speculate. The chief shouted an order. Tarzan did not understand the phrase. But the tree being climbed was next to the one on which their quarry was hiding. Tarzan had to decide whether to keep hiding in the fungal mass or make a break for it. Four of the riflemen had been sent aloft. Two were on the ground.

Tarzan looked for and found Rahb. He was on the same tree as the hunted man. He was, however, on a much higher branch. And he was partly hidden by a mass of intertwined lianas, flowers, and gigantic leaves.

Tarzan managed to catch Rahb's eye. Rahb showed the ape-man that he held in his hand the big hunting knife stolen from the village. He was ready to fight armed with the blade, his gorilla-strong body, and his wits.

Tarzan quickly decided to take action. He removed his bow and quiver from their casing, strung the bow, and fitted an arrow to the string. Leaning out from the fungus, he chose his target. His shaft pierced the side of a climber's neck.

Silently, the dead man plunged from the side of the trunk where he had been climbing up a tree which grew from the fork between two huge branches. His rifle fell with him. Both struck the jungle floor a few feet from the chief.

The chief jumped. A few seconds later, he yelled more orders. The two riflemen hastened to stand by him.

Meanwhile, the three surviving climbers came out of their paralysis and scrambled upward. One was too hasty. He lost his hold. Screaming, he fell at least sixty feet. By the time that he had hit the ground, another arrow had been loosed.

It drove through the shoulder of a rifleman by the chief. Though the shaft probably did not hit any vital organs, its shock power knocked the rifleman out. *Out* was the operative word. The stricken man was no longer in the action and would not be for a long time, if ever.

The chief and his rifleman ran away. Not until they were partly shielded by a great tree did they stop. Then they stuck their heads out far enough to get a good look. Tarzan ignored them. He had fitted another arrow to the string and was about to shoot at the last rifleman on the tree.

But he was startled by gunfire. It came from the ground, and it was not the bang!-bang!-bang! of bolt-action rifles. It was a continuous fire, a stutter as of a machine gun. Before he even located its source, he knew that it was from the Italian machine carbine. A glance confirmed that. It also told him that the chief and his bodyguard were dead or wounded.

And now Helmson was spraying his carbine fire on the climbers. He stopped only to slip in another magazine.

One of Helmson's white partners, the red-haired man with the foxish face, was shooting slowly and methodically with an Enfield rifle at other climbers. Between the firepower of the two white men, they had already brought down three riflemen and six spearmen. These lay at the foot of the tree. Among them was the last of the men on the tree.

Suddenly, the gun roar ceased.

The safari trackers and askari swarmed around the tree. They drove spears through the wounded, and they mutilated the dead. The white men did not try to stop them.

By then, Tarzan had raced from his tree to the next. As agilely as Manu the monkey, he descended to the branch on which the black man lay quivering. Without saying a word, Tarzan lifted him to his feet. Then Tarzan spun him around and hit him on the chin with his fist. He lifted the unconscious man over his shoulder and carried him up to the highest terrace. The hippopotamus-hide case swung by the strap from the man's shoulder. Rahb followed them.

They did not stop until they were long out of earshot of the safari. Rahb asked them, "Ashowmakesawhelmsonpota?" Rough translation: "How did Helmson get here?"

The ape-man said, "I don't know."

By then, the black man was stirring. Mumbling, he opened his eyes. It seemed to Tarzan that the mumbles were in some Bantu language. But the native, seeing the two standing over him, quickly closed his eyes. Under the dark skin pigment, he was pale. He muttered something, and this sounded somewhat familiar to Tarzan. Then the man opened his eyes again. What he had seen would not go away.

Tarzan pulled him up to a sitting position. The ape-man smiled, and he spoke soothingly in the tongue of the Waziri. Since he was the chief of the Waziri tribe, he knew that Bantu tongue well.

The man could not keep his eyes off Rahb. His teeth chattered.

Tarzan told the bear-man to move past the man so he could not see him. He did not blame his captive for his terror. Rahb was a scary creature to see. It was, perhaps, his half-human face that made him so fearsome in appearance.

The man could not keep from trying to look behind him. After a moment of this, the ape-man placed both hands on the sides of his head and restrained it. The man said something. His tone and expression said that he'd quit his annoying movements if Tarzan would release his head. Tarzan did so.

Then, to Tarzan's surprise, the man switched to the Ki-Unjuga dialect of KiSwahili.

"The language you spoke to me seems to be related to KiSwahili, a language I learned in Kenya. Ah, I see you understand it! Very well. I am Waganero of the Half Weasel clan of the tribe of Deenga, which is far far away from where I was born and where I lived until I was a man. But am I truly a man in the sense of being brave? I do not think so. On the other hand . . ."

Waganero seemed to realize he had been chattering.

He paused, then said, "Who are you? And what is the thing that stands behind me?"

The ape-man replied in KiUnguja. "I am Tarzan."

The man started, and his eyes widened. "Tarzan? The white demon whose mother was an ape?"

"You have heard of me?"

"Yes, when I was for several years on the coast, far from my land, which is hidden from the white men and most black people. But . . . I did not believe that you existed. I thought . . ."

"Never mind what you thought," the ape-man said. "Behind you is the Ben-go-utor who calls himself Rahb. He won't hurt you . . . unless you deserve it."

"Ben-go-utor?"

Tarzan ignored the question. He said, "Where did you come from? What are you doing here? In short, what is your story? Keep it as brief as possible. We are in a hurry."

Waganero pointed southward. "There is the land of The More than Dead, of Rafmana, The Toucher of Time, and of many more marvels and terrors. It is behind the mountain that has on the side toward the Deenga the image of The Great Mother of Snakes. She sometimes comes alive. Or so people say. She . . ."

"I saw her," Tarzan said.

"Yes. The mountain is a long way from here, though it is so large that it looks near."

As he spoke, the light began to dim. From far off came a rumble, the war rumble of Pand the thunder. A breeze began to flutter the leaves. Soon, the clouds would cover the sky. Then the thunder would bellow, and the lightning would crash over the forest ceiling. The army of white-hot bolts would smash through the canopy and the upper terrace and kill trees and any life on them.

Tarzan interrupted the man's ramblings and told Waganero and Rahb they must move on. They found a relatively rainproof shelter under a particularly thick mat of vegetation. There, while the thunder roared like Numa the lion, a very hungry and angry Numa, Waganero continued his tale. But he had to shout, and he was often interrupted by Ara's talk. Ara made the sky and the earth shake and spoke louder than the forest gods themselves.

However, the storm did not last long.

Waganero resumed his account.

"My people live south of the land of Rafmana, she who sees everywhere and sees the present, past, and future through the roots of The Glittering Tree. Just north of my people, the Deenga, is the mountain which is the most southward extension of the range which begins on the north with the mountain of The Great Mother of Snakes. Do you follow me so far?"

"Yes," Tarzan said.

"In between the two mountains, far away from either, live the Rafmana, the people of Rafmana. She is also called The Toucher of Time, the guardian and holy priestess of The Dark Heart of Time, which lives within The Glittering Tree. North of Rafmana but south of The Great Mother of Snakes is the vast swamp where dwells

The Ghost Frog. I knew about these places because I heard of them from the elders of my village.

"Many generations ago, my people came to the land where we now live. Long before they arrived there, The Toucher of Time had lived there. She was the daughter of The Good Twins . . ."

"Keep it short," Tarzan commanded tersely. "Stick to the essentials."

"I will try. But I am a kagafona. You are a British citizen. You speak English or so I've been told. A kagafona is what you English call a bard. I have been trained to tell all, to sing about what must be sung about."

"Untrain yourself. Now!"

"I will try. My male ancestors were always singers, players of the tawango . . ."

"The what?"

Waganero pointed at the case. "I'd show you, but if I took it out of its case, it would get wet. Rain is not good for it."

He explained that his grandfather and father had been famous artists. Accompanying themselves on the tawango, they sang the genealogies of the great chiefs, who were descended from Apwu. Apwu was the hero who had led his people from a faraway land to the land where they now lived. They also sang the love songs and the war songs and the epics of the tribe of Deenga and its related tribes and neighbors, the Tumuola and the Sashaki. In this tradition, Waganero studied to be a kagafona.

Tarzan thought that the kagafona would be like Homer of the ancient Greeks or the bards of some West African tribes.

Now, Tarzan understood what the case enclosed. It was the Deenga version of the harp.

"But I asked Nasakwee, the chief of my clan, the Half Weasels, if I could marry his niece, Lutsu. The chief didn't like me. He . . ."

"Why not?" Tarzan said. Despite his impatience to move on from here, he was intrigued by Waganero's tale.

"He said I talked too much. I wouldn't shut up . . . he said . . . and I drove him as crazy as if I were a hornet trapped inside his ear. That was enough to reject me . . . he said. But, however, and also . . . he said . . . Lutsu, the woman I wanted to marry, his niece on Lutsu's mother's side, was related to Wintusa, an ancestor descended from The Great Dog-Man, Basessi of the Many-Colored Waters. I was descended from Basessi, too, and that relationship, though very distant and thinned by time, was enough to force calling in The Sniffers-Out of Incest. He wanted nothing, nothing at all, to do with them. Neither did I or Lutsu. In addition . . ."

"Enough of that," Tarzan said. "I am beginning to understand why Nasakwee, your chief, didn't like you. Tell me, and keep to the essentials, why were those men trying to kill you?"

"It's a long story, O Demon-Sired One."

"Call me Tarzan. It's a short name, and I like my tales short. Try hard to please me. Otherwise, Rahb and I will leave you now, which we may do anyway."

Waganero rolled his eyes. He said, "If you would allow me to play on my tawango while I sing my story, you would be enchanted."

"There are men looking for us right now," the ape-man said. "Do you want them to find us by following the sound of your voice and of the tawango?"

"No," Waganero said. He breathed in deeply, as if he found the ways of nonartists to be just too perplexing to deal with.

He continued, "The chief also claimed I was off-key, a terrible insult to me and all of my clan. Before I could claim the right to a trial, my bride-to-be, Lutsu, was carried off by men from the other side of the mountain. That is, if you remember, the land of Rafmana. The land where no one from our land ever wishes to venture. The chief consulted a witch, a summoner of visions. She said that she saw Lutsu being taken in a dugout far to the north. The men who took her away were carrying her to the tribe which lives north of Rafmana's land. There Lutsu would be sold to the witches, the drinkers of blood, who sacrifice people to The Ghost Frog. Do you understand me?"

"Well enough for now," Tarzan said.

"Those who get thrown to The Ghost Frog are swallowed by that monster. But they do not die. They join those others in the belly of The Ghost Frog. In that vast belly is the land of The More than Dead. Lutsu would become one of them. She would lament her awful fate with the others. And their weeping and wailing and lamenting would become as one. Their united voices would become one voice."

Waganero paused. Obviously, he was waiting for dramatic effect.

Tarzan said, "Well, what is that one voice?"

"It is the terrible sound known as The Voice of the Ghost Frog. When the witch was through with her visions, she was paid off. Then my chief said that I must go north and rescue Lutsu before she was fed to The Ghost Frog. Or, if I got there too late, I must slay The Ghost Frog and bring Lutsu out of the land of The More than Dead."

Waganero choked then. Tears dripped down his cheeks.

"Telling me I must do that was telling me that I was as good as dead. The men who abducted Lutsu would be given safe passage northward by Rafmana to the swamp where The Ghost Frog dwelt. But I would be caught by her warriors and sold to the abductors long before I could get to the swamp.

"Even if I could get to the swamp, was I Apwu himself,

the great slayer of demons and ghosts and of The Elephant Who Ruled the World? Even Apwu might have hesitated to attack The Ghost Frog.

"And then the chief insulted me by saying that I should play the tawango and sing to the monster. That would surely kill The Ghost Frog. The chief laughed so hard that he almost died. And the tribe laughed with him.

"Then he gave me weapons and put me in a dugout and told me to paddle up the river. Not until I brought Lutsu home would I again be part of the clan and the tribe. So, while my aunts and uncles wept for me and the kagafona of other clans sang of my great deeds, all of which were yet to be done, I paddled by boat upstream and out of sight finally of the mourners and the praisers.

"But . . . I was and am a coward! That night, I sneaked past my village and southward on the river. I went on the boat until I left my native land. Then I traveled east on foot through the terrible jungle. Then over mountains and then onwards to the east.

"Since then, years have passed, and I have become well acquainted with the great plains and the seacoasts and even a little with the white men who ruled the eastern tribes. But I decided to return home. Perhaps the chief was dead. Perhaps my people had forgotten me. In any event, I longed for home. But on the way back, I was captured by slavers. I escaped, and then you, O Mighty Tarzan, and that half-man beast appeared. I do indeed thank . . ."

"Enough!" Tarzan said. He spoke more loudly than he had intended. "The time for talk is over. We leave now! You may come with us for a little while, until we're far away from those who are hunting us. But you must promise not to speak unless it's absolutely necessary! And I mean . . ."

Tarzan himself stopped speaking, as gunfire sounded, not at all far away. Waganero's mouth hung open with astonishment. Rahb said something which Tarzan did not understand.

Then there were cries of men interspersed with more gunfire. It seemed to him that some enemy force had attacked Helmson's safari. Whether the newcomers were more of the tribesmen who had been chasing Waganero or another band of warriors that had blundered into the safari, the ape-man did not know.

However, there were too many of Helmson's men nearby to descend to the ground just now. He started through the highway of lianas intertangled with tree branches. A glance below him and behind him showed that Rahb, despite his bulk and weight, was proceeding swiftly. Waganero was trying hard to keep up with them, but he was losing ground. And then he was lost to sight in the thick mesh of vegetation.

Tarzan thought that there were far more people in this small area of jungle than there should be, that is, in normal circumstances. And he suspected that this was because Waganero was here.

It seemed to the ape-man that the bard had always been, now was, and ever would be a source of trouble and turmoil. Only a very small part of Waganero's odyssey had been told. Yet, that tiny part was enough for Tarzan to know that the man was a magnet for stress, anxiety, and things going wrong. The sooner Tarzan and Rahb got away from him, the better off they'd be.

I owe him nothing, Tarzan thought.

He slowed down until Rahb caught up with him. Then he said, "Now, we go as swiftly as we can. The black man is on his own."

The bear-man pointed ahead of them.

"I agree with you," he said, "but what about those?"

17

TARZAN LOOKED IN the direction at which Rahb was pointing. A green flood was flowing toward them through the upper terrace. It flowed and swelled and shrank. It seemed to be a giant light-green amoeba with yellowish-white stripes and yellowish-white spots.

Then Tarzan's eyes refocused. What had been confusing and chaotic became understandable and distinctly formed. It was no longer a shape-changing and oozing mass. It became at least a hundred green-and-white men crowded together. They were very little, shorter by twelve inches or so than the Ituri pygmies. The painted green and white stripes and spots covering their heads and bodies made them blend into the sun-dappled foliage.

They were entirely unclothed. Their weapons were hollow bamboo blowguns, flint knives, short flint-tipped spears, and short wooden bows. The quivers strapped to their backs held arrows only half as long as Tarzan's. He suspected that the blowgun darts and the arrows were coated with poison.

As the crowd moved closer, it became less packed. The intruders were spreading out. Some were climbing higher, confident that the thinner branches would bear their lesser weight. Some climbed down via vines and lianas to the middle terrace. Their agility matched or exceeded the ape-man's.

In this world, being small and light was not always a handicap—far from it.

Rahb growled. Then he said something. Tarzan did not understand the phrase.

Waganero's voice trembled. "It's the Shelaba!"

"What are the Shelaba?" Tarzan said.

"They are tiny beings, not human, though they look like humans. They were made by Kaasamana, the woman-crocodile, the Creator, in the first days of shaping the world. She rejected them as not being up to her standards. She threw them to the Tree Crocodiles to eat. But some survived and hid in the deepest forest. Which is where we are now. On the edge of it, anyway. The Shelaba live high in the trees in nests, and they seldom come down to the ground. When a Shelaba dies . . ."

"Enough," Tarzan said. "For now, tell me one thing only. Are their darts and arrows dipped in poison?"

"It is said that they are," Waganero replied. "It is also said that they are cannibals."

"You don't really know much about them," the ape-man said.

Perhaps the strangest thing about the Shelaba was their blowguns. Tarzan had read that these tools of the hunt were known only in southeast Asia and in South America. But here they were in central Africa. However, the people using them were also unknown to science. And judging from the fact that he had never heard of them, there must be very few natives who knew about these creatures.

He turned to look behind and below, and received the answer to one of his questions. Two of Helmson's safari had been climbing a tree. Suddenly, the small white fluffs at the end of the darts were flowering on the men's skins. Then the men loosed their holds and fell to the ground.

They did not scream as they hurtled downward. They were already dead.

Immediately afterward, three of the men on the ground crumpled. Helmson, the other white men, and the blacks ran into the jungle. Tarzan doubted that they would be back.

Within a minute, the little painted warriors surrounded him and his companions—above, below, and around them. He did not understand the jabbering of the man who seemed to be their leader. But the chief made gestures that plainly indicated that the three should surrender.

They could do nothing except to hold their hands high. Their weapons were taken away from them. For a moment, the chief seemed about to drop Waganero's harp from the branch. Waganero protested loudly. The chief shrugged—who knew what he was thinking?—and handed the case-enclosed instrument to a warrior.

Following the signals made by the chief and some of his men, the three captives climbed higher.

Looking downward while ascending, Tarzan saw that a dozen or so Shelaba were on the ground. Their knives were busy cutting out pieces of flesh of the slain men and severing heads, arms, and legs. Perhaps, they were taking the heads for trophies. But the limbs? These must surely be for eating.

Another of the ape-man's questions had been answered.

They passed through the intertangling vegetation of the highest terrace from tree to tree. Abruptly, they came to bridges constructed out of roughly hewn wooden planks for foot passage. These were held up by lianas attached to the branches above them. Lianas also provided handholds. The entire bridge network integrated big branches as part of it. Tarzan was sure that this network would be invisible from the ground or even, at most points, from the middle terrace.

They came to the first of the outposts. After the guards had passed them through, they came to the first of the enormous Shelaba-made nests. These were much like bird nests except that some here and there had thatched roofs. None had walls. The roofs were supported by four to six vertical branches.

The prisoners came to an area consisting of many dozens of broad platforms secured by grass ropes and lianas. This, Tarzan assumed, was a meeting place, the Shelaba equivalent of a town hall. The platforms, all close together, were filled with middle-aged or old Shelaba males. They were also painted green and white, but their buttocks were painted purple. Around their heads were leather bands in which were stuck the large canines of leopards and other predators. The chief of the chiefs— or so Tarzan assumed he was—wore three fish-eagle beaks in his headband.

The women and children stood on bridges or branches or in their nests and looked down on the assembly. Even the nursing babies were camouflaged with green and white markings.

The wrists of the captives were bound behind their backs with leather bands. These burned the prisoners' skin, making Tarzan think the leather was coated or soaked with some toxic substance.

Long leather ropes were strung beneath their armpits, then the three were lowered to a platform which swung from thick bands secured at each of the four corners. The platform was thirty-five feet or more from the branch to which the upper ends of the bands were tied.

The Shelaba dropped one end of each of the ropes beneath the men's armpits, and the ropes were pulled upward.

Tarzan, bending his back and looking upward, could see the Shelaba staring down at him. By the side of the chief, who was a middle-aged man, stood a very old man. His long white hair was arranged around his face to form a halo. His nose was painted red, and his lips were painted bright orange.

He looked long and hard at the captives. Then he spoke. The ape-man was surprised to hear a Bantu language. It differed somewhat in pronunciation, vocabulary, and grammar from any he had ever heard. But it was reasonably intelligible.

"I am Kurigi, he who speaks four tongues," he said. "I know my native speech, that of the Shelaba, and two other languages, those spoken by the Big Very Brown Lumps. I learned them when I was a captive of the Big Very Brown Lumps far from here."

He made a vague gesture indicating, perhaps, the east.

Kurigi pointed at Rahb.

"We have heard of his kind, the monogarenadulu, but we have never seen one. The tales of our ancestors say that, once upon a time, there were many. But they lived in a valley behind the mountain known as The Python."

That, Tarzan thought, would be the same as the mountain which Martillo wrote down in his manuscript and map as The Great Mother of Snakes, the mountain he, Tarzan, had seen.

"These hairy beings, the monogarenadulu, were, we thought, long dead and long gone. Yet, here is one."

He pointed then to Tarzan.

"I am old, very old, and this is the first Big Part-Pink Lump I have ever seen, though it is true that we have heard about them. But we did not know that, like us Shelaba, they went naked and lived in the trees. Can it be that this being here is not just a Big Part-Pink Lump but that he is related to us Shelaba?"

The chief, scowling, said something to the interpreter. Kurigi replied, though in such a low voice that Tarzan could not hear him. But Kurigi's tone sounded apologetic. Apparently, the chief was telling him to get to the point.

Kurigi pointed down at Rahb.

"No village of the Shelaba has the head of a monoga-renadulu. Now, the village of Suwakidi, our great chief of chiefs, unfortunately sick in his nest, will be honored. Shelaba from every other village will come to us to see the skull of the monogarenadulu, and they will bring gifts and food to us."

The interpreter pointed down at Waganero.

"Our great chief says that the Big Very Brown Lump will not be eaten. Not as yet. First, we will determine if he can entertain us with his, ah, musical thing."

Apparently, the Shelaba had no word for harp, though they knew what its purpose was.

"If he does that well, we will allow him to live for a while. The skull of that one"—he pointed at Rahb— "will bring us fame and fortune. The music of the Big Very Brown Lump will soothe and entertain us and also bring many visitors. If he is no good . . ."

Kurigi did not need to describe what would happen.

He pointed down again at Tarzan.

"We will keep the Big Part-Pink Lump in a cage. As long as he draws visitors to see him, he will live. When people are tired of looking at him and talking about him, we will fatten him up. Then we will feast on him and the Big Very Brown Lump."

The upper terrace rang with cheers, whistles, and the clapping of hands. Also, many Shelaba beat on big hollow bamboo tubes with sticks. When the noise died down, the chief said something to Kurigi. He, in turn, spoke loudly to the crowd.

"The great chief has changed his mind. We will wait a while before we kill the hairy beast-man. He, too, will be on display. Then, when the Big Lumps are eaten, the monogarenadulu will also be eaten. Our warriors will become very strong with the flesh of the beast-man and of the Big Part-Pink Lump in our bellies."

Then the old man spoke directly to the captives.

"Do not try to chew each other's bonds apart. There is a poison in the leather. It will burn your lips, gums, tongue, and throat. Your saliva will burn all the way to your stomachs. You will suffer as if a flaming torch had been thrust into your guts. Then you will die screaming, though only after a long time.

"But if the poison only touches your skin, it will not kill you. Nor will it burn worse than it is now burning your skin."

There was more cheering and beating of sticks. The gourds were passed around, and everybody, including the little children, drank from them. Some had dripped from above on him, so Tarzan knew that it was some sort of beer and very strong beer at that.

Just where these people made beer or how they did it in the trees—if they did brew it in the trees—Tarzan did not know. It was enough that they seemed to have an endless supply. It was also obvious that the party, like every native party he'd seen, would last all night.

He told Rahb what was going to happen. Or, at least, he tried to convey to him as much as his still-limited knowledge of the bear-man's speech allowed him to do. He could not use gestures or signs as aids because his hands were tied behind him.

But Rahb seemed to understand. He snarled loudly at the Shelaba and said something. That was all. As for Waganero, he had understood most of what the interpreter had said. Oddly enough, if he was shaken by it, he did not seem to be so.

When the evening rain came, it dripped steadily from the leaves and drenched the three captives. Waganero and Rahb shivered with the cold. Tarzan never shivered.

The downpour, however, only slowed the party for a while. When the rain ceased, the merriment was renewed full blast. The Shelaba made small fires on top of the big branches. Tarzan could not see what the sticks burned on, but he supposed that the firewood was on places so deeply charred that they would not burn at all. Or it might be on piles of dirt.

Halfway through the night, while the din and the drinking made the forest clamorous, Tarzan lay down. On his side, his hands still tied behind him, he slept. It was an uneasy sleep. Several times, he was startled awake by an unusually loud noise from the partying Shelaba. The second time, Rahb was lying snuggled close to Tarzan's back. And Waganero's back was up against Tarzan's front. Feeling warm, the ape-man dropped into sleep again.

At dawn, he awoke. The only noises were the snoring of Rahb and the cries of the day animals and birds. He managed to get to his feet without the aid of his hands and despite the numbness of his right arm. Rahb snorted and muttered something in his sleep. Waganero groaned. The platform swayed.

While the blood started to run through his limbs, Tarzan ignored the pain. He looked around. If there was a single subpygmy awake, he was not visible to Tarzan. Doubtless, everybody was lodged deep in a drunken stupor.

Before starting to drink, the Shelaba had been sure that their captives could not escape. How could they climb with their wrists bound together behind their backs? It was true that they could jump to their deaths from the platform. But the Shelaba expected their captives to keep themselves alive as long as they could. That was the nature of men, small or big.

Tarzan awoke the other captives by nudging their ribs with his big toe. Then he spoke slowly and softly.

18

T HE PLATFORM ON which the three stood was approximately seven feet long and five feet wide. It was suspended from a medium-large branch thirty-five feet above the platform. Four thick leather ropes had been slung over the branch, and the ends of each one had been secured in holes drilled through the roughly hewn planks at the corners.

The rope ends had been inserted through each of the holes there, and then the rope ends had been knotted on the underside of the platform.

Close to the platform, horizontal ropes had been tied to the vertical ropes to make a rough but serviceable safety fence. These would keep the captives from falling off.

From the platform to the ground was a straight drop of about 160 feet. Thus, if the captives were to escape, they would have to haul themselves up the ropes to the branch.

That would not have been easy to do if their hands had been free. But they were bound together behind their backs.

The medium-large branch from which the platform was suspended was six feet wide. The closest branch to it was approximately seven feet distant and ran almost parallel to it. But it was a smaller one, about two feet

136

wide. And it was perhaps four feet lower than the other branch.

There seemed to be no escaping via the platform's leather support bands. Nevertheless, Tarzan was going to take the only way available.

In a few words, he told Rahb and Waganero what he planned to do. Waganero whined softly that their situation was hopeless. No plan would work. Tarzan's certainly would not. Tarzan stated flatly that he would make it work. Anyway, if he failed, he, not Waganero, would die at once. Of course, Waganero was doomed to die relatively soon if Tarzan did not now succeed.

Waganero shrugged, and he said he would do whatever was needed. Rahb had said nothing during this conversation. But he did as the ape-man ordered. He moved with Waganero close to the platform end pointing eastwards. They presented their backs to Tarzan and then crouched. After which they leaned far forward. Their backs were almost level with the platform floor.

The ape-man studied the situation for several seconds. Then he ran from the opposite end of the platform to the end where they crouched. Despite the swaying that resulted from their actions, he leapt from the platform and planted one foot firmly on the harpist's back and one on Rahb's.

Using their backs as springboards, he leapt almost straight upward from the platform. It rocked hard. But he bent his head sidewise, and his teeth closed on the thick leather band attached to the southwest corner of the platform.

For a few seconds, he hung there, supported only by the strength of his teeth and his jaws.

Below him, the bear-man and the harpist braced themselves against the swaying of the platform. They had now moved so that they were back to back. They were still crouched. If the ape-man should fall, he might drop onto their backs. That would soften the impact of the fall and, perhaps, keep him from going over the side ropes into the abyss.

Just before Tarzan closed his teeth on the band, he had bent his knees. His right foot was just above the left foot. But Tarzan had opened the gap between his big toe and the long toe next to it on both feet.

He did not have the big toes of an ape, which were almost at right angles to the other toes. Nor could he bend his foot as far as an ape could. Thus, unlike the ape, he could not use his foot as an efficient hand. Nevertheless, by biting down on the band, he could carry his weight enough to keep the toes from sliding back down. The combined grip of teeth and both toes was enough to keep him from slipping back down.

However, if he was to progress up the rope, he had to release his bite for a second—for less than a second. At the same time, he had to straighten one leg and thus thrust himself upward. For a moment his only hold on the band would be by his toes.

Then, his head cocked far to one side, he would have to bite down again on the rope. Immediately thereafter, with very little pause, he would have to bring up his legs with knees bent and grab the rope between the big toes and the long toes of each foot. And then he would have to clamp the band again between his teeth. And on and on.

This all had to be done very very quickly. It was extremely tiring, though he could rest now and then between moves. Not for very long, though. Strong as his jaw and secure as his teeth were, they could give out under the great strain.

It was a procedure that no one but Tarzan could have accomplished. The world's greatest athletes had not been raised from the age of one in the rain forest by great apes. And, though it had not been scientifically proven, it was possible that the ape-man owed part of his superior strength and quickness to a beneficial genetic change, or, as it was called, a mutation. Or so Tarzan had been told by an Oxford University botanist with whom he had once dined.

The botanist had admitted that not much was known about the science of heredity. Yet, he theorized that part of Lord Greystoke's muscular ability had to be genetic. Greystoke's life in the trees could not explain *all* his more-than-human physical powers.

Just now, whether they were partly due to a mutation or not, the ape-man was testing his physical powers to a very high degree. If he failed, he would drop to the ground. And no amount of strength or of luck would help him. He would be a shattered corpse.

Slowly and painfully, Tarzan went up the band. His lips, gums, and tongue were bleeding. The blood and saliva slickened the leather. When he closed his toes on the wet places, he tended to slide back down when he had to open his mouth to make another lunge upward for another bite.

By the time that he reached a point just below the branch, he was breathing very hard. If he had had to climb another six inches, he might have been too exhausted to do so.

He halted. Four feet above him, the band was snug against the side of the branch. Past that point, he could no longer grip it with his teeth. And, of course, he could not use his hands to grip anything at all. But he did not plan to get onto the big branch. Not just yet, anyway.

He could not look down at his companions nor could he utter a command. The two captives would have to work on their own.

A few seconds later, swinging his legs began to pay off. He felt the band from which he was hanging begin to move. It went an inch or two one way. It stopped briefly, then went the other way. Down below, Rahb and Waganero were moving the platform like a swing. He had to hang on until they could bring the platform to the top of the arc described by the rope.

It was slow work, so slow. Tarzan hoped that the Shelaba would stay in their drunken sleep long enough for him to carry out all he planned to do. If they did not, if one awoke and saw what the captives were doing, it was all over.

For the time being, anyway. As long as he lived, he would not quit.

He thought of Jane and wondered where she was. He was glad that she could not see him now.

At long last, just as Tarzan felt as if he could hang on no longer, he swung to the height he needed. Whether it was or not, he had to release his teeth and toes from the rope just as he reached the apex of the swing.

He did so. And, lent momentum by the outward movement of body and leather band, he soared toward the smaller branch.

It wasn't much of a flight, but he just had time to whirl himself half around. Less than a second after he completed the turn, he fell against the branch. It slammed into his belly, and it knocked the wind out of him.

Then he was gasping for air, and his stomach muscles hurt. Some of the skin on his belly, chest, and thighs was scraped off, though he did not allow himself to feel the pain then.

Unfortunately, he had landed more on the side of the branch than on its top. He began sliding backward.

He slammed his chin down against the branch. It caught on a small projection, a broken-off branch, not much larger than a sharp twig. It was enough—for a short while. The point dug into the flesh just back of his chin bone. It held, though his neck muscles felt as if they would stretch to the snapping point.

Taking a moment, he managed to recover his wind. He

overrode the agony the loss of breath had caused and made every subtle move needed to keep from falling.

The two watchers below saw something they had never seen before and probably would never see again. They saw him swing to his left side for about six inches. They could not see the projection digging deep into the place just behind his chin. But they could see that something was keeping him from falling off. Nor could they see the blood pouring out from the wound and along the side of the branch. And they could not feel his pain.

Tarzan swung the other way. He brought up his right leg and gripped the bark near the top of the branch with the back of his heel. Then he pulled himself up onto the branch with his leg. The back of his heel lodged in a slight depression in the branch.

This effort made his spine crackle.

Suddenly, he was face down on the branch. The blood from the gouge behind his chin ran swiftly. However, he had no time to rest or to staunch the flow. He got to his feet, still without the use of his hands. For a moment, he tottered and came close to falling sideways from the branch.

But he regained his balance. Then he turned around and walked on top of the branch to the trunk. Near it was a small nest. One of the tiny women lay sprawled on her back on layers of moss in the middle of the nest. Her breath was very beery. She held a very small and naked baby to her breast. Though the infant was nursing, the mother seemed to be sleeping. By her side were several tiny weapons, a flint-tipped spear, a quiver full of arrows, and a flint knife.

Tarzan stepped inside the nest. The woman stirred. The baby continued to suckle. But when the ape-man reached past the two, the blood from his chin fell on the baby's back. The baby started. But it did not quit sucking.

Quickly, Tarzan straightened up, dripping more blood

on the baby's back. A few drops also fell on the woman's leg. She opened her eyes. But Tarzan was crouching down near her. All she had to do was to turn her head to see him. Then, he would have to kill her before she could cry out. But how could he do that with his hands tied behind his back?

The only way would be to press his foot on her mouth and hold her down with it. He had never asphyxiated anyone with a foot. But, today, he had accomplished a number of things he'd never done before—things that, in a calmer time, he might have thought impossible for him to do. He began to lift his foot.

The woman closed her eyes. The baby continued to feed. Tarzan waited for sixty seconds, after which, he brought his raised foot down. He was very careful not to make the twigs beneath the moss snap. He sank to his knees, then bent his back toward the nest, balancing himself, hoping that the great drain of energy from his body had not weakened him too much.

After all his efforts, to come this far and then fail . . . it would indeed be laughable. His smile was grim, for no one found irony more humorous than Tarzan, especially if it was directed at him.

His body shook as his shoulders almost reached the top layer of moss. His hands, groping behind, finally felt the knife. He got it between his fingers without cutting himself. Or so it seemed to him. The edge of a flint knife could be sharper than the finest surgical tool. He could have cut himself on it, without feeling pain for quite some time.

Slowly and cautiously, Tarzan raised himself to a standing position. He looked around, and he listened. There was the usual racket made by the upper-terrace beasts and birds in early morning. But he could neither observe nor hear any awakening Shelaba.

Then he saw the column of large ants approaching the nest. They had smelled his blood, and they would soon be swarming on the baby and the mother, biting them. That was a sure guarantee that they soon would be screaming.

His hands were still bound behind him. He did not have time to saw through the ropes before the ants got to the nest. But he could go around the nest to the head of the column. There, he could stomp on the insects and foot-brush them off the branch.

They would keep coming anyway. But he just needed enough time to sever the binding leather bands. In a few seconds, he had cleared the insects off the top of the branch. Several managed to get on his foot, though. Their bites were painful. He swept them off one foot with the other foot. Though he had to stand on one leg to do this, he found it possible. His balance already was better than a moment ago.

Holding the knife with one hand, he swiftly severed the tough bands. By then, the ants were beginning to come up again from the under part of the branch. He went to the nest and pulled up chunks of moss. The woman slept on without even twitching. And the baby had fallen asleep, too. Perhaps, the alcohol in its mother's milk had knocked it out.

He used the moss to staunch the flow of blood from his chin. Though he was also bleeding in other places, he thought that he was not losing enough blood from those areas to bother now with the moss.

The knife held between his teeth, holding the moss against the chin wound, he made his way up and around the tree to the big branch. None of the Shelaba he passed stirred, though they snored loudly and beerily. When he got to the big branch, he saw that the platform had stopped swinging. The bear-man and the harpist were looking up at him. Waganero's teeth showed whitely in his deep brown face. Rahb's face was limited to fewer expressions than a human's. Nevertheless, he managed to look pleased.

Tarzan took a short length of leather band from a nest. The sleeping occupants, five in all, did not stir. After discarding the blood-soaked moss he'd held against his chin wound, he removed the comparatively clean moss from the nest. While holding it on the wound, he managed with one hand to bind the leather band around his chin and the top of his head, thus securing the moss to the wound.

There was nothing to stop him now from getting out of this area as swiftly as possible. The light was getting somewhat brighter. Soon, some of the Shelaba would be up, and they would see him. Then the alarm would sound. He should leave with great haste. But, if he did that, he would be deserting the harpist and the bearman. It was true that they had no true claim to his loyalty. But he felt they did, and that was all that mattered.

First, though, he had to work out the method for getting the two free. He could go down to the platform on one of the bands slung over the top of the big branch. Then he could sever the bands binding the wrists of the two. And they could climb back up the rope by which he had descended.

But when they reached the point where the ropes lay snugly against the side of the branch, how could they get to the top of the branch? The weight of the platform would pull the ropes very tightly against the six-foot-high sides of the branch. The climbers would not be able to insert their fingers between the ropes and the branch. They would not be able to pull themselves up along it. They would be stuck there.

The method Tarzan conceived to solve this problem would take a little time, perhaps more than he would have. But, he reflected with a degree of fatalism, if events turned out to be against him, that was the way it would have to be.

He did not find the long bands he was looking for until at least four minutes had passed. They were on a branch six feet above and a foot to one side of the branch holding the bands from which the platform hung. This branch was smaller in thickness than the one below it.

The bands were in a sort of storehouse, a large nest with a thatched roof. He knotted three of the ropes together to make one long one, then tied one end of the three-length band to an end of a long bamboo blowgun. He lay face down on the branch, and extended both arms down the sides of the branch.

After several failures, he succeeded in swinging one side of the weighted band far enough to be caught with the other hand. He stopped twice in his efforts, though, because a nearby Shelaba was groaning. Then the man went back to his snoring.

Very swiftly, Tarzan untied the blowgun and put it to one side. Then he tied the band together and dropped the long free end down to the platform. Its end dangled a few inches above one side of the platform.

He quickly lowered himself down the band. He passed the larger and lower branch by a few inches. When he got to the side of the platform, he had to swing himself a little to grasp one of the ropes supporting the platform.

In a few seconds, he was on the platform. He lost no time cutting apart the bonds around his companions' wrists, though the platform was swaying again, making any action difficult.

He led the way back up the band down which he had come. When he was opposite the top of the big branch, he extended one leg and planted his foot on the top of the branch. A few minutes after he was on the branch, the others were by his side.

Five minutes later, armed with knives and blowguns,

with quivers full of arrows or darts strapped to one arm, they left the village high in the trees. Not, however, without the harp. Waganero saw it while they were climbing around a big nest that housed the Shelaba chief. Near him was the case that held the harp. Tarzan would have ignored it, but Waganero stepped into the nest before the ape-man could stop him. Tarzan kept silent, though he made gestures at Waganero to get out of the nest before he woke up the chief or the three women and two babies sleeping nearby. The harpist ignored the ape-man. He picked up the instrument in its case and slowly and silently departed. He was grinning, quite satisfied with himself. Tarzan could only express his displeasure by frowning. Before he could do more, someone discovered the empty platform.

19

A FEW DAYS before Tarzan and his companions had encountered the Shelaba, the safari had been called to a halt by Helmson. His gun bearer, Rakali, had found the knife that Tarzan had taken from the slain askari while escaping from the tent.

Helmson thought that Tarzan could have been traveling via the trees. He sent a tracker far up the tree to look around for signs that the ape-man had been there. The man saw some tufts of long black fur caught in the bark of a branch. He brought some samples down and showed them to the other trackers and to the white men.

The natives, Fitzpagel, and the other whites said that they did not know from what animal the fur had come. Helmson admitted his ignorance, too. That was for show. He knew at once that the fur was Rahb's.

He knew that both the ape-man and the bear-man had been here. But what had happened then? Why, if Tarzan had dropped his knife, had he not retrieved it? Was Rahb still following Greystoke? Did Rahb intend to capture him and bring him back to the man who held Rahb's mate as a hostage?

Or had Rahb somehow made peace with Tarzan and told him all he knew? That seemed unlikely to happen. However, Helmson could not be sure.

Two hours later, the safari had halted in its northwestward progress. It had come to the place where the earthquake had broken open the ground as if a thousand cannons had fired explosive shells into it. The underground river had gushed up from the earth and soared outward as high as sixty feet. Then it fell into the water and was still gushing. The ground on which the awed safari men stood was at the edge of a flood. It was so broad that its other side was not visible.

Somewhere in that rage of water was the original river.

Fitzpagel had asked Helmson what he intended to do now. Helmson had replied that he did not know. But it was possible that Tarzan, if he were still alive, had been swept downriver by the flood. The Irishman had said that it was just as possible that the ape-man had been killed by the quake or the flood.

Or he could have escaped. If so, he'd be heading northward. That was where Lady Greystoke and her abductor, Lieutenant Erich Obergatz, were reported to be. But it didn't matter which direction the ape-man had gone. He was lost to them. He could not be found. That was that.

Fitzpagel had said that they should return to HQ. They could wait until they heard something definite about Tarzan's location. Then they could go after him.

Helmson had angrily replied that that could take a year, maybe two years—maybe forever.

Fitzpagel had said that he knew that as well as any man alive. The chances were good that the project would eventually be called off. He, however, intended to pass a word or two on up the line. They would go to Himself, the unknown originator of this search. They would say that he, Fitzpagel, would be willing to wait for a long long time. That could be in Nairobi or any other place. Meantime, as long as his expenses and a reasonable salary were paid, he would be patient.

"What if I say no to that?" Helmson asked. "What if I order you to continue?"

Fitzpagel's smile made it obvious that he knew, and Helmson knew, who was actually in control.

"I'll be going back with my men. Ye may do as ye please. However, if ye'd reveal to me and me only what method ye used to track down Tarzan, then it'd be a salmon of a different shape."

Helmson had grimaced. At that moment, he felt much like strangling Fitzpagel.

But he said, "Let me think about it."

"Ye have an hour," Fitzpagel said.

Thirty minutes later, Helmson went to the Irishman. He was sitting on a folding chair and smoking a pipe.

Helmson held a brass cylinder in his hand. Its brass was old and tarnished and looked as if it were centuries old, which, indeed, it was. Without saying a word, Helmson began unscrewing its cap. Fitzpagel straightened up and removed the pipe from his mouth. He knew that Helmson was about to reveal something very meaningful to him.

The American carefully and slowly pulled out several rolled-up sheets of parchment from the cylinder.

He said, "I'll let you see these in a minute. Be careful how you handle them. First, I'll tell you the story. It's a strange one, and you may not believe it. But it's true. And it'll show you why we'll be going south, down the river."

Fitzpagel said, "Does this have anything to do with why you were able to track down Tarzan so surely? Until recently?"

"No," Helmson said. "But what I'm going to tell you is just as strange as what I could tell you about my . . . locator. And it'll bring us a vast fortune."

He told Fitzpagel all he knew about the Spaniard and about the manuscript and the map. Fitzpagel listened without comment until Helmson was finished.

Then, he said, "I can read Spanish well enough to get the gist of Martillo's tale even if it's in the lingo of the

1500s. Let me have it and the map. I'll be very careful handling it."

When he had done with the manuscript and the map, he handed them back to Helmson.

"Very intriguing," he said. "But where's your proof of Martillo's veracity? Do ye have any samples of the gold found in great abundance in so many places? If ye can believe his narrative and the map, that is? How do I know it's not all the Spaniard's fantasy? Or a fever dream he had? It certainly sounds like it."

With that thought, he became openly agitated. "City Made by God! The Great Mother of Snakes! The Voice of the Ghost Frog! The Toucher of Time! The Uncaused Causer! What are those?"

"I don't know," Helmson said. "But I intend to find out, even if I have to do it alone. However, I know gold when I see it. Now, I'll tell you why I think there's some truth to the story and why I think it's possible there may be a lot of truth to it.

"Years ago, I ran into an old white trader in a Nairobi tavern. His name was Horn. Among the tales he told was one where he had himself seen, from a distance, mind you, this mountain which bore a gigantic image of a red snake. This old man said that the natives called it The Great Mother of Snakes. As soon as they saw that, they stopped. They refused to go on. Since the expedition was short of supplies and it was lost, far away from its original destination, Horn turned back northward.

"He meant to return someday to the mountain with another expedition. But he never did."

Fitzpagel relit his pipe and puffed out a few clouds. Then he said, "How do I know ye're not making this up?"

Helmson, his face red, shouted, "You don't! So, forget it! I'll go on myself, and all of you and your kind be damned!"

That outburst seemed to convince Fitzpagel that Helmson was sincere. After asking Helmson a few questions about what he planned to do, Fitzpagel said that he would go with him. Perhaps there was something to the Spaniard's story. First, though, if they found gold, he and Helmson would split it, or any other profits to be made.

Thus it was that, some days later, they came around the bend of the very wide river. And there, coming toward them, was Tarzan in a dugout—Tarzan, whose possession would give Helmson a great fortune, though no fame. There were also two others: Rahb, one of the last two of the beings that called themselves the Shong; Rahb, who with his wife and future child, would be shown to an amazed world, three beings who would bring Helmson great wealth and fame; and a black man Helmson did not know.

Helmson's cry was more than that of surprised recognition. It was joy. To come across the two persons that he wanted to capture so much, the two he had thought he would never see again, that was ecstasy.

But now . . . now! Helmson cursed. Once more, Tarzan and Rahb eluded him. They outraced their hunters to the forest. And, Helmson did not doubt, the two would be quickly lost again in the forest.

Also, there was Fitzpagel to be considered. He had asked Helmson to tell him what the huge bearish thing with Tarzan was. No doubt, he was already suspicious about Rahb. He had probably guessed that the unknown creature had something to do with Helmson's uncanny ability to track Tarzan down. And he had probably guessed, too, that Helmson had lost control of the creature.

Just now, Helmson had no time to explain anything to the Irishman. But he could put that off only so long.

After the boats had been dragged into a shallow place, Helmson ordered a dozen bearers and several askari to stand guard over them. They would be left unloaded until later. Meanwhile, he and Fitzpagel led the rest of the party through the thick riverbank growth and on into the rain forest proper. The three they pursued had left a few unmistakable footprints near the edge of the riverbank. There were also three sets of prints deeper in the woods.

But, at the bottom of a huge tree several hundred yards inland, the prints vanished. Though the trackers searched diligently in ever-widening circles from the base of the tree, they found no sign of their quarry.

Helmson did not expect them to come across any. He was sure that the ape-man and his companions would have taken to the trees as soon as possible. After a half hour of the frantic search, he called it off.

And then he heard, far off, gunfire.

He had no idea who was shooting or who was being shot at. There was a very small chance that Tarzan was involved. However, Helmson could not ignore it. He gave the order to push on. When they got close to the area of the explosions, they slowed their pace. Presently, the two white men were looking at the strangers from behind a tree. Helmson soon discovered that all these men were blacks. A few wore some tattered European trousers or vests; one wore an old stovepipe hat—trade goods. Their rifles were Martinis, 1870 vintage. These would also be trade items.

Helmson asked Rakali if he knew the identity of the strangers.

Rakali said, "No."

He pointed upwards and to his right.

"There! Tarzan!"

Helmson glimpsed a patch of white skin. Then he saw briefly the silhouette of a monstrous figure.

He turned around to order his men—and Fitzpagel's—to shoot at the black strangers but to make sure they did not hit the white man and the Shong.

While the two white men banged away with their firearms at the blacks on the ground and those climbing the trees, the askari and the trackers charged out with their spears and knives. They killed all those on the ground and then began slashing the corpses.

A few minutes later, they were retreating headlong. At least half of them were dead from the poison on the tips of the darts and the tiny arrows. They did not stop running until they were sure that they were far away from the little green-and-white-painted men.

Once he had recovered his breath, Helmson cursed his bad luck.

Fitzpagel said, "No, me bhoy! We were indeed fortunate! We got away with our skins intact and our lives. What more could we ask for, considering the circumstances? Though the basic question is, What do we do next?"

"I didn't mean I was going to give up!" Helmson said loudly. He glared at Fitzpagel. "OK! Let's unload the boats! Then we'll see how many men we've got left! We'll load the bearers with only the most essential supplies! The things without which we just can't survive! And then . . . !"

After a long silence, the Irishman said, "And then?"

"We go back to where we ran away like yellow-bellied cowards! And we find Greystoke! Somehow, we'll track him down!"

"I don't think we were cowards," Fitzpagel said coolly. "As the Bard himself said, 'Discretion is the better part of valor.' However, I've still not gotten from ye an explanation of what in the divil that black beast, that antediluvian-looking thing, is. It seems to me the ape-man keeps very strange company. I insist ye enlighten me. It's fer me own safety and protection. The black divil looked very dangerous to me. So, what was it?"

"I don't know!" Helmson shouted.

Even to himself, he did not sound convincing.

Fitzpagel looked angry.

Helmson thought, *What can the Irishman do about it? He certainly can't report his suspicions about me to Mister Big, whoever he is. In fact, we'll be doing no reporting for a long time . . . if ever.*

Bevan waited until his employer had finished reading the decoded message. This text was far longer than most of those that had been sent out of Africa.

Stonecraft put the two pieces of paper down on his desk. He did not look happy. He sat back in his office chair, closed his eyes, and steepled his fingers. His face looked calm.

Bevan's long experience with his boss told him that Stonecraft was raging under his skin.

Bevan waited. The sounds of Fifth Avenue traffic came up through the closed window. And then—where had it come from?—the buzzing of a fly filled the room.

Stonecraft opened his eyes. But he still said nothing.

Suddenly, Bevan had a mental picture of his boss's tongue shooting out of his mouth. Like a giant frog's tongue, it went on and on, halfway to the entrance door. Then it touched the fly, wrapped itself around it, and shot back into Stonecraft's mouth.

The fly kept on buzzing.

Bevan thought, Stonecraft is a big fat frog who's devoured legions of flies. He's never failed in any of his projects.

Except for the fly John Clayton, Viscount Greystoke, Tarzan the Ape-man, Waziri, chief of the Waziri tribe and who knew how many others?

Would it keep on buzzing no matter how long the frog's tongue was?

His boss sat forward, his eyes open. He rested his elbows on the desk.

"Well," he said. "I suppose that Africa is a very large estate."

Bevan said nothing.

"And the Ituri forest, if I remember correctly, has an area of more than 24,000 square miles. A rather large place, equivalent to the square mileage of the states of Illinois, Iowa, Missouri, and Indiana and perhaps more."

Bevan still kept silence.

Stonecraft looked upward.

"I usually have you or some specialist research what I want to know. But, last night, having some time for my own purposes—my wife was off to some charity fund-raising or other—I did some reading in my library."

Bevan said, "Yes, sir?"

"Do you realize that the 24,000 square miles or more is only on the ground? But in the rain forest, there is a middle continent, as it were. And there is an upper continent, as it were. That is, the middle continent is the vegetation halfway from the top of the forest. And the upper continent is near the top of the trees."

He leaned back again and closed his eyes as if he were trying to vizualize the entirety of the rain forest.

"Thus, there are three areas containing plant life, animal life, insect life, and bird life, each of approximately 29,000 square miles. That, Bevan, makes an area of . . . ?"

Without having to think about it, Bevan said, "An area of approximately 87,000 square miles, sir."

"Unless I'm mistaken, and I never am," his employer said, "the man I want is loose somewhere in all that three-tiered territory. This latest report is from the small and very fast expedition that followed the blazed trails left by Helmson and Fitzpagel. They found an area which, apparently, those two with all their men had entered. A great earthquake had ravaged that area. And then the trail came to an end."

"Yes, sir. An end."

"Now we don't know if the earthquake killed all of them, that is, Tarzan and the men I sent to find him. Or if they were swept away by the underground river which was brought to the surface by the earthquake. Or whether or not they survived being swept away. If they are alive, where are they? We don't know if they went northward. Or if they're somewhere in the south. Or if they're even in the Ituri. Or if they're where all dead men go."

"We don't know, sir."

Stonecraft opened his eyes and looked hard at Bevan.

"What is the answer? How do we solve this problem?"

The secretary did not hesitate.

"I don't know, sir. In the past, I usually have had some good answers for you. When I didn't, you answered your own questions. Now . . ."

Stonecraft said, "The only thing that occurs to me just now is to send out another expedition to find the lost men. But that is a very inefficient and a very expensive way. And it might take years. Years, I say. Now, I don't mind the expense. Well, actually, I do. But I can endure losing half of my fortune or more to find that man. But the time? I may not have the time. Men die, Bevan. Though I'm the wealthiest man in the world, I am a man. Therefore, I will die.

"Just when, I can't say. Only He above knows."

For perhaps the fiftieth time, Bevan wondered why Stonecraft wanted so desperately to capture Greystoke.

Some day, he thought, *someday Stonecraft will slip up. And I'll know then. Meanwhile, I can only wait. And if I find out . . . whatever it is, I'll profit from it.*

20

TARZAN, RAHB, AND Waganero ran as fast as was possible through the thickly vegetated forest. Now and then, glancing backward, Tarzan saw the Shelaba. Many had come down to the jungle floor for the chase. Others were above on the upper and middle terraces. All were intent on killing or, at least, recapturing the three fugitives.

But these were still ahead of the pack by several hundred yards. However, the Shelaba, despite their much shorter legs, were very swift. Tarzan estimated that, within ten minutes, perhaps sooner, the hunters would be within blowgun-dart and arrow range.

A moment later, the three, their skin scratched and torn, burst through the barrier. They were at the edge of the great, brown, greasy, and stinking waters of the flood. Breathing hard, they glanced around. Rahb was the first to see a dugout, half-hidden by the bushes and smeared with mud. Crying out and pointing, he lurched toward it. The others followed. But Tarzan stopped to pull up a paddle from the mud left by the flood.

The seven-foot-long dugout was bottom up. The three pulled it over so it was right-side up. They dragged it through the mud and into the river. The ape-man looked around for more paddles. There was none that he could see. Nor was there time to probe around in the mud for others.

Rahb climbed into the stern of the boat. He held the

paddle. The others got in quickly, though the dugout rocked violently. Rahb used the end of the paddle to push the boat out into the stronger current.

At the same time, several of the green-and-white-painted subpygmies emerged from the bush. And what had seemed long logs in the grass on the other bank began moving. Within a few seconds, they were in the river.

Gimla the crocodile was here—one more danger threatening the quarry. But they would be as happy to eat the Shelaba as the men the Shelaba were chasing.

Tarzan had been about to order Rahb to paddle up the river. But the Shelaba were too close to them. And going against the current would slow the boat down. There was nothing to do but to paddle as hard as possible downstream. However, Rahb had sized up the situation and was already doing that.

Also, he was heading toward the opposite bank to get the boat as far away as possible from the darts and arrows.

Tarzan feared that Rahb might ground the boat on the opposite bank so that they could continue their flight on land. He used what he knew of Rahb's language and also used signals. His message said plainly, "No! We go down the river! We try to outrace them!"

That was their only chance for escape. To flee on the jungle floor or even to take to the trees would enable the Shelaba to catch them soon.

Rahb understood the ape-man. And, indeed, he may have come to the same conclusion as Tarzan. He steered the boat to the middle of the river and then turned it southward.

Meanwhile, at least several dozen of the Shelaba were along the bank. They began slipping through the dense vegetation along it. They halted now and then to shoot darts or arrows at the men in the boat. This was at least sixty feet away from them. Several darts and arrows did come close to their targets. Most, however, fell wide or short of the three.

Rahb dug the paddle into the water with the strength of a gorilla. The boat sped over the water.

Then, suddenly, two small dugouts, each containing four paddlers, appeared behind them. Evidently, the Shelaba had had boats hidden along the river. These seemed to skim like dragonflies over the muddy waters. Tarzan estimated that they would overtake his boat within twenty minutes. Perhaps sooner.

The pursuers had relatively long-range weapons. These included throwing spears. Tarzan and his companions had the blowguns, darts, tiny bows and arrows, and the small flint knives they had stolen.

By now, the warriors on the bank seemed to have dropped behind. Thus, the only ones he and his companions would have to deal with would be the eight Shelaba in the two dugouts.

He waited until his boat rounded a long lazy bend in the river. The Shelaba were now out of sight. He spoke quickly to Rahb and Waganero in their languages. He made gestures to Rahb to make sure that he understood. Rahb drove the craft onto the bank. The ape-man stepped out and began climbing up a tree which leaned over the water. Waganero and Rahb dragged the dugout up the bank. They left it so that it would be easily seen by the pursuers. Then they hid in the foliage nearby.

The Shelaba slowed their boats when they saw the abandoned dugout. By then, Tarzan was lying face down and flat on a large branch twelve feet up and extending twelve feet over the stream. The leaves and vines hid him. Or he hoped they did.

Here came the Shelaba. They were cautious. Probably, they feared a trap. If so, they nevertheless slid into it. Before they passed into the shallow water, a big white body dropped from the branch overhead onto the boat in the rear. It was Tarzan, landing on his feet on the bottom of the dugout. Just before he struck, he yelled to add to the surprise and the confusion.

As he fell between two paddlers, he slashed out with his knife. Its very keen edge severed the jugular vein of one. And, as he went over the side of the tipping boat, he slammed a fist into the neck of another Shelaba.

Then, he was in the water. So were the two survivors of the craft. That had turned over completely and was now floating away along with the paddles the little men had dropped.

Tarzan, the flint knife now between his teeth, burst up out of the water. He jerked a paddle from a Shelaba in the other boat and brought its edge down on the head of a Shelaba struggling in the water. Quickly, he was under the dark surface again. He had glimpsed two Shelaba standing up in the remaining boat to blow darts at him.

Because he could not see through the murky water, he had to guess where the second boat was. He came up just where he had hoped he would. That was alongside the middle of the boat. He grabbed the side. But, instead of trying to turn it over, he gripped the side with both hands. And he was up and over the side and in the boat.

All except one of its previous occupants had been spilled into the river. That one was clinging to the side of the boat. He died at once.

By then, Rahb and Waganero had come out of the bush as if they were catapulted. They waded into the shallows. Their longer legs, trunks, and arms gave them an advantage over the very short Shelaba. Three of the tiny warriors were still trying to get into water where they could stand up. They did not last long.

Other survivors swam away toward the opposite bank. Tarzan let them go. When their tribesmen on land caught up with them, they would hear the tale of how their fellows had been ambushed. This might discourage the pursuers.

These two, though, would not be able to speak to anyone about their misfortune. Before they got to the bank, they disappeared, leaving only a swirl on the surface. Tarzan had seen the crocodiles just before they dived to seize their prey.

Now, other giant reptiles, drawn by the odor of blood, were in the river and headed toward the fight.

Not one to linger when events demanded action, the ape-man got the big dugout into the river and himself and his companions into the craft. Now, they also had a paddle for each of them, although two were smaller than those they were used to.

Tarzan had planned to go on down the river for approximately ten miles. By then, the Shelaba, if they were still on the track, would be even more behind them. Then, the boat could be hidden in the bush, and the three could make their way northward on land.

Or, at least, Tarzan could. What the other two did was not going to interfere with his plans.

Before he had gone a mile along the winding course, he heard gunfire. It was upriver and seemed fairly close.

He said, softly, "Mon Dieu!"

Tarzan was not in the habit of swearing even mildly. The great apes among whom he had been raised had no expletives, blasphemies, or obscenities. When frustrated, angry, or frightened, they screamed or bellowed. However, the ape-man had heard plenty of swearing when he was among the French, the first humans with whom he had had extensive contact. But he had not picked up the habit from them. Nor had he adopted the swearing he had learned from the English later on.

His very mild oath, "Mon Dieu," showed how frustrated he was now.

He thought that the likeliest origin of the explosions

was Helmson and his men. The members of the other
party with firearms, the blacks who had shot at him and
Rahb and Waganero, were all dead, but they could have
been part of a larger force. These newcomers might be
doing the shooting.

Given the number of parties that seemed to be popu-
lating this part of the jungle, it was possible that a third
and entirely unknown party could be firing, Tarzan realized with a great deal of irritation.

What should he do?

His decision came quickly. Whoever the strangers
were, they would keep the Shelaba from continuing their
chase. So, this was the best time to put in at the riverbank
and take to the forest.

He motioned to the others to head in toward the bank.

A second later, he said, "Zut!" And then, "Putain!"

These two expletives, comparatively restrained in
French, would have been stronger in their English equiva-
lents. He was not even conscious that he had uttered them.

Just ahead and to his left, three men had appeared out
of the bush. Then, one by one, others came out of the
jungle. Ten in all. They were tall black men dressed, he
supposed, in war regalia and painted with warpath symbols. All had necklaces composed of jawless human
skulls. Seeing him and the others, they screamed what
were obviously threats. They shook their long stone-
tipped spears at the three men.

Waganero groaned.

Tarzan said, "Who are they?"

"They are the Krangee, the tribe who live near The
Voice of the Ghost Frog," the harpist said. "They must be
on a raid to get slaves. That is the only reason they leave
their land. Most of the slaves they get, however, will be
passed on down the river to the people who live in The
City Made by God, and . . ."

Tarzan had seen the dugouts being dragged out from

behind bushes by the Krangee. He said, "Start paddling! Fast as you can!"

Though he churned with impatience and frustration, he had to accept what reality gave him. At the moment, he must keep on traveling southward. There was nothing else he could do, though it meant that he would be getting even farther from Jane.

And he would soon be in the land of the Krangee. There, if Martillo's manuscript was right, those unfortunates who heard The Voice of the Ghost Frog were always eaten. But Martillo had not described The Ghost Frog.

Beyond that land lay The City Made by God and those other enigmatic and sinister things and beings the Spaniard had described. The More than Dead, The Dark Heart of Time, Rafmana the Toucher of Time, and that enigmatic being with the sinister title The Uncaused Causer, also called The Unwilling Giver of the Unwanted.

21

ONCE AGAIN MEETA the rain and Pand the thunder galloped from the west unexpectedly early. The sun, before the clouds suddenly covered it, had been only several degrees past its zenith. By now, though, this strange land had conditioned the ape-man to expect the unexpected.

The bellies of Tarzan and his companions had been growling for hours. The three adventurers were also getting weak from lack of food and their incessant paddling. The ape-man was losing his strength faster than the others because of loss of blood, especially from his chin wound.

Just before the rain began, the Krangee had dragged into sight two five-man dugouts, and the pursuers were a half mile behind them. They had been lost to view in the darkness brought on by clouds and the almost solid downpour.

Tarzan at once told the other paddlers to head for the right bank. There they could conceal the craft, and there they could hide until their enemies had passed them. But things changed just too swiftly to do that.

The brown river suddenly became blue. It was a thick and dark blue, poisonous looking. When this happened, Waganero cried out with fear.

"It's The River of the Color of Death! Now, we'll soon

be in the swamp where The Voice of the Ghost Frog is heard! We're doomed!"

Tarzan supposed that the river now passed over a place where the bottom was rocks containing a pigment washed into the current. That seemed to be the only reasonable explanation he could think of. In any event, he was not going to argue with the harpist.

Now, the river suddenly narrowed. The dugout immediately picked up speed. The banks, which had been only a few inches higher than the surface of the water, were now two feet higher. And then the river seemed to plunge. The banks flew upward. The day became even darker. The river boiled around them. The boat rocked. The bow dipped, then tilted up, then dipped again.

Now, the channel became even more narrow. Dark though it was, Tarzan could see both banks. They were only twenty feet apart, and they were cliffs that soared up into the unseeable. Water began to fill the dugout. Part of it was the rain. Part of it was the surging stream spilling over the sides into the boat.

Tarzan called out through the smashing sound of rain, the roar of the very agitated river, the boom of thunder, and the explosions of lightning. He ordered them to scoop out the water with their hands.

He did not know if they heard him. By now, it did not matter. The rain was shooting off the projections of cliffs to form waterfalls. These torrented over the paddlers and filled the boat too quickly to be bailed out. He looked behind him. He could not see Waganero, though the harpist was only a few feet behind him.

At that moment, his only consoling thought was that the boats behind him would be in as dangerous a situation as his craft.

Unless, of course, they had gone ashore before getting to this perilous passage. They knew this territory. It seemed likely that they would climb the hills lining the river. They would then come out on the other side into their native land.

But they would not be waiting at wherever this river left this narrow rock-filled river. They could not climb swiftly enough to overtake this boat. The river was like a stream of water under great pressure spurting out from a fire hose. It hurtled the boat along at such a rate that its occupants could do nothing to control it.

That thought, however, did not cheer him. Just now, the Krangee were of no importance. The rocks his boat sped by were his only concern. Should his boat strike one, it would turn over and probably be shattered.

Less than twenty seconds later, the boat suddenly quit rocking and plunging so violently. It shot out of the narrow channel. But where were they?

He turned his head and yelled as loud as he could. Waganero leaned forward and tapped the ape-man's shoulder.

"What did you say?" he screamed.

"Tell Rahb to start paddling again! We're out of the turbulent waters, for the time being, anyway! I'll give you directions for changing our course! You relay them to Rahb!"

A moment later, he saw the right bank. It was again only a few inches above the surface. He relayed his orders to the black man. The boat veered away from the bank. Just as it did, Tarzan saw the rain-blurred figures of tall men approaching on the land.

These would be Krangee. But he did not know if they were the pursuers who had somehow gotten through the cliffs—a tunnel?—or if these were new opponents. In any event, the thing to do was to get away from here at once, which they did, on Tarzan's orders.

This rain lasted a long time. Hours later, it was still falling as heavily as when it started. The thunder and lightning, however, had eased off, so there were only far-off flashes and rumblings. By now, even Rahb's grizzly bear strength was enfeebled. Tarzan ordered that the boat be put into shore.

The river waters had ceased to be troubled. They seemed to be smooth except for the ripples caused by the rain drops.

Waganero commented that they should be in a lake. If his estimations were correct, they were close to the great swamp which led to The Voice of the Ghost Frog. Of course, he had never been here. He knew only what he had heard about it.

No one he had talked to about this terrible place had actually been here, he admitted. They had been relaying stories from the very few involuntary visitors who claimed they had been lucky enough to escape this place. They had lived and died before his great-great-grandfathers were born.

"What do the tales say about this Voice of the Ghost Frog?" Tarzan asked.

"It is said that those who hear The Voice will die. But they are fortunate if they do, because those who see The Ghost Frog itself will be eaten by it. They will then become The More than Dead. These will not die as others do. They will suffer the worst of pain as the acids in The Ghost Frog's stomach burn them, burn as the worst of fires burns. Their flesh and bones are entirely burned away, except for the soul bone. Nothing can burn that to ashes.

"A new body grows from the soul bone. Then, this will be almost burned away again. Only the soul bone will be left. Then, the body will grow whole again. This lasts forever. Those eaten by The Ghost Frog never die. Their torment will last until the world is worn away to dust. During this time, the numberless people that The Ghost Frog has eaten swell its belly.

"However, it is true that The Ghost Frog may be

charmed by the sound of a harp played by a great kaga-fona, which I am, despite what my love's father has said. And it is claimed that the man who charms The Ghost Frog with his music can summon from The Ghost Frog's belly one, only one, of The More than Dead.

"My love has been eaten by The Ghost Frog, and she has been suffering great pain in The Ghost Frog's belly. But I will play my harp and I will sing, and she will be vomited out from the belly. And . . ."

Tarzan spoke very softly to Waganero.

"If these people heard The Voice and were eaten, how were they able to tell others about their death? And how do you know that your love was eaten? Did anybody see this happen?"

Waganero was almost invisible in the darkness and the rain. But his voice sounded puzzled.

"I do not know. I just tell the tale as it was told to me."

"And you never thought to question it?"

"No. Why should I?" Waganero said.

Tarzan did not reply. He had come across this phe-nomenon before in the jungle, and in the great cities. The uncurious and the gullible were everywhere.

Whatever the truth was, he would have to find out for himself. However, there could be something solid and probably dangerous in this legend. It would be better to avoid the swamp, but the ape-man had a feeling that he and his companions could not do that. Like it or not, they would have to go on toward the south.

Just now, they had to fill their bellies. And they would have to find some place to hole up and to rest.

After a while, Tarzan saw a dim light flickering inland. Despite the fact that a light rain was still falling, it seemed to be firelight. Still speaking softly, Tarzan ex-plained that he was going to investigate, and suggested that they accompany him. They agreed that his course was the best. They paddled the boat to the dimly visible riverbank.

On the bank were about a dozen dugouts in a line. After beaching and hiding their own boat, the three pushed the others out into the water, letting the current take them away. First, though, Tarzan took from one boat paddles better fitted to their hands than the tiny Shelaba paddles. They put the paddles in their boat.

Following the light of the fire, they came to a village not far inland. They made sure that there were no dogs there before they approached.

The light came from a dying fire inside an open structure with a thatched roof. The man apparently entrusted with the job to tend it was snoring away.

Ten minutes later, still unobserved by the local citizens, the three left the village. They carried woven grass bags containing millet, fruit, and pieces of smoked meat. They ate these in their boat as it drifted downriver. Later, they put ashore again, and found a dead tree with a hollow just large enough to hold them.

They crawled into the cavity and again slept huddled together for warmth. In the morning, the rain stopped. But the clouds did not go away. And the river was still as blue as The Hideous Hunter's lips.

It was gloomy country in which they ate breakfast. And, not long after, they saw boats far off to the north, coming swiftly. Presently, the mass separated into a dozen long dugouts manned by many Krangee warriors.

Once more, the chase was on. During it, Waganero provided some interesting but at the moment irrelevant information. River tribes elsewhere, he said, ate tortoises and turtles. But the Krangee refused this food. They thought that if they ate the meat of these slow beasts, they, too, would be slow.

After a long time, the Krangee narrowed the gap between the hunters and the hunted, until only sixty feet separated them. Then, the Krangee suddenly upended their paddles.

"Why are they stopping?" Tarzan said to Waganero.

The harpist pointed ahead. He spoke in a quivering voice.

"I do not really know. But I suspect, indeed, I am almost certain, that we are entering the swamp where The Voice of the Ghost Frog is heard. The Krangee are said to be very brave and fierce warriors. But ahead is a place where they will not go."

"So the Krangee are no longer a danger to us?" the ape-man asked.

"The Krangee, no. But . . ."

The chase had gone through a lake, a river about three miles long, and on into this lake. Now, the lake had broadened into a swamp, and the flow of water was suddenly reduced. Far ahead, the peaks of mountains were visible on the horizon. The upper part of the peak of The Great Mother of Snakes was also visible. Its one red eye looked baleful.

It seemed to Tarzan now that the image of the serpent was part natural and part artificial. Surely, long ago, some artists had seen that painting certain areas of the mountain and joining them to certain mineral-streaked areas would result in a complete image. It must have been a gigantic undertaking and had probably taken a dozen generations.

According to Martillo's manuscript and map, this very place, about where the dugout was, marked the limit of his travels southward. He had not found the gold he had so fanatically sought. The local tribesmen—apparently not Krangee at that time—had told Martillo that there was much gold beyond the place of The Voice of the Ghost Frog. They were certain that part of The City Made by God was gold.

"Have you been there?" Martillo had asked the tribesmen.

They had replied, "No. But some of our ancestors were. And they came back with many tales of the wonders there."

On the other hand, the tribesmen had told him that no one who went into the swamp had ever returned.

Sick with fever and starving, Martillo had had enough of Africa. Even if he had found much gold in the land behind the mountain, he would have had no means to get the gold back to the coast.

However, he realized that his fortune could be made in the form of a book of wonders. Should he be able to return to Spain, he could write a chronicle describing his adventures and the marvels he had witnessed in this far-off and dark land.

He would have been able to make much money if anyone believed his tale, and perhaps even if it was not believed.

So Martillo had turned around and headed northward. After still more hardships and adventures and many dangers, the giant Spaniard had ended his epic exploration in the desert. There, the magnificent warrior— Tarzan thought of him as that—had died. And Tarzan, three hundred years later, had come across Martillo's bones. He had found the metal cylinder containing the rolled-up manuscript and map.

Which manuscript and map, Tarzan thought angrily, were now in the hands of Helmson.

22

A T A QUARTER to ten in the morning, while at his office, James D. Stonecraft got sick. He turned pale, and, shortly thereafter, vomited. Bevan immediately summoned his personal physician, who was in an office down the hall. Bevan made sure that not a word of his boss's attack would get to unauthorized persons. If the news got out, it would deeply affect the stock market and other vital business organizations.

An hour later, Stonecraft was taken to a private hospital, one of three he owned. Though the outdoor air was hot, the magnate wore a coat and a hat. He kept a handkerchief pressed to his face.

Later that day, Bevan, dressed in overalls and carrying a big, round, metal lunch bucket, visited his employer. He had to pass two security guards at the lobby desk and two guards stationed at the door of Stonecraft's room, which was huge enough for ten patients. The ailing man was attended by Doctor Springer, two female nurses, and a ticker tape machine.

Stonecraft was sitting up in bed. He did not look sick. But he did appear to be worried.

As soon as Bevan stepped into the room, Stonecraft asked, "What have you heard from Africa?"

"I'm sorry to say I've heard nothing," Bevan said. "How are you, sir?"

"Never mind that. I'll be back at the office early to-morrow morning. Springer assures me that my main trouble is indigestion. It caused symptoms resembling those of a slight heart attack, but my heart is as sound as the U.S. dollar. He wants me to rest for a few days, but I'll not be kept from work. You have, of course, not told my wife and children?"

"I won't unless you instruct me to do it," Bevan said. He was thinking, *Although if you die, it'll be too late to tell me anything.*

"Come closer," Stonecraft said.

Bevan approached his employer, stopping when his legs bumped into the bed.

Speaking very softly, something he seldom did, the magnate said, "Bend over. Keep your voice very low."

Bevan looked around quickly. The doctor was in a corner and talking to the nurses. Bevan bent down until his nose almost touched Stonecraft's. His employer's breath smelled like licorice.

"Is this close enough?"

"Yes. Now, Bevan, we've got to do something about Project Soma. I've very dissatisfied with the slowness of its pace, and its expense. Very dissatisfied. In fact, un-happy. Very unhappy. We've got to do something to speed it up, bring it to a much quicker and satisfactory conclusion. I don't want to . . . ah, I won't say . . . die be-fore this is done . . . but . . ."

His voice trailed off as he sank back onto the pillows and closed his eyes.

"Are you all right?" Bevan said. "Should I call the doctor to come here?"

Stonecraft muttered, "Is this a wild-goose chase? A quest for El Dorado? What if it's blasphemy, a defiance of God's way, of His plans for us?"

He began mumbling. Bevan leaned so close his ear

almost touched the magnate's lips. But he could make out nothing except unintelligible sound.

Bevan raised up, and he said, sharply, "Doctor!"

Stonecraft opened his eyes. His hand shot out and seized Bevan's hand.

"No! I don't want him! Do as I say, Bevan! This is to be a very private conversation, do you understand?"

Having made sure that Springer had moved back out of earshot, Bevan leaned over again. His heart seemed to be bouncing around in his chest. Perhaps his employer was going to reveal what this African operation was about. God knew it was more than time for it.

"It would be ironic if I died now," Stonecraft said. "Just when I have a chance, a very good chance . . ."

Bevan waited for several seconds. Then he prompted, "Yes?"

"Someday, I'll have to tell you what this is all about. I know you're dying of curiosity. But I can't . . . not just now, Bevan. First, we have to capture Greystoke, then . . ."

Bevan tried to keep the disappointment and anger out of his voice. "Yes, sir?"

"We've done all that could be done to expedite this matter. Yet . . . there must be more. But what? I want you to think very hard about this, Bevan. Come up with something we've not thought of, some way we've been blind to. We have to make things happen faster. Put a cattle prod to this project."

No one can hurry Africa, Bevan thought. *No one's big enough to do that. Africa goes at its own pace, very slow but very sure. Irresistible.*

But he said aloud, "You mean we must get our hands on that man in Africa?"

"Yes, of course! Don't pretend to be stupid, Bevan!"

"Sorry, sir! But there are so many serious matters that

need dealing with. They can't be put off. There are the Venezuelan oil rights, there's the Shawnee land suit . . ."

Stonecraft squeezed Bevan's hand with a strength surprising in a man supposed to be very sick.

"Tyler and Jones can handle those! I want you to solve this problem! I thought I had time, plenty of time! But I'm not at all sure now, Bevan! 'Man is but a flower, and he's cut down . . .' "

Once more, the magnate began mumbling. Bevan listened intently. Again he heard only nonsense. He straightened up and called to the doctor.

23

MEETA THE RAIN suddenly ceased. And, as often happens in the tropics, the sky was clear within a few minutes. It was as if a titan had whisked away the clouds the way a waiter whisks away a tablecloth.

Now, Hul the stars began to twinkle. The face of Goro the moon was almost full, and he spread his silvery smile over the land. Tarzan did not feel like smiling. To him, the swamp seemed to be a grisly fist unfolding and folding, unfolding and folding. It beckoned, but this was not an inviting gesture. At least, Tarzan did not think so.

Behind them, the Krangee sat silently in the moonlight. They were distant shadow-shrouded figures. But Tarzan knew that they were watching the men who had eluded them. They would make sure that these did not try to sneak back upriver past them. And they would probably keep a close watch for several nights and days.

Near the right bank, in the river, a large herd of Duro the hippo had been snorting and yawning, bobbing up, then sinking back. Before long, they would swim to the edge of the blue river—black in the moonlight—and they would begin eating the land plants.

In the shallows near the flood edge, gray herons as tall as the ape-man had been stalking. Now and then, their heads and snakish necks dipped. These came up with fish between their beaks. The birds were of a species he had never seen before. When Kudu the sun had not yet retired, Tarzan had seen the heron's scarlet-rimmed eyes and their bodies and wings, black as evil itself.

Crocodiles, their bellies in the mud, had been lying on the banks. A few of the great reptiles were cruising in the river and in the swamp, only eyes and nostrils and, occasionally, parts of a long gray body or tail were visible. Now, Gimla was silent and out of sight, hidden by the night despite the bright moonlight.

In that time between pure day and pure night, the owls had begun to fly over the forest border. Among them was a large black-and-green fish-eating owl. Unlike most owls, it did not hoot. It mewed like the kitten of Malskree the golden cat.

Black bats flapped from the forest. Along with the night birds, they soared and dipped while chasing insects.

A few sleek otters were still diving for fish. But they would soon be seeking their homes.

Suddenly, the Krangee were singing. Tarzan could not make out the individual words. If he could have done so, he probably would not have understood them. It seemed to him, however, that the voices were laden with the spirit of farewell, of saying good-bye forever. Curiously, there was no hatred or enmity in them. They seemed genuinely sad, and at the same time horrified. It was as if, for that moment, the Krangee felt that the beings they had been chasing were human beings, not just prey to be killed. And the Krangee were ... doing what? ... consoling those who were doomed to an almost unthinkably horrible fate?

Waganero was sitting just behind Tarzan. He spoke in a low voice.

"It would be better to go onto the land and then try to sneak back upriver. Anything is preferable to going into the waters where The Ghost Frog waits for his victims."

Tarzan also spoke in the soft voice that the swamp

somehow seemed to demand. His tone was not scornful, but his words were.

"What happened to your desire to charm The Ghost Frog with the music of your harp and your singing, so that it would vomit your love out? Why are you so suddenly very backwards about confronting it?"

Waganero was silent for a moment. Then, he swallowed audibly, and he spoke.

"You do not say so in so many words. But you accuse me of cowardice. In any other place or circumstance, I would try to kill you for that, even though I would be sure to be killed. But you are right. I am afraid! I am afraid! Who in their right mind would not be terrified? Yet, Tarzan, your words shame me. They remind me that I am not only a kagafono, I am a warrior, and my ancestors were all very brave warriors.

"Therefore, I will draw on the great courage of all my ancestors. I, like them, will be brave. I will not flee from the fearsome spirit that has my love in its belly. I will free her from the flames."

"I knew you would say that," Tarzan said. "But if you try to play your harp and sing, you might attract other beings, say, enemies who are not afraid to venture into this swamp or creatures with appetites as large as The Ghost Frog is reputed to have.

"No, do not strum your harp or sing. If you do, I will snap your neck."

"We shall see what the moment brings," Waganero said.

"I do not make idle threats," Tarzan said.

By now the jungle noises had died away. The only sound, when they were not speaking, was the chunking of their paddles.

Dead trees rising from the dark and slowly moving swamp waters had become more numerous. Moss hung in great swaths from the dead branches, though there were few branches. As far ahead as the three could see, which was not far, the darkness overcame the moonlight. The trees seemed to huddle together. Yet, when the three put a half mile behind them, the trees around them still were no more numerous.

But the trees ahead seemed to move closer together.

Everything suggested ruin. And the swamp stank of decay.

Waganero's teeth began chattering. Apparently, the fear of the things that bloom in the night, of creatures that prowl seeking the blood or the souls of human beings or both, was working on Waganero.

Tarzan did not have this fear, but he did not laugh at it as Europeans did. The Europeans had their own superstitions, though they usually differed from those of the blacks. He understood how this fear terrified the natives. They had been hearing the stories of ghosts and things from the other world since they were able to understand speech.

He also thought that the boat had gone far enough now away from the Krangee. He said, "We'll paddle toward the west now. We'll keep on until we come to dry land."

"And then we go west on land and then north, away from this witches' world?" the harpist asked hopefully.

"If we can," the ape-man answered. "The Krangee will probably be watching for us on both sides of upriver. They might expect us to backtrack. You don't have to go with us if you are really determined to seek out The Ghost Frog. After we're on the land, you may take this boat wherever you wish."

They swerved the boat to face what should be the west, though they could not determine the exact direction in this closeness of naked trees and a light as pale as milk much diluted with water. Anyway, it was in a direction at right angles to the one they had been following. That was enough for the moment.

Then Tarzan, who never ceased his vigilance ahead or behind, to either side, or down or up, saw a nest. It was a huge construction of branches in the lofty top of the dead tree. Something twittered far above them. When the emitter of the birdlike sound looked over the edge of the nest and down at them, its head did not seem to be a bird's.

He dug his paddle deeply into the water, and he thrust with all his strength. So did the other two. There was something about the bird that was not a bird that made them get away from it as quickly as possible.

When the boat was fifteen minutes or so from the nest, Waganero spoke.

"That must surely have been a ghost devil. It is said . . ."

"Don't talk unless it's to warn us of something dangerous," the ape-man said.

Then he said, "Stop the boat."

They did so. No one spoke. He listened to the airborne sounds. After a few minutes he broke the silence.

"I will be getting out of the boat to lie on that stump there."

He pointed to the black and broken-off remnant of a tree. It rose to a foot above the surface.

The others did not question him then, though they must have been very curious. But when he had slid out of the boat and pulled himself up and onto the jagged top of the stump, Waganero spoke.

"What . . . ?"

"I will be putting my head under the water," Tarzan said. "If you see anything I should be warned about, smack the water with the palm of your hand."

Before he could be questioned, he thrust his head down into the swamp water.

He had first done this when he was a child, perhaps nine or ten years old. He had been by the bank of a creek playing with Taug. Taug was a Mangani of Tarzan's size though not of an equal intelligence or curiosity.

Tarzan had told Taug to watch his back while he thrust his head beneath the surface. Taug was to warn him if he saw Sheeta the leopard or any other danger.

Then the young ape-man had peered into another world. It was a very strange world there. He could not see far, and what he did see was somewhat blurred. The worst thing was that he could not smell. Deprived of that sense, he was only a half Tarzan.

But sounds had come to him, sounds he did not hear when his ears were in the air. Later, after he had submerged his ears many times in creeks, pools, and rivers, he had come to know what he was hearing. The first time he tried this feat, though, he was not at all sure of what he heard.

Now, in the still waters of the swamp, he heard the swishing noises Pisah the fish made by swimming. Pisah seemed to be heading in one direction, away from the boat. He also picked up the tiny clicking of the claws of many crustaceans. Usually, this was a relatively slow clicking. But now the snapping noise suggested agitation, alarm.

Tarzan could also feel the differing pressures made in the water by various denizens of various sizes. The larger the fish or snake or crocodile or swimming animals, the greater the pressure, the louder the noise.

He lifted his head, breathed the foul air out, breathed in deeply, and dipped his head again. Now, he could identify what sounded like a dozen of his old enemy, Gimla. Not only the pressure their bodies made displacing volumes of water but their belly sounds assured him of the nature and number of the reptiles. These sounds, he had learned, were the means of communication Gimla used.

He could tell by their quick repetitions and their high-pitched noises that they, too, were agitated.

And, like them, the fish, crabs, and crawfish were alarmed.

He also heard a very faint yet identifiable rumble, the several belly voices of Kota the turtle. These, too, advised flight at once.

Whatever was coming, it was scaring every living thing in the immediate area of the swamp. It was large, very large, and it was fast.

He raised his head. Before he had got his breath, he was up and off the stump and into the dugout.

Then he said, "Something is coming, something we should look out for."

"What do we do?" Waganero said.

"We go ahead. There is nothing else we can do at the moment."

A few miles more toward the hoped-for west bank, they were forced to stop. In front of them and springing up from below water level, grew a wall of very black thorn-bearing plants. Their leaves were numerous, glossy, poisonous-looking, and fleshy. The bushes themselves grew at least twenty feet high. They extended horizontally as far as the boatmen could see in the weak light.

The bushes did bear a few fruit. These were orange-shaped and orange-sized and black.

Seeing them, Rahb became excited. He spoke rapidly, though not loudly. Finally, Tarzan understood him. Rahb wanted the boat brought around so he could lean out and pick the fruit.

The ape-man agreed to do this since there seemed little else to do at that moment. Then the great black-furred creature plucked two dozen of the fruit and quickly devoured them.

Tarzan managed to ask him about them in Rahb's native tongue. After several attempts, Rahb corrected Tarzan's speech. The ape-man repeated his question.

"I can eat them," Rahb said. "But they are not safe to eat for you. They poison sleeshintush."

"Sleeshintush?" Tarzan asked. A few seconds later, he came close to laughing aloud. He understood the word now. Freely translated into English, it meant "The Stinking People."

To Tarzan and Waganero, Rahb stunk very badly. But, according to Rahb, the odor of human beings insulted his nostrils.

A moment later, the boat was moving along the edge of the bush wall. It seemed to be going south, though Tarzan would have preferred the opposite direction. He hoped that the thick growth of the plants would not continue, and the boatmen could then get to land. But the barrier seemed to be endless.

"Like it or not," he said, "we should sleep in the boat. We're too tired and hungry to go on. But . . . I think it's best that at least one of us stay awake at all times."

He fell silent. So did the others. The only sound now was a singing in the ears. They could have been at the bottom of a deep cave.

Then Waganero whispered, "Have you noticed something strange?"

Tarzan strained to hear. How could this man have heard something he had not heard? No man had senses as keen as his.

"The odor," Waganero said.

The ape-man sniffed. He could only smell decaying vegetable matter floating in the water and the effluvia of the moss hanging from dead branches.

Chagrined, he asked, "What?"

"It is not something to smell," the harpist said. "It is what does *not* stink."

Tarzan sniffed again. Not until then did he understand what the harpist was driving at.

Rahb had lost his sickening odor.

"It's gone!" Tarzan said.

He turned around and spoke slowly to the bear-man.

Rahb replied, "It is the harskanen. What I ate from the bushes. If I eat those, I do not smell so bad to others. Also, I have more success in hunting."

"Then this land is where you were born and raised?"

"No. It's west of here. Far from the swamp."

"You ate the harskanen," Tarzan said. "Is there any food grown here which is not poisonous to us? We're very hungry."

Rahb had no chance to answer Tarzan.

A vast croaking came like an evil wind through the trees and over the water. It was not loud enough to deafen them. But it certainly startled them.

There was a three-second silence. Then, the croaking as of a frog bigger than three elephants grown together boomed through the swamp. Now, Tarzan could distinguish another sound accompanying the croaking. It seemed to be part of the sound, a sort of undercurrent. It was made of voices, many voices, human-seeming voices. It was as if a multitude of people were talking in wailing tones, tones empty of gladness or hope.

The harpist did not scream. But he said, too loudly, a word. It might have been the name of some deity or powerful spirit or a heroic ancestor.

Tarzan said, "Quiet!"

Though he did not believe in a Ghost Frog, he had to admit that the croaking sounded as if it came from a frog. However, that amphibian would have to be much larger than any he had ever seen or read about. And if the vast creature did exist, what did it eat? Its appetite would be prodigious. Hence, its prey would be large. Not many human beings, Tarzan was sure, ventured into this desolation of desolations.

What lived here in large enough numbers to feed this leviathan, this behemoth, if indeed it was such?

Breaking his own command to keep silence, he spoke, though very softly, to Rahb. He did not know enough of the Shong language to phrase his question clearly. But he tried.

"You come from this area, if not from this land. What is The Voice of the Ghost Frog?"

Rahb said, "I don't understand you."

So much for that.

The croaking continued. After a while, it seemed to be getting louder. The sound of many voices of men and women at the bottom of a well increased in volume. Of all the eerie feelings Tarzan had experienced, and they had been many, the impression caused by these voices was the eeriest. He thought that this phenomenon should be called The Ghostly Voices of the Frog, not The Voice of the Ghost Frog.

Tarzan told the others that they must get ready to defend themselves. They should use the poisoned darts and arrows first. But it seemed likely to him, though he did not say so, that the poison would not affect it. Indeed, the skin of so large a beast or whatever it was would probably be so thick the darts and arrows wouldn't penetrate it.

For some time, he and his companions sat and waited. Presently, the croak became deafening.

Tarzan looked ahead and behind him. Then he watched as Waganero suddenly snatched up his leather case. He began to open it.

Tarzan turned all the way around. He tore the case from Waganero's hands and threw it over the man's head. Though Rahb must have been caught by surprise, he grabbed the case with one hand. Then he put it behind him on the bottom of the dugout.

Tarzan drew a finger along his throat. The harpist nodded. He understood.

A wave came and lifted the boat slightly. It was followed by more waves, each higher than the previous one.

Waganero said. "We are going to die! Or we'll be swallowed and kept in flames in its belly forever. Even The More than Dead will not suffer so!"

Tarzan said nothing. He would do what had to be done when—if—The Ghost Frog attacked them. He might suffer from fire, but that would be the digestive juices of the creature's enormous belly. And he would not suffer long. Tarzan did not believe in genuine ghosts.

He thought of Jane then. What would she do if he failed to find her?

If he did fail, what happened would happen. He had something else to think about just now.

A croaking to shatter all croakings filled his ears. The boat rose on the highest wave yet.

Tarzan wanted to scream defiance, to challenge it, to tell it that he, Tarzan, was the worst enemy the thing had ever faced. But he knew that would be foolish. Perhaps, the thing was just going by. It might be unaware that three tasty bits sat nearby, just out of reach of its sight and smell.

Then, the bear-man yelled.

24

SOMETHING UNSEEN PULLED down on the left side of the dugout. For a moment, the boat was straight up from the side, at an angle vertical to the surface of the water. The violent movement catapulted Tarzan out into the stinking water.

Tarzan went down deeper than he had thought he would since swamps were usually very shallow. But the earthquake-inspired flood had raised the water level. At this point, the bottom was at least seven feet below the surface. He felt the oozy mud of the floor on his hands, and then he spun and shot upward.

When he came to the surface, he heard a loud splashing, a sound as of a giant flail beating the water. He made several strokes forward. Then his fingertips touched the boat. It was still rocking, though the movements were decreasing. The Ben-go-utor and the harpist were silent, but some smaller splashing noises indicated that his companions, too, were in the water.

On the other hand, he realized, those splashings might have a sinister significance.

Suddenly, the loud crashing noises ceased. At the same time, Tarzan's hand closed on something else floating on the surface. He groped along it. Then he recognized that it was a paddle. Holding it, he stroked forward until he could firmly grip the dugout. He placed the paddle in it, then pulled himself smoothly and powerfully into the

187

boat. It turned on its side while he was doing this, but it did not turn over.

He called softly. "Waganero! Rahb!"

They answered in equally soft voices. A moment later, he was helping them get into the boat without capsizing it. Rahb still had his paddle in his hand. And he was holding the leather strap of the harp case.

Waganero said, "What happened? What grabbed the boat? What made that thrashing noise? What. . . ?"

Tarzan ignored him. He spoke to Rahb.

"Why did you cry out?"

"You would have done so, too, if you had felt what I felt," Rahb said. "Something rose from the water. I heard it come up very swiftly, felt it for a moment just as its jaws closed on the boat. It was not the mouth of a frog."

Tarzan waited for a few seconds. Then, impatiently, he said, "What was it?"

"Unless I am mistaken, what I felt was the long snout and some of the teeth of an enormous crocodile."

The ape-man said, "Crocodiles do not croak like giant frogs."

"True. But perhaps this Ghost Frog or whatever it is eats crocodiles."

"Why do you say that?"

"Because I felt, and I could dimly see, and even more, I could smell something I had never smelled before. The creature was gigantic but by no means slow. It seized the crocodile, which had clamped its jaws on the side of the boat and pulled that side down. I know it was a crocodile because I smelled it. And then that Frog gulped half of the crocodile down. I could make out that much in the dark. Then it sank back—I felt the water rushing into the hole left in the water—and it and the crocodile were gone."

Tarzan translated this story for Waganero.

The harpist said, "The Ghost Frog has eaten the giant

crocodile which was going to eat us! Let us thank Eemabobo for saving us. And then let us get away from here as soon as possible. The Ghost Frog may still be hungry."

Tarzan still was not certain that the thing that had saved them was what Waganero believed it to be. It might be something else. Whatever it was, it was a creature completely unknown to him. And he didn't care to have any more to do with it.

They had lost one paddle. Their supplies of food and the spears, blowguns, and archery equipment were on the bottom of the swamp or floating unseen somewhere. Tarzan did still have a flint knife and sheath he had stolen from the village. They pushed on slowly and as quietly as possible with the two paddles.

Finally Tarzan said that they had gone far enough away from the place where they had been attacked. Now, they could sleep.

Dawn finally came. The skies were a gloomy blackish gray. The pall that the swamp seemed to exude still hung over the three. Not very refreshed because of their fitful sleep, they paddled on more or less southward for several hours. The bamboo-like plants with long-thorned boles and long-thorned branches bearing the glossy black fruit still barred the dugout's way to the right.

Rahb ate many more of the fruit. After a while, Tarzan stopped the boat and once again got on top of a stump. He put his head under water and listened. The noise that reached his ears indicated business as usual in the aqueous element. The sinister pressure, and the very strange noise as of many people talking, were gone.

Then he heard a large specimen of Pisah the fish approaching. He grabbed it as it swam headlong into his outstretched and still hand. He pulled it up. It was black-and-white striped, green finned, and a foot and a half long. He had never seen its like before.

Tarzan got back into the dugout. He cut off Pisah's head with the flint knife. Then he sawed through the backbone at two places to make three pieces. Waganero did not like it that he would have to eat his portion raw and bloody, but he did so anyway.

The ape-man decided that the impenetrable and thorn-studded wall on their right might run on for days. At his order, they changed direction. They would cut as straight as possible to the left. Perhaps there would be relatively open land there.

But as they paddled eastward, they noted that the current was speeding up. Before they had gone two miles toward the left, they had to paddle much harder to keep from going southward. Suddenly, they found that they had run out of swamp. Once more they were on a river, a narrow one. Its pale blue color became once more a deep blue.

Before long, they heard the rumble of a rapids. Tarzan and Rahb stepped up their paddling rate. The river had become a chute forty feet wide. The banks on both sides had become limestone cliffs the tops of which rose higher and higher. The gloomy skies soon became a narrow ribbon of comparative brightness far above them. The boat, now out of the paddlers' control, whirled. It banged several times against rocks in the boiling water. Somehow, it did not smash up or turn over.

They heard the roar of a waterfall ahead of them. Mists blinded them. Then they were falling.

Tarzan dived out of the boat as it tilted downward. He came up in seething water and was whirled around and around. Then he was completely under the water. He did not know which way was up, but he swam in what he hoped was the correct direction.

Something struck his head.

* * *

When he awoke, he had a very painful headache. He was, however, no longer in the water. He was lying on his back on soft mud. First, he saw the same gloomy sky. Then, a face appeared suddenly above him. Its black skin was painted with white circles and X's. It wore a broad-brimmed and high-coned hat of woven grass. A three-foot-long, white, black-edged feather rose from the top of the hat.

The head's lips moved. The speech issuing from them made no sense. The language did not even sound related to Bantu.

The man straightened up. Under a coating of rancid grease, his body was painted with various designs. His knee-length kilt was of antelope skin. A skull hanging from a belt made a queer sort of sporran. The belt also bore a scabbard from which the wooden handle of an iron or steel knife protruded. In the man's hand was a long spear with an iron leaf-shaped head.

Other black men, similarly dressed and armed, crowded over him. They jabbered for a while. Presently, they lifted Tarzan to his feet and bound his wrists together in front of him with thin leather strips. Near him were Waganero and Rahb, also standing, their wrists bound together. Three warriors with spears were guarding Rahb. They seemed uneasy and not at all eager to get near him.

One of the warriors carried the case-enclosed harp. Tarzan wondered how the strangers had managed to retrieve it. Perhaps Rahb had never let loose of it.

Tarzan said, "Waganero, who are these men?"

"I do not know."

The men around the ape-man were startled when he spoke. Apparently, they had not been sure that he was human. That did not surprise him. These people had probably never seen a white man until now.

Rahb spoke, and for a second time the captors were startled.

He said, "I have never seen these people nor have I ever been in their land. But I have heard of them. These are the Saweetoo people. It is said that they live in The City Made by God, though those who built it long ago have gone to The Shadow Land."

The captives were marched along the river over rolling terrain with many bushes and clusters of trees here and there. The land sloped very gradually upward. After an hour, they halted. The captives were fed dried meat and fresh fruits during the stop and given water to drink.

Then the three were coated with the stinking grease. It stung Tarzan's wounds. But, within fifteen minutes, the sting was gone. An hour later, he felt as if the grease was healing his wounds. Certainly, they no longer bothered him.

They came to a village. It was small, but it was protected by a wall of white-painted bricks. Round watch towers were spaced along the top of the wall. Then they came to a road made from flat stones and mortared bricks. After a while, they came to a fortress of bricks and stone.

The group halted for a few minutes while several tremors shook the land. These were not strong. After a few fruitless minutes of waiting for more, the captives and captors continued southward on the road. They passed around a number of walled villages and some areas where the villages became small towns. At all of these, the citizens crowded around to stare at the captives. They chattered among themselves and pointed with obvious awe at the ape-man and the bear-man.

At one of these villages, the soldiers stopped for a while to drink water and beer and to eat small loaves of millet or barley bread. The captives shared their food.

While eating the dense and coarse but good-tasting bread, Tarzan looked at an elephant nearby. Its two front legs were manacled. These were attached to big iron chains connected at their other ends to big stakes driven deep into the reddish earth.

The beast was neither a pygmy Tantor nor a forest Tantor. She was the giant of the savannah. She rocked back and forth and swung her head as if she would charge at the slightest provocation. Tarzan listened to the sounds seemingly issuing from deep in her stomach. Actually, they were in her throat. The ape-man knew that they were the words of Tantor. Tarzan called the language Tantor-gogo, elephant-talk. It was very simple. A linguist might have said it consisted more of signals than words as humans perceived them.

But Tarzan had been a friend and companion to this ancient lineage of proboscideans since early childhood. He walked boldly up to the she-Tantor, and uttered sounds unintelligible to the other humans. He put his hand on her leg. She stopped swaying and turning her head back and forth. Her eyes did not look so wicked now.

"I am Tarzan."

"We know of you," Tantor said. "My mother and her sisters knew of you though they had never seen you. Everywhere, we know Tarzan, and we know that you, though a mere male and a human, are our friend."

That translation was a loose one and much expanded beyond the limited text of her speech. But it was a true representation of her communication. For the word *Tarzan*, she used a sort of code of long and short rumbles to form a concept. That meant: He Who Knows Tantor.

"Have these puny vermin harmed you?" Tarzan said.

"Puny vermin" was a more or less literal translation of a rumble word used by Tantor everywhere to describe all human beings except Tarzan.

"Not so far," Tantor said. "But I do not know what to

expect. I am from far away. I was captured by the puny
vermin of the plains. And I have been given by one group
of puny vermin to another to another to another for a
long long way until I came here. I doubt I am through
being moved."

Tarzan believed that she was probably destined to go
to the capital, The City Made by God. But that was a concept she might not understand.

He said, "If I am ever able to help you escape, I will
do so."

Tantor said, "I know you will, He Who Knows Tantor."

"Until then," Tarzan said.

"Maybe," she said. Tantor was a pessimist and a
skeptic, that is, a realist.

The march began again. The road ascended gently
until it had topped a very high hill. Tarzan heard the
trumpeting call of the elephant and knew that it was
Tantor's farewell.

The soldiers halted for a moment. The clouds dissi-
pated quickly. The sun shone brightly.

Tarzan looked down the long valley until he saw a glittering in the middle of a large lake near the river. The
glittering was caused by an enormous white dome rising
from a great pillar in the middle of the lake. It was
formed of twelve curved and broad arcs, widely separated from each other, soaring out from the top of the
pillar and then down to the lake shore and plunging into
the earth.

Tarzan had seen many exotic and wondrous cities in
his thirty years of adventurous life. But he had never
seen anything to match this.

"The City Made by God," Waganero murmured.

The captain of the detachment struck the harpist
across the back with his club. Waganero cried out once
with pain. Though the captain said nothing, he did not

have to speak a word. The captives were to be silent until told they could speak.

As they went down the hill, they saw the beginning of the large city that surrounded The City Made by God. Hundreds and perhaps thousands of square houses of wood, stone, or brick. Square! Tarzan thought. Not the round houses of the jungle-dwelling blacks. These were square.

Then he heard the sounds of hammers beating on metal, and the ringing of metal against metal. One large open building showed smiths working on white-hot artifacts near hearths of glowing coals. Other smiths were working foot-propelled bellows.

Shouts arose from the many dwellings. Men, women, and children stood along the road. They screamed what seemed to be threats and made hostile gestures. But they did not step over the invisible line that the soldiers had established.

Many of the crowd wore white woven garments much like Roman togas. The small children, however, were naked. The women's raiment covered only one breast. The exposed breast was painted in red and white.

Presently, the road was on level land. Other roads, Tarzan noted, ran off at right angles from it. They were wide and paved. But along their way, and along the main road, were tall cross-shaped structures. Tied to these or sometimes nailed to the horizontal arms were animals with their limbs tightly bound together. Not all of them were as yet dead.

Also on the crosses were men and women and even some children. These, too, had been tied or nailed to the crucifixes. Some had not yet given up the ghost. From the bloated bodies of others drifted a stench Tarzan had smelled too many times. Ska the vulture wheeled above them. Others of Ska's kind were on the ground below the crosses. A few were clutching the cross arms and, bending down, picking at the flesh of the hands and arms of the dead or, here and there, stripping off the flesh of those not quite dead but alive enough to groan or scream.

The ape-man wondered if the victims were prisoners of war or sacrifices to some spirit or other.

He also wondered if the fate of these unfortunates was to be his.

If so, so be it. Meanwhile, he still lived. He would make the most of it.

25

THE CAPTIVES WERE taken into a large stone building. Here they were bathed, and their hair was washed by young women. These were very nervous when they laid hands on the bear-man and the ape-man. However, the warriors had their spears ready, and the captives' wrists were still bound in front of them.

After being dried off with cloth towels, the three were well greased. During this, the ape-man noted that those of his wounds that he could see were healing at an almost miraculous rate. The worst wound, the deep gouge behind his chin, had long ago ceased to bleed. He felt it. There was a crust on it, but that was peeling off.

Necklaces formed of scarlet flowers were hung around their necks. A little later, they were marched by many warriors to the foot of one of the great shiny arcs which spanned the lake from the apex of the pillar to the shore. An immense and noisy crowd awaited them.

Not until then did drums beat, horns blow, rattles shake, and harps thrum and plink. The three began walking up the very wide steps carved into the shining stone of one of the great arcs. There was nothing along each side of the steps to keep people from falling off. Spear-bearing warriors marched on all sides of the prisoners.

On reaching the apex of the pillar, they halted. The circular floor was the top of the shining dome that rested on the pillar that rose up from the center of the lake. It was huge—big enough to hold easily a thousand standing people. In the middle was an altar of what had been white stone. This they approached. Most of it was now covered with dark brownish-red streaks, the dried blood of sacrificial victims. Several men whom Tarzan assumed were priests stood before the altar. Their faces were painted dark blue, their robes were long and white, and they held short sharp knives.

Here is where we'll be sacrificed, he thought. *But it should be quick. Better that than the very slow and very painful death on the cross.*

He estimated that the top of the immense pillar was at least a hundred feet above the lake. From where he stood, he could see the array of the downward supports that curved from the edge of the pillar to the lakeshore.

Near the bottom of the steps up which the ape-man had come, a river left the lake. Though Tarzan could not see part of the opposite shore, he did see the river coming from beneath the edge of the pillar top. This flowed from the opposite side of the dome.

Before he had started up the steps, he had seen many boats on the lake.

The drums, which had been booming the entire time, suddenly became a staccato. The horns blew a long flourish. The harps and the rattles ceased their noise.

More steps reached the rooftop at forty degrees from those Tarzan had just ascended, and heads appeared above the edge of the great circle of the pillar. Then the bodies rose into sight, and the newcomers were approaching the prisoners. Officers shouted commands. The soldiers came to attention.

The chief of the party coming toward the altar was a very tall but very fat middle-aged man wearing a cap sporting the feathers of several different birds, a sort of necktie encrusted with rubies and diamonds, a long scarlet-and-white kilt, and a skull sporran. This was the skull of a huge Bolgani the gorilla. Fierce-looking warriors formed his bodyguard. Close behind him stood several fan bearers and a man carrying a large parasol made of leopard skin. The chief waddled toward a huge four-legged stool which had been set down by the side of the altar.

The drums, horns, and harps fell silent. One of the priests by the altar, a very old white-bearded man, faced the king. He got down on his skinny knees and kissed the stone floor three times. The king gestured at him. The old man rose to his feet and began shouting at him. Obviously, he was describing these three captives—though they were standing within eyesight—and was also describing how and where they had been taken prisoner. Judging from the king's expression, Tarzan was sure that he had already been told about this event.

During the long speech, a servant handed three large bottles of beer to the king, which he quickly drank. This impressed Tarzan. These people were not only workers in iron but makers of glass.

However, he was not here as a tourist. He had plans to get out of this country as quickly as possible. They were desperate plans and had to be carried out very soon.

Twice, he spoke quietly to the Shong and the harpist in their own speech.

"I am going to jump. I'll have to knock over the guards on my left. You follow me. Don't think about this. Just do it."

The warriors ranked around the prisoners were still at attention. They stood stiff and straight backed, the butts of their spears on the floor and leaning at forty-five degrees to the horizontal surface. Their eyes looked straight ahead.

Tarzan spun to his left, lowered his head, and charged. He had only a few feet to go to get to the nearest soldier. Before that man knew what was happening, he was knocked hard against the next man. That man also went down.

Behind the ape-man, Rahb bellowed.

Tarzan, still bent over, propelled his legs as if he were trying to push a mountain aside. He could not see what the two men at the end of the file were doing. Suddenly, the way was open.

He leaped over a fallen man and landed on the edge of the top of the pillar. Rahb's cry rose above the shouting of the soldiers and the screaming of the onlookers. Without hesitating, Tarzan sprang out into the void.

He was falling toward the blue lake a hundred feet below. The wind screamed in his ears.

He saw boats large and small on the lake, sailing boats and dugouts propelled by paddles. Fortunately, none were directly below him.

Immediately after jumping, he managed to straighten out horizontally. Thus, he would present as much surface to the air as possible and slow his fall somewhat. But, just before he struck the surface of the lake, he had to twist himself so that he would be vertical. Then, his legs held together, his arms up, he would have to pierce the surface as if he were a spear dropped at right angles to it.

Even so, the impact would be very great.

He hoped that none of his companions would fall on him before he was far enough down into the water.

The crash knocked him half unconscious. His fear that the lake might be shallow at this point was unjustified. He plunged deep, deep, yet did not touch bottom. Then he rose, though instinctively—he barely knew that he was doing so. His head broke the surface. He gasped for air. Near him, Rahb's black-furred, half-beast, and half-human face thrust up from the surface.

Tarzan's and Rahb's flower necklaces were floating on the surface. They had been stripped off them by the impact.

So far, there was no sign that Waganero was in the lake.

A long dugout, paddled by three men, was making toward them. Tarzan's senses came completely back to him then. Though his wrists were tied together, he swam as best he could away from the boat.

He called to Rahb. "Dive! I'll take one side of that boat! You take the other!"

He turned toward the oncoming boat, drew a deep breath, and swam downward, then onward. The sun was bright enough in the clear water for him to see the bottom of the boat cutting the water above him. It was not going so fast now. The men in it were backpaddling. Two were leaning over the side, looking for him. Doubtless, the other was staring down over the other side of the boat.

Tarzan could not see if the boatmen held spears. It did not matter. He had to attack.

Then the boat tipped on its side toward the ape-man. The two men were thrown into the water. Rahb had gotten to the enemy first.

Tarzan swam up in frog fashion. He ignored the two men thrashing around. By now, the boat had regained its normal position, though it was still rocking. With his two hands, still bound together with a long band, Tarzan grabbed the edge of the craft. He pulled himself up from the water and into the boat with one smooth and powerful movement. Then he sat up in it.

Rahb was treading water by the craft. The third man was nowhere in sight. Either he was swimming away underwater or Rahb had killed him.

Tarzan spared time to glance upward. The edges of the steps and the circle were rimmed by black faces.

He looked around. A number of boats were headed toward him. And now he could see Waganero swimming toward him. He called to Rahb, "Bring those two paddles. They're floating behind you."

It did not seem likely that they could escape. But he intended to try as hard as he could. For Tarzan, trying hard often meant doing the seemingly impossible.

Rahb, though handicapped by his bindings, got the paddles. He pushed them ahead of him until he came to the boat. Tarzan took the paddles, then he helped the huge and clumsy Shong get aboard. They almost turned the boat over.

"Now!" the ape-man cried. "Paddle! That way!"

He pointed with the paddle end at the outlet to the river on the south side of the lake.

But they had to stop to help Waganero to get into the boat.

A few minutes later, Rahb spoke over his shoulder.

"The boats ahead will cut us off from the outlet. Anyway, the drums will notify those down the river to intercept us. You can hear them sending messages now."

"What do you propose we do?" Tarzan said.

"Let us three stand and do battle with the paddles as our only weapons. We shall surely die. But we may kill some of them. They will know they were in a fight."

The shouting and cries of the men in the boats became louder. The beating of drums along the shores and up on the steps of the arcs increased. A large war boat with at least a dozen paddlers appeared in the river close to the lake. Its prow bore a figurehead which Tarzan was not near enough to see clearly. But the war canoe would soon be in the lake itself.

The man sitting just behind the figurehead stood up. His tall plume of feathers waved in the wind. He raised a big brass horn to his lips and blew three long notes.

Those sounds were like magical words uttered by a sorcerer. The people in the boats around them quit paddling. Their mouths fell open, but they did not speak or cry out. Some people on shore ran away, seemingly in a panic. The drums and the horns fell silent. There wasn't a sound except for the cries of the birds wheeling over the lake. There was no motion except for the current and the wind blowing on the feathered plumes and shaking the leaves.

Rahb, like Tarzan, quit paddling. He whispered.

Tarzan said, "What?"

Before the Shong could answer, they heard the chunking of the paddles. Now, the newcomers were so close that the ape-man could see the boat's long figure-head. It was green-painted wood carved into the image of Histah the snake with the end of its tail in its mouth. Tarzan knew that this image of his ancient enemy represented a symbol of eternity, or of the cyclic nature of time itself. It also had been used by the Vikings, some of whom were his ancestors, as the figure of the Midgard Serpent, the giant evil snake that circled the world. Various peoples, ancient and modern, used this symbol all over the world. Thus, it was no real surprise to find it in this remote and exotic land.

The snake boat slowed. Once again, the man standing in the prow blew his brass horn. It was curved and flared open at one end, and around the mouth was set a ring of gold. The man wore many bracelets and anklets of gold, and his headband was of thin beaten gold.

The Spaniard's tale about the abundance of gold in this area seemed now to have been validated.

The prow bumped very gently against the side of Tarzan's dugout. He did nothing because the man with the horn had held up one hand, palm out. That normally was a sign for peace.

Anyway, these men were not of the same tribe as their captors. Their skins were not glistening with rancid grease. Only sweat made them shine. Their long and kinky hair had been shaven on top of their heads to form an image of a snake. Tarzan saw this when several of them bent forward and he saw the Histahs made of hair.

Not only that. The men's lips were painted crimson.

Their eyes were circled in yellow. Thin vertical black marks were painted over their eyelids and below and above their eyes. These clearly stood for the slit pupils of snakes. On the chest of each man was painted a tail-in-its-mouth green serpent.

Their only clothing were loincloths made of the skin of the python.

All this was too much Histah for Tarzan. He loathed and detested snakes.

The man with the horn studied the ape-man and his companions for a moment. When he spoke, he did not use the gibberish Tarzan expected.

His speech was of the Bantu language family. Though it must have been long separated from other Bantu tongues, it was still somewhat intelligible to Tarzan and Waganero. With the aid of signs, the interpreter made himself understood well enough.

"We have come for you. But we were almost too late."

26

BEVAN WAS SURE that Stonecraft was in a coma. Perhaps it was wishful thinking, but he was also certain that it would be the prelude to the death of his employer.

Indeed, Doctor Springer assured Bevan that there was no doubt about it. Stonecraft had gone into a fatal coma. Springer, ordinarily a cautious man, would stake his reputation on it.

Therefore, Bevan thought, he would have to act swiftly. He must keep this information as his secret for as long as he could. He would be able to make a very large fortune before the news got out.

He told the doctor, "Take care of him. But don't tell anyone except me what his condition is. It's absolutely necessary that everybody keep mum about this for a while. For business and legal reasons, you know."

Doctor Springer stared hard at Bevan through his gold-rimmed pince-nez. He said, sharply, "I am not in the habit of disseminating information to unauthorized persons unless my patient tells me to do so."

"I am sure of that, and I didn't mean to insult you," Bevan said soothingly. "But it's vital that no one knows his condition. Not now, anyway."

"What of his wife?"

"I'll be the one who keeps her informed," Bevan said. "You examine Mr. Stonecraft. I'll be back in a few minutes to get the results."

He left the room swiftly. He went to his own room and picked up the phone. After several minutes of telling his stockbroker, Hitcham, what and how much to sell and to buy, he said good-bye. He had made Hitcham swear that he would not divulge anything to anybody about the identity of the man who was making all these purchases and sales.

Bevan knew, of course, that Hitcham was aware that something was up. The broker also knew better than to ask Bevan about it. But Hitcham would be selling and buying, too. He would make a fortune riding on Bevan's back. It would all have to be done subtly. No one must notice. Not for a while, anyway.

Bevan, who seldom smiled, was grinning broadly as he came into his employer's sick room. He was going to make a killing, and . . .

He halted just after he stepped through the door. His smile was as unchanged as if it had been painted onto his face. But, inside him, he felt as if a noose had been placed around his neck and he was falling through a trapdoor.

Perhaps, in a sense, he *was* being executed.

The magnate, his very sick and comatose employer, was sitting up in bed. The paleness was gone. His face, in fact, looked flushed as he talked with the doctor.

Bevan finally broke loose from the metal mold around him. He walked toward Stonecraft. He said, "I . . . I . . . I . . ."

"What in the world is the matter with you, Bevan?" the magnate said.

"I . . . I am very surprised . . . I thought . . ."

"You thought I was going to die, didn't you?" Stonecraft said. "Well, Bevan, so did Doctor Springer, though the quack didn't say so in so many words. But something happened. It could be a miracle, though Springer assures me that such things do happen, and naturally. But what, really, do I care what he thinks? I'm going to fire him.

Anyway, here I am, come back, you might say, from the bourne from which no one ever returns."

Bevan stopped at the foot of the bed. It was an effort, but he kept from goggling. His head seemed to rise high, to stretch his neck toward the ceiling.

"It is a miracle, sir!" he said too loudly.

"Whatever it is, and I don't deny that God may have had a hand in this," the magnate said, "it did happen."

He leaned back against the high-piled pillows. "I think I'm being saved for a very important reason. I may be the very first . . ."

His voice trailed off as he closed his eyes.

"The very first, sir?" Bevan said.

Stonecraft opened his eyes. "Never mind. But, now that this has happened, I'm very sure that a higher power wants me to succeed in my . . ."

Hesitating, he glanced at the doctor, then continued. ". . . African project. God himself has said so. Not in so many words, you understand, but in effect."

Bevan did not understand. He thought, *When in God's name is he going to tell me what this business is all about?*

He was given little time to keep wondering.

Stonecraft smiled. Bevan, who knew his boss well, knew that this smile was cynical. And it contained, perhaps, a hint of evil. Though the evil might only be in his, Bevan's, mind.

"Now, Bevan, I think you should make haste to get to your private telephone and advise your broker to buy back what you sold and to sell what you purchased. Better do it fast."

The secretary's knees turned to water. He shook. But he did not argue. Though he felt as if he would fall on his face, he managed to turn and to walk out of the room.

Behind him, Stonecraft chuckled.

* * *

Three mild tremors had shaken the earth under Helmson's and Fitzpagel's feet. They had also sent wild waves through the river. After a while, the tremors seemed to have stopped, and the river started to settle down.

But, suddenly, the surface of the river plunged, literally plunged. Within five minutes, the level had sunk at least a foot and a half. The two men stared in amazement. Neither had ever seen such a phenomenon.

From far down river, a faint bellow sounded.

"Saints presarve us!" Fitzpagel said. "What do ye think it is?"

"I don't know," Helmson said. "Maybe—I'm just guessing—some chasm south of here has opened up, and the river rushed into it. I don't know."

Now, the rate of sinking slowed down, but the water was still dropping. The top of something round appeared. It was approximately thirty feet from the two men. They waited. In another five minutes the face of a fearsome-looking being appeared. It had the carved features of a half monster, half devil. The statue seemed to be made of some unknown material. Its identity would have to wait until the mud covering it was wiped off.

They walked out into soft mud, which stank of dead flesh and dead vegetation. The mud was up to a few inches above their ankles. At every step they took, the mud threatened to suck the boots off of their legs.

Flies swarmed around the mud as if they had just hatched from tens of thousands of eggs. They buzzed and hummed and keened. But the men had donned mosquito netting over their helmets, and their hands were in thin gloves.

After a lengthy silence, Helmson resumed talking.

"Two men dead from cobra bite. One snatched away by a crocodile. Three so sick with fever they have to be left behind with two others to nurse them."

"We really can't spare those two men," Fitzpagel said.

"No, we can't spare them. I agree with you on that. But . . ."

Helmson stopped talking and glared at the Irishman.

"Leaving the sick without someone to care for and guard them . . . that wouldn't be good for morale! You want the rest of them to desert us? That'd be a sentence of death for us!"

"We may be under that now," Fitzpagel said. "I don't know . . . this country . . . it's strange, very strange. Can't you feel it? It's somehow different. There's something unnatural about it."

"Is it your Celtic intuition tells you that?" Helmson said. "To me, it's just Africa, though that's saying a lot. The whole damned wonderful continent is strange. And deadly. And that's enough to make you wonder what in hell a man's doing here. White or black, if you're in this jungle, you're facing a deadly beast.

"But there's gold for all of us. Gold, gold!" he added gleefully. "And we know the way to it! The manuscript and the map tell us that."

The remaining porters had been busy loading the supplies into the dugouts. They had stopped because of the swiftly receding water. They could do nothing except wait for the river to quit dropping. Then they would drag the boats down to the new edge of the river. And they would resume loading.

Under normal circumstances, they would have been talking loudly or singing. Now, they were as silent as possible. Askari were guarding the perimeter of the camp. Yesterday, the safari had been attacked by a fleet of the locals as Helmson and his crew had paddled around a big bend in the river. The locals had been driven off, with heavy losses to both sides.

But the jungle was the greatest enemy.

Fitzpagel scowled for a minute. Then he said, "What if

the map isn't a true one? What if Martillo was preparing a big scam when he got back to Spain? What if . . ."

"We've gone too far to back out now!" Helmson said. "If the map is correct, and I believe it is, we should soon be in sight of the mountain he called The Great Mother of Snakes. Then we'll know for sure he wasn't lying."

Fitzpagel was staring at the statue. He said, "And if we don't see it? For all we know, we may have gone past the point where we could see its face. We could have done so when it was raining so hard we couldn't see more'n three feet away." He pointed at the mountain that was looming above the jungle trees. "Maybe that's the side of The Great Mother of Snakes?"

"Whatever you do," Helmson said, "I'm going on. I'm no quitter."

"Don't get insulting," the Irishman said.

His face was red, and his hands were clenched.

"I'm as good a man as most and better than some I could name. But I'm also rational, and I know when to throw in the cards. I'll give ye two more days. Then, if we see no such mountain, I go back with me men. No arguments, no ifs, no buts. I go!"

Helmson started to put his hand on the butt of his .45 Colt automatic pistol. But he withdrew the hand. Now was not the time to threaten Fitzpagel. Helmson knew that, despite his bold words, he would be very handicapped if Fitzpagel and his men left the safari. There was no telling how many savages stood between him and his goal or what nonhuman dangers infested this land.

He choked back his anger and said, "The map isn't according to scale. Why not give this four more days, at the very least?"

"Two days. Two days is all. Then we part."

Fitzpagel's red-shot eyes looked determined.

Helmson saw a vision. He was alone in the jungle with Fitzpagel. The others were off some place. Without hesitation, he pulled the gun, gripped it by the barrel, and slammed the end of the butt into the back of the Irishman's head. Then he used his knife, the one he'd taken from Tarzan, to cut the unconscious man's throat, after which, he dragged the corpse to the river and dumped it into the water. Crocodiles quickly took care of the body.

It was a very satisfying fantasy. But what would he do after the murder? How would he explain Fitzpagel's disappearance to the blacks? Actually, he thought, he didn't have to explain. He would just say . . .

That wasn't going to happen. The Irishman was never alone with him. When he was with Helmson, some of his men were always in view or within earshot. That Fitzpagel made sure of this told Helmson that Fitzpagel did not trust him.

But that was to be expected. Helmson did not trust Fitzpagel either. He knew that, if they discovered gold or, somehow, captured Tarzan again, Fitzpagel would try to kill him. Though Helmson had no proof of the man's treachery, he was one hundred percent sure that his partner would attempt to murder him.

After all, he himself intended to make sure that he did not have to split any loot or rewards with Fitzpagel. Meanwhile, he needed his partner.

Fitzpagel spoke excitedly. "There! Look there!"

He pointed at the statue. There was mud around it up to its waist. Beyond it, the river was still falling.

"What? Where?" Helmson said.

"That arm! The arm!"

Helmson looked. Of the four arms of the statue, that nearest to them was stretching toward them. The long-taloned hand had lost its coating of mud. The bare streak on it glinted yellowly.

Fitzpagel tried to dash toward it. But the mud came higher and higher up his boots. He slowed down. Very shortly, he had sunk down almost to the top of his boots.

They came off his legs. But he struggled on until he reached the statue. Now, he was up to his knees and slowly sinking. But he brought his knife out and began scraping away what looked to Helmson like metal.

Even before Fitzpagel began howling out his discovery, Helmson knew what it must be.

Gold! Gold! Gold!

27

"WE HAVE COME for you. We were almost too late."
Tarzan had not been told why he and his companions had been rescued. Thus, he did not know what fate was planned for them. However, his saviors seemed to be in no hurry to take the three to wherever they planned on going.

Tarzan and Waganero were hauled aboard the first war canoe. There they sat among the paddlers.

Rahb was taken onto the second war canoe. His wrists were left bound, and two spearmen sat directly behind him.

Then they waited. Tarzan watched as a dozen warriors left the third boat and started climbing up the steps to the top of the dome. After a while, a warrior came back down. He carried Waganero's encased harp.

A few minutes later, all the men in the canoes looked upward. Tarzan did so, too. He saw nothing to stare at. Then he heard a scream, and a man hurtled down from the top of the pillar. A spear stuck into his back waggled like a reproachful finger. He quit screaming halfway to the surface of the lake. By then, the ape-man recognized the executed man.

He was the king—the late king.

Whatever Tarzan had expected to happen, he had not expected that.

Within a few minutes, the warriors came back down

the steps on the double. They got into their canoe, and the paddlers headed it into the mouth of the river.

The ape-man took a last backward look at the lake. The corpse of the fat king was being hauled onto a boat.

Tarzan asked the man with the horn to answer some of his questions. The man spoke a few words. Though the ape-man did not understand all of them, he had no trouble interpreting the two phrases. Tarzan had been told he was to ask no questions until he was given permission to do so.

The drums, harps, horns, and voices from on top of the pillar had been silent. Now, as the war canoe carrying Tarzan started to go around a bend in the river, they all burst forth. They seemed to be celebrating some event. The execution of the king? Announcing a new king? Or both?

The canoes sped past farms and orchards that lined both banks and, every mile or so, a stockade fort. Then the jungle again took over. More and more of Duro the hippopotamus surrounded them. And there were many more of Gimla the crocodile sunning on the tops of ridges of earth left exposed by the sinking of the river. Suddenly, the hippos and the crocodiles were left behind.

The river became even more narrow. Tarzan could have reached out to either side and touched the end of a drooping branch.

The current kept on accelerating. Before long, the canoes put into a shallow creek that had a weak flow of water. The boats were hauled ashore and beached. The captives were marched on a dirt road up a steep hill. After going down into a valley and then up an even higher hill, they came to the river again, as it shot out of a tunnel in the hill, and into another lake.

Here were canoes tied to stumps by the bank. Everybody got into the boats and started in a general southwest direction. It was difficult to be certain of the direction, though, for it was near dusk, and a heavy rainfall had started. Nevertheless, the canoes did not stop until they had put many miles behind them, traveling in the dark.

They stopped among the first of the hills past the mountain called The Great Mother of Snakes. After all had gone ashore and settled down for the night, Tarzan had a chance to speak to the Shong. Both were side by side on the ground. Tarzan whispered to Rahb.

"Helmson has your mate, and he has made you a promise. If you tracked me down by my scent, so that he could capture me, he would give you both your freedom. That is, after I'd been delivered to whoever it is that wants me. Am I right?"

"Except in one thing," Rahb said. "My mate was with child. By now, it should have been born. Thus, he has two in his power. I am doubly bound to obey him. But . . ."

"Yes?" Tarzan said after a long pause.

"We three are the last of our kind. The very last. I am sure of that. Even if he has not killed them for my betrayal, even if we get free of the evil white Stinking Man, and others do not capture us or shoot us, what future do we have? If we had more children, they would feel compelled to mate with each other, brother with sister. That would mean, eventually, that sick and monstrous children would be born. Then our kind would die out, anyway. So . . . why strive to live? The main reason I still cling to life is . . . I want to kill Helmson."

"You don't know that there are no others of your kind," Tarzan said.

Suddenly, tears ballooned in the bear-man's eyes. The ape-man was surprised. He had not expected such a creature to be able to weep. Then he thought, *Why not?*

Tarzan lifted his hands and placed them on Rahb's massive and hairy shoulders. The sorrow of this creature had touched something in him. Perhaps it was the memory of his own deep grief when his foster mother,

Kala, the tender and loving great ape, had been killed.

"There is always hope," he said. "I promise you I will help you find the place where your mate and child are imprisoned. We will free them. And we will kill Helmson. Of course, though, I must do all this after I have found my own mate and taken revenge on those who abducted her."

Rahb spoke in a quavering voice.

"By the time we found your mate, if we ever did, my mate and child would have been taken by other Stinking People. They would be caged and put on display until they died. Then they would be cut apart, their organs studied and then their skins would be stuffed and put on display."

"Helmson told you that?"

"Yes."

Tarzan considered this for a moment. "Could you find your way back to where your mate and child are kept?"

"No. But they would be someplace else even if I could find it. Helmson told me that my mate and the child would be moved from place to place from time to time. So, I would not be able to find them . . ."

"I don't believe he would move them," Tarzan said. "Now, I have another question. It seemed to me that you meant to throw Mitchell off the branch. But he tripped trying to get away from you. Obviously, he had never seen you before. Yet . . ."

"Helmson had told me that I should kill Mitchell the first chance I had to do so. Helmson believed that Mitchell was a spy for whoever had, ah, had . . ."

"For whoever had ordered Helmson to capture me alive," Tarzan said.

"Yes. Nobody except you saw me on that branch. All except Helmson believed that you killed Mitchell."

28

THE NEXT NIGHT, following a hard, all-day voyage, the captors and the captives slept in a large longhouse by the river. Tarzan and his companions were so carefully guarded that they had no chance to escape.

All night long, drums near and far were beaten, and horns were blown. At dawn, after eating and bathing, the party got ready to push on down the river. But, before they could get in the boats, more tremors shook the ground. The river waters were upheaved somewhat. The party waited a while for more and larger shocks. When these did not come, the waters settled down. Then, the chief gave the order to push the boats out and begin paddling.

Shortly afterward, the chief deigned to introduce himself to his captives. He said his name was Oyabatu, and his tribe was the Ataka. It was the "elder brother" of the Saweetoo, the people of the land where the king, Eshawi, had been executed.

Tarzan asked him several questions.

Why was the king executed?

Because, Oyabatu replied, the king had lied. He had tried to hide from their ruler, Rafmana, that he had captured three strangers, two of whom were extraordinary indeed. No one lied to The Toucher of Time, The Masked One, The Eye of the Glittering Tree, The Feeder of the Dark Heart of Time, without suffering death. Though King Eshawi had finally sent a message to Rafmana, he had been far too late doing so. In addition, King Eshawi had obviously planned to sacrifice the three strangers to his ancestors. He should have sent the strangers on to Rafmana so their ruler could determine how and when to dispose of them. But he had not done so.

However, Rafmana had known at once the very moment that the strangers had been captured, perhaps as soon as when they had entered the land of the Krangee.

So, King Eshawi, who already had been behaving in an increasingly arrogant manner, had been sentenced to die at once. He would be an example to his people and to his successor.

"The City Made by God," Tarzan said. "It seems to me that the Saweetoo, though they work in iron, are not capable of making as marvelous a structure as that. No people in the world are capable of doing that."

"That is not the genuine City Made by God!" Oyabatu said. "Though the Saweetoo claim it is, the real city is in our land. The Saweetoo are liars and always have been and hence will always be inferior people. But we permit them to claim that they built that city. Rafmana is amused by that.

"In reality, the Saweetoo city and the one in our land, The City beneath the Waters, were built by people who came from up there."

He pointed upwards.

"They came from the land beyond the clouds, beyond the skies, beyond the sun. They were not human, yet they were not spirits. Nevertheless, they begat children by humans. And Rafmana is descended from them. So, as a matter of fact, am I. But I do not brag about it. It is not good to boast about one's self when spirits or demons may hear you."

At that moment, the canoe passed a giant tree that stood fifty feet inland from the right bank. All except for the captives stood up, faced the tree, and sang some sort of chant. Hanging by their necks from the branches of the tree were at least thirty dead men, women, and children. Ska the vulture was in large number there. He was very busy stripping off the rotten flesh from the bones.

When the boats had passed the tree, the men stopped singing, sat down, and began paddling.

In reply to Tarzan's question, Oyabatu said, "That is a sacred tree, though not nearly as sacred as the one on Rafmana's tower. The people hanging from that tree are sacrifices; they died willingly. They gave up their lives in honor of The Masked One. As a reward, they will live forever in perfect health in a trouble-free world."

"The Masked One?" Tarzan said. "You mean Rafmana?"

"No. Rafmana is The Other Masked One."

Tarzan asked Oyabatu what he meant by that. The chief just grunted. For a moment, Tarzan was silent. He still did not understand the complexities of the local religion. But then he did not understand much of any religion, though dozens of people in the "civilized" world had tried to explain them to him.

By now, however, he did know enough to believe that all these mysteries could be wrapped up inside a single thought. That is, if the Creator revealed the Truth, all present religions would vanish instantly.

The ape-man was curious enough about The Uncaused Causer to ask Oyabatu about that enigmatic being. To Tarzan's surprise, Oyabatu did reply.

"It was long long ago prophesied that, some day, a strange creature would come from the north to our land. It would have no evil in its heart toward us. But the goddesses, including The Great Mother of Snakes, had decreed that the half beast would be the focus and the bringer of great destructive forces. It would cause the ruin of our land and its people. Yet, it would not know that it was destined to do this.

"That is why we call it The Uncaused Causer, The Unwilling Giver of Unwanted Gifts, The One to Avoid."

Tarzan thought that, if these people really believed that, they would kill every stranger who came to their land.

"How will you recognize The Causer?" he said.

"Only Rafmana can recognize it. But Rafmana can only do so by consulting The Tree when The Causer is touching The Tree and Rafmana is also touching it. I do not know why this is. Perhaps, The Tree tells Rafmana. But I do know that The Causer comes from the beasts and is itself a beast. Or so says the ancient prophecy. However, Rafmana does say that not all prophecies are true prophecies. Some may have been uttered by The Evil Twins, The Sayers of Lies. We will discover the truth when it appears, though it may then be too late for us to do anything about it."

At noon, just after a hard-driving but brief rain shower, the river widened into a large lake. On both sides, as far as Tarzan could see, were very high cliffs. On top of them were giant statues. Oyabatu said that they were images of Penago, the four-armed god of Time. Some said Penago had only one face. But these had two faces. One looked ahead. The other looked behind. Each statue had a hollow core, but each was very heavy because it was made from pure gold.

Oyabatu stood up and began blowing on the horn. Its long and eerie notes ascended to the skies. The clouds began dissipating. The fierce tropical sun beat its golden light into hot air.

Ahead there appeared a high cone-shaped island. Its blackish-red stone cliffs bore three painted and gigantic images on the side toward Tarzan. They were rock pythons forming a circle, their tails in each others' mouths. A tower at least three hundred feet high was built on the top of the cone. It was formed of huge black stone blocks.

Something on top of the tower glittered. Tarzan could not see what it was. Then they neared the base of the island, and the bright object was lost from his view.

The canoe entered a large dark opening in the side of the cone. From there, it plunged into increasing darkness. After a while, the light from the opening disappeared, but some of the canoe men lit torches, and these illuminated their slow and silent passage.

Suddenly, light shone ahead. They increased their speed as the opening grew larger. Then they came out into full daylight. They were deep within the hollow interior of the mountain, which might have been a dead volcano. The sun was visible just above the edge of the top of the tower wall. As the sun sank beyond the edge, far above them, the sky remained bright blue.

Oyabatu blew his horn again. The notes bounded off the straight up-and-down sides of the great well. When these ceased, a horn blew far above them. The canoe stopped. A large floating platform offered a landing place. From there, Oyabatu led the captives and warriors to a steep stairway cut out of the blackish-red rock. It corkscrewed around the inner wall. They climbed up the steps slowly, their left shoulders frequently scraping the stone.

Halfway up, Tarzan saw the first of many windows carved into the walls of the cone. Light shone dimly through them. But he could see the guards' white eyes and teeth and white feathered headdresses. These windows afforded passage for missiles launched by the guards stationed deep within the walls.

They came to wooden platforms and stairways attached to the walls. After going up these, they came to gently slanting tunnels that had been cut out of the rock. And then they were on the top of the round island and continuing up the interior of the tower. After this steep climb, they emerged on the very edge of the top of the tower wall. Here, near the outer part of the rim, was the thing the glittering of which had caught Tarzan's eye.

It was a tall, wide tree with many branches and many leaves on the branches. But it seemed to be made from a single crystal. And its roots were sunk into the stone as if they were sucking food from the rock.

Moreover, near the translucent surface of the crystal floated large light-green objects. Or they seemed to be within the tree though it was hard to be certain that they were not on the surface itself. The objects were as broad as his hand. But when they wriggled and fluttered and turned to present their edges, they looked as thin as a razor blade.

The ape-man's gaze passed on, though reluctantly, to a three-story building made of worked stone. It perched on the rim of the tower wall. From its flat roof a metal pole rose. Near the top of that was a large flag spread out by the strong wind.

It bore the image of a python poised to strike.

Oyabatu barked orders. The warriors assembled in military file. A tall man stepped out through a doorless opening. He was clad in a brass conical helmet, an iron cuirass and greaves, and python-skin sandals. His triangular wooden shield bore a python image. His left hand clutched the shaft of a long iron-tipped spear.

He spoke loudly, bidding Oyabatu to announce who he was and what he was doing here, though he must surely have known the answers to his questions. There were more of the time-mossed ceremonies. Presently, the warriors were told to be at ease, then the officer wheeled and strode into the house.

More time passed. Tarzan looked around and decided that there was no way he could escape this place, not yet anyway.

The officer emerged from the building. Oyabatu called the warriors to attention. A horn blew. The ape-man looked upwards. A giant black man on the rooftop was doing the trumpeting. When he stopped, a long ululating cry soared up from the top of the tower.

A masked woman appeared.

She wore only sandals and a knee-length kilt of snake skin, grayish green and marked by reddish circles. Her blue-black body was well shaped, though, to Western eyes, rather broad hipped. The triangular mask was split on a vertical line. The left side was malignant, a demon's. The right side portrayed half of a smiling and gentle black woman's face. Above the mask rose a mass of kinky hair cut into the shape of a coiled python. Shining grease held the hairs into a cohesive form.

Tarzan was surprised. Nothing so far said to him had indicated that Rafmana was female. And men had been in charge—up to this point. He had assumed that Rafmana was a man. He had been wrong, and it was his own fault. After all, he had been in more than one society, including several black tribes, in which a woman was the supreme ruler.

Rafmana spoke in the language of the Ataka. The voice behind the mask was a pleasant contralto.

"Bring the strangers up so that Rafmana, The Other Masked One, The Toucher of Time, may speak to them!"

A minute later, the captives and their guards were in a large room on the second story. The woman sat on cushions on a mahogany chair on a stone dais. Behind were soldiers and, seated on stools, an old woman, a middle-aged woman, and a young woman. These were in white robes which left one breast bare. Each held in her hand an iron sickle.

He supposed that they were priestesses.

Draped over Rafmana's shoulders was a python about six feet long. It moved its head from side to side while its forked tongue flicked out, flicked in, flicked out and its lidless yellow eyes stared at the three captives. Though it may have been his imagination, the ape-man thought that it gave him a special regard.

Though Tarzan did not fear it, he had never gotten over his horror of Histah the snake. He had felt this since he had seen his first snake. He had been an infant, sitting on a high branch, his back against the trunk of a tree. And he had become aware of Histah, a great python, moving on its belly plates toward him.

He had cried out then, and he had been paralyzed. But Kala had heard his cry, and she had come in time to seize its tail with a strength equal to that of Bolgani the gorilla. She had plucked it from the branch and hurled it to its death.

Ever since, Histah had held a strange fascination for Tarzan. There was something about him that whispered evilly of the ancientness of his feud with humanity. That feeling, Tarzan knew, was not rational. He also knew that many snakes were not only harmless to man, but were actually beneficial.

Nonetheless, he and Histah would always be enemies.

The eyes behind Rafmana's mask moved from side to side. That went on for several minutes. Then she broke the silence.

"I know you! The black beast that talks and walks like a man! The white man who was raised by apes! The black man who feared to face The Ghost Frog so that he might sing to it and bring back his love from The More than Dead!"

The three captives had been warned not to speak until The Other Masked One permitted them to do so.

She was silent for a minute. Far far away, an eagle screamed. Or was it a human being under torture?

Before the cry had faded away, Rafmana spoke. "You came into our land uninvited. The law says that you should die for this."

The three women on stools held up their sickles. And they said in unison, "Die!"

"But," Rafmana said, "none of you would have come here if you had not been pursued by your enemies. Therefore, I, Rafmana, The Toucher of Time, The Great Mother of Snakes, may pardon you."

She paused, laughed, then added, "Or not!"

"I am the law! I may do what I please because my ancestors were the beings from beyond the stars. They decreed that I should rule this land for almost forever, and that I should touch time and see the past, the present, and the future through The Dark Heart of Time!"

Whatever that means, Tarzan thought.

She said, "The men who chased you are led by two white men. I do not know why they wish you evil. But I . . . we . . . will find out why. Soon.

"Meanwhile, your enemies, the two white men, will be allowed to pass unmolested and unhindered through our land. When they get here, they too will be judged. No one has forced them to come here."

The face behind the mask turned toward the ape-man.

"Or am I wrong, Son of the Great Ape?"

"You are not wrong!" Tarzan said.

"Well spoken. Those who tell me I am wrong wish they had said otherwise. Now, you may speak, if you so desire. It pleases me to answer some of your questions."

She rose from the throne, the snake still on her shoulders. After turning around to speak a few quiet words to the three women, she turned again toward the captives. The three women, holding their sharp-edged sickles high, walked in single file around the dais three times. Then, the old one halted in front of Tarzan. The middle-aged one stopped in front of Rahb. The young one stopped in front of Waganero.

Tarzan knew no more what to expect next than did his

companions. The sickle was a symbol of good crops. It also stood for several other things, including death.

Each woman made signs that the captives should hold their hands out. They did so, though Tarzan was waiting to snatch his hands back. But no men had grabbed the captives' arms to hold them steady. That seemed to him a good sign.

He held his wrists parallel with the floor. They were also pulled apart as far as the bonds would extend. But he still could not be sure just what the women intended to do.

The sickles flashed downward, and they cut true. The bonds were severed.

He sighed with relief. So far, good.

The three women marched back to their original places behind the thrones.

Rafmana said, "Now we feast! Then we talk! In the morning, we consult The Tree!"

29

"IS THERE TRULY a Ghost Frog?" Tarzan said.

Rafmana had not yet taken her mask off, so while her words were loud, they sounded hollow.

"There is a voice. A voice cannot exist without a voicer. So, there must be a Ghost Frog."

"A voicer, yes. But how do you know that there is an animal or a thing such as The Ghost Frog?"

Rafmana said, "You heard The Voice. And you felt its bulk in the water. The bear-man saw it devour a huge crocodile."

Tarzan thought, *How does she know all this?* But he said, "Something swallowed it, but I saw no Ghost Frog."

"You are indeed lucky," Rafmana said. "It has been said that he who heard The Voice will surely be eaten by The Ghost Frog and become one of The More than Dead. Now, because of your experience, we know that it is not always true. But, Ape-man, if you are allowed to go home, do not pass through that swamp again. The second time, you may end as the crocodile ended."

She paused, then said, "Stranger, I get the feeling that you are a great doubter."

Tarzan said, "Yes."

But he was thinking of what she had said about his being allowed to leave this place. On what did the permission depend?

He, Rahb, Waganero, and three chiefs, males, had

moved to the stone roof of the house on top of the tower wall. There they were sitting on a circle of furs. Rafmana sat on a small stool outside the circle. She was facing Tarzan. All except Rafmana were eating, using their fingers to pluck the food from the large mahogany bowls before them. They devoured crocodile and hippopotamus steaks, tender barbecued goat ribs, plantains, yams, and many kinds of fruit and nuts. They drank beer from large gourds. The smoke from nearby cooking fires swirled around them.

Rafmana did not pass food under her mask. The apeman supposed that she might have eaten earlier in her apartment. There, she could remove her mask without being seen.

He wondered if it meant death for anyone to see her face. He knew that, in the past, in some sub-Saharan societies, the king never set food on the ground. A carpet was always unrolled before him to ensure that it would not happen. If it did, the ones held responsible for this sin were killed at once.

Most likely, this was what happened to the unfortunate who accidentally glimpsed Rafmana's face.

Rafmana had said nothing since Tarzan had admitted that he was indeed a doubter. Ten minutes passed. Then, she arose and made a gesture. Servants immediately took the bowls and gourds away. Others brought bowls full of water and cloth towels for the feasters to wash their hands and faces. Everybody then went down the steps and remained outside the house.

Tarzan wondered what was to come next. A trial? Judgment? Execution?

Instead, Rafmana beckoned to him to stand with her before the crystalline tree that grew out of the stone roof. As he did so, he looked upward. The tree was at least forty feet high. Its lowest branches, all transparent, started at about seven feet from the roof. They spread out at least twenty feet on all sides from the transparent trunk.

The morning wind shook some of the shining leaves, and they tinkled. Yet, the sound was not quite like the tinkling of glass pieces on a chain. He thought that he could hear faint voices mingled with the crystal sound.

The dark shape-shifting things he had seen at a distance yesterday were still swimming around inside the trunk and the branches. Now that he was closer to the tree, he saw that they were as large as his hand. They fluttered and swam under the surface of the shining stone, up and down the trunk and along the branches.

Rafmana's hollow voice spoke behind him. "These are The Eyes of the Glittering Tree."

Tarzan looked around. The most distant spectators were forty or so soldiers to his right and the same number to his left. Their helmets were of wood encased with snake skin. The helmet fronts were carved and painted to resemble the spotted python's head. The warriors held triangular shields with their left hands; each shield was painted with the image of the serpent with its tail in its mouth. Their right hands gripped short stabbing spears.

The upper halves of the chiefs' bodies were painted a bright blue; the lower halves, scarlet.

The edge of the roof of the house was lined with bowmen. These had greased bodies which shone in the sunlight.

Somewhere close by, a large drum slowly thumped. Then the deep whirring sound of a bull roarer began. The drum beat picked up its pace. A score of large rattles began to shake.

Rafmana spoke again.

"In the center of The Tree is The Dark Heart of Time. It beats like a heart, but its blood is Time itself. Distance also flows with Time in its arteries."

Tarzan looked intently at The Heart. Though he could see it pulse, he could not make out its exact shape. It kept changing form, and it also seemed blurred.

"Stranger, you who are called Tarzan, also called the Ape-man, put the palm of your hand flat against The Tree. You will be allowed to keep your hand there for only a short while. To touch The Tree too long will drive you mad. Your soul will soar into the void and be forever lost."

Tarzan did as he was ordered. At the same time, the drum and the bull roarer increased their tempo. The rattles shook even faster. A horn joined in.

The stone felt very warm and greasy beneath his bare feet.

As soon as his flesh came into contact with The Tree, the dark form-changing things that were floating inside the tree—or seemed to be floating inside—began to move more swiftly. And after a minute or so, they were racing along like dried leaves blown by a strong wind.

"Keep your eyes on The Heart," Rafmana said.

Tarzan did so. He also mentally counted the beats. Though he had no watch, he did have an excellent sense of physiological time. It was his sense of social time, of time as something vital in dealing with people, that had never developed.

He counted eighty beats per minute. And then he became aware that the thing in the center of the tree was pulsing at the same rate as his own heart. He was sure that it had not been doing so before he had put his hand on The Tree.

Suddenly, the dark things racing through the tree slowed down. One slid beneath his hand but did not go past. Though he could not now see it, he knew that its form exactly matched the outline of his fingers and hand.

The music of the drum, bull roarer, horn, and rattles became louder. Then sweet notes, the silvery sound of harp strings being plucked, added an undercurrent to the roar and banging of the louder instruments.

From beneath his hand, long dark threads shot along the surface. Some of them seemed to turn inward. They touched The Heart and then merged into it. They were like bloodstream conduits connected to the pulsing shape.

He became dizzy. The entire planet seemed to rock beneath him. The rapid to-and-fro tilting sent waves through the cold, cold reaches between the stars, between the galaxies. Space now had a skin, though he could not have described the skin to anyone. The skin wrinkled. And the blood of Time shot through the skin. They, Space and Time, were one.

Or so it seemed to him.

Then, if his mind could be said to have feet, he stepped forward. His mind, that is, advanced one pace. Though it was only one step, it was immeasurably long. He was at a doorway of some indescribable kind. He knew that if he passed through the doorway, he would be where Time had not yet come into being. Nor would Matter as yet have come into existence.

He would be in a non-Place where non-Time and non-Space were. But, if Nothing was, how could he be there?

Of all the enormously stimulating feelings Tarzan had ever experienced, this seemed the strongest—and the strangest.

Dimly, he heard Rafmana.

"Keep your hand against The Tree!"

He started. Her hand was now resting on his shoulder. Or was it not Rafmana's but someone else's? And now the doorway was closed. A mingled sorrow and relief from The Dreadful, The Abstract Dreadful, swept through him.

"Your sight will dim," she said. Was it her voice or

someone else's? And how could his sight become even dimmer without his going blind?

"But your eyes will also see a light never seen before by you! Do not lift your hand from The Tree!"

Tarzan did as she commanded.

"Now! Think of the face of the one you would most like to see! Whether that one is dead or alive—it makes no difference! Think!"

Tarzan had no idea how anyone could visualize the face of an unborn person. Now, of course, was not the time to ask questions.

He bent his mind into the shape of the person whom he most desired to see. He also tried to envision the place where she was. He hoped that it would not be in the dark of a grave or among bones on the ground.

"The one you seek may be in the past or the present. Wherever and whenever you wish to see the one . . . it makes no difference in the perception," the voice of Rafmana said. "But you must think of the time, whether you wish it to be today or in the past."

All was dark around him. Then a strange light shoved out the darkness as if the darkness were a solid object, a block of stone being moved from the middle of a wall made of blocks. The light illuminated objects just as ordinary light did. But it was a different kind of light, though he would not have been able to describe in what way it varied.

At first, he was half-blinded by the glare. Within a minute, however, he could see clearly. All this while, he thought of the present, of this exact minute. Of course, the present was becoming the past even as he was concentrating on staying in the now. But he, being alive, was moving with the flow of Time.

He shook a little, and his lips moved slightly. What he was looking at certainly was not where he was. But through whose eyes was he seeing?

The windows of someone's eyes. No doubt of that. He could see part of that person's nose, his nose. And ahead there was a jungle clearing. In it stood a white man wearing a dirty and torn uniform. Once, it had been the clean military uniform of an officer of the German Empire. The man's face was gaunt and fatigued, and he badly needed a shave.

A rifle was slung over his shoulder by a leather band, and an automatic pistol was in a sheath hanging from his filthy belt. Held by his belt was a large knife.

Tarzan had no control over the eyes of the person through which he was seeing the German. What that person saw, he saw. And Tarzan could not hear. He saw the man's lips moving, but nothing audible came from them. It was like watching a silent movie—lots of action but no sound.

Then, the eyes looked down. They saw, and so did Tarzan, the swell of a woman's breast. He also saw the woman's hand. Though it was dirty and its fingernails were broken, it was instantly recognizable.

Tarzan murmured, "Jane!"

She was still alive. But where she was, and in what kind of situation, Tarzan could not know.

The man had to be Lieutenant Erich Obergatz, the officer appointed by the German High Command to take Tarzan's wife, Lady Greystoke, into the Belgian Congo. With them had been Obergatz's company of native soldiers. But the soldiers were nowhere in sight. Judging from Obergatz's appearance and from what Tarzan could see of the dirty hand and the ripped dress, the two were in a bad way.

Suddenly, strong hands seized his wrist, and his hand was lifted from The Tree. Everything he was seeing through her eyes rushed away. He became aware that two muscular warriors had grabbed his wrist.

He cried out, "Jane!"

Rafmana spoke behind him. "You may tell me what you saw when you are through with The Tree. Today, you have one more touching of The Tree. You may think of someone else, someone you deeply desire to see. What you will see may be in the past or in the present. It will be as you wish. Place your hand on The Tree again."

The two warriors released his wrist and stepped back. Shortly thereafter, a dark leaf-shape hovered once more under his hand. Tarzan hesitated.

He wanted to evoke Jane again, or, rather, see through her eyes. But that would tell him nothing about her location. What about his son? Where was he? The last time Tarzan had heard of him, his son was in France, fighting in the trenches.

It was then that the ape-man felt his hand flatten out. It was as if the shadow shape had exuded some sort of magnetic pull. It held his palm firmly. Tarzan knew, without being told, that something was pulling his mind toward . . . what? He did not resist. Again, the light dimmed, then was replaced with the peculiar light.

Abruptly, he was looking through a person's eyes. But they were his own eyes. Though he could not say why, he knew that they were not the eyes of someone else. He seemed to be lying down. Above him was a branch and a sun shining through a tangle of leaves. Then a great black-furred hand came into view. His whole being soared with joy. A huge head appeared, covered with black fur except on the face. That showed a low forehead and huge supraorbital ridges and out-thrust jaws. It was a fearsome face. But he loved it. It was the face of his foster mother, the female ape who had taken him as her own after Tarzan's parents had died.

For twenty years, she had been the only being whom Tarzan had loved deeply. She had nursed him with her ape's milk, had protected him from all dangers, including some of her tribe, had loved him as much as he had loved her.

Tarzan knew that he was looking up at her through his infant eyes.

"Kala!" he cried. He sobbed as he had sobbed when he had found her dead, slain by the black tribesman Kulonga. She whom he knew had been killed years ago by Kulonga's arrow was alive. His grief and his anger of long ago shook him now as then.

Suddenly his wrist was gripped again, and his hand was lifted away.

"That is all for you today," Rafmana said. "It is the turn of the harpist and of the beast-man."

"What about tomorrow?" Tarzan said.

"That depends," Rafmana said. But, despite Tarzan's urging, she would not say on *what* it depended.

30

LATE IN THE afternoon the safari had camped in the forest a mile eastward from the riverbank. The only native village the men were aware of was on the west bank, and was several miles up the river.

The group was behind a ridge of earth. Helmson and Fitzpagel were sitting on a log. Both had their shoes off. All their luxuries, large tents, folding table and chairs, towels, and bottles of booze, everything that would tend to slow the safari down and that could be dispensed with, had been left behind.

Deprived of these, the white men had become irritable, dirty, and scratchy. They had also found it hard to sleep at night in the alternately noisy or silent and brooding jungle. They were very jumpy and very tired.

Two of the whites had already died. One had succumbed to a cobra bite. The other had infected his hand, though no one knew what had done it. His arm had swelled, and nothing Helmson did with his medicines had helped the man. He had died shortly before dawn of the previous day.

That left Helmson and Fitzpagel as the only whites.

Moreover, more than half of their porters, askari, and trackers had deserted them. They had left quietly the previous night in the dark, taking with them much of the food supplies, guns, and ammunition. The faithful ones claimed that they had not heard the deserters. Neither of the whites believed them, but they knew why those who remained had kept silent. They had not wanted to get into a bloody fight by trying to restrain the deserters.

Also, those left behind were probably thinking of abandoning the safari themselves. One of these nights, they would. Some of them had no doubt overheard the whites talking about the mysterious dangers ahead. Not even the assurance that there was much gold ahead, far more than that in the statue, had fired up their courage.

So it was that Helmson and Fitzpagel got gloomier and gloomier. If the rest of the men abandoned them, they would have to follow them back up the river. Without support, they doubted they could make it alive back to their starting point. And, if they stayed, they certainly were done for.

"We'll still be able to organize another expedition," Fitzpagel said. "We can make it a big one and armed with machine guns, hand grenades, maybe flamethrowers. We can roll over any opposition. And we'll have enough men and enough boats to carry the gold away. Enough to make us all rich as American oil magnates. Richer!"

"Yeah, sure," Helmson said. He stared into the fire. "But what about Greystoke? What about the reward money?"

"Greystoke?" Fitzpagel said. "We don't need him. But if I had him in my sights, I'd blow his head off. Wouldn't hesitate a second. He's the one got us in trouble. It's his fault we're in this mess. I ain't going to forget him. Someday, after all this is safe behind us, I'll hunt him down and kill him. Don't ye make no mistake about that!"

Helmson was astonished. The Irishman's face was twisted with hatred.

"You never said anything before about hating him!" Helmson said. "You acted like getting him was just a job. Just like me. It was a professional task. You . . ."

Fitzpagel rose from the log. He stared down at the American. "There's much ye don't know about me," he said. "There's much ye'll never know."

He stooped and picked up his boots. With them held by one hand, he began walking away. And then he stubbed his toe on a rock.

"Auwa!" he said loudly.

He almost fell, but he recovered after staggering for a few feet. Then he stopped.

Helmson gaped at him. A few seconds later, he rose swiftly. While doing so, he drew his automatic pistol from his holster.

He clicked off the safety and aimed the gun at Fitzpagel.

"Hold it! Don't move! Hands up! I'll shoot if you don't do as I say! I mean it!"

The Irishman did as ordered. He was facing away from Helmson. But he said, "Are ye daft? What're ye doing?"

"Auwa! Auwa!" Helmson shouted.

By now, the blacks were standing up and watching the white men. They seemed to be completely puzzled. Some of the askari, however, had their rifles in their hands. They did not know what to expect next, but they hoped to be ready.

Fitzpagel said, "What do you mean? Auwa! Is that what you said?"

"Auwa! Auwa!" Helmson howled. "If an Englishman or an American stubs his toe and hurts it, he says, 'Ouch!' It's involuntary! But if a German does the same, he says, 'Auwa!' He can't help it! But you, you German swine, you gave yourself away! You're no more Irish than I'm Paddy's pig! You're a German! And you're a spy!"

Tarzan stepped back from The Tree to give Rahb his turn. Rafmana stood closely behind Rahb, as she had done with the ape-man. She placed her hand on his thick-furred shoulder while she half-chanted the instructions for using The Tree. After each phrase, Tarzan repeated them in the Shong's language.

Rahb said nothing during the procedure, but he did

grunt several times. And he cried out near the end. When he turned away from The Tree, he was weeping. The tears ran from his large brown eyes and down the part-bear, part-human face.

The beast who weeps, Tarzan thought. And then he corrected himself. *No beast weeps for sorrow or joy,* he thought. *Rahb weeps for sorrow or joy. Therefore, Rahb is not a beast.*

As Rahb passed him, Tarzan spoke softly. "What makes you cry?"

Rahb stopped. He sniffled, then wiped away his tears with both hands.

"I saw my mate. She was outside a hut which looked like those the black men make. Far off to the east, according to the shadows cast by the sun, was a tremendous mountain, white on top. She was chained by the neck to a post. She walked back and forth at the length of the chain. Three armed men whom I have never seen before were watching her. One was white. Two were black. I do not know where she was . . . is. But she is alive."

Tarzan did not wish to hurt Rahb. But he had to ask.

"Where was the baby?"

"It was held in the arms of a black woman. I could see only parts of her."

"Ah!" Tarzan said. "You saw her through the eyes of your child?"

"Yes."

The ape-man had expected the Shong to be confused. But evidently he was even more intelligent than Tarzan had supposed.

"A great mountain which is white on its top?" Tarzan said.

"Yes."

The ape-man turned to Rafmana. "O Great One, may I speak?"

The mask turned toward him. Her hollow voice came from behind it.

"You may speak if it is very necessary."

"It is to Rahb and to me," Tarzan said. "And it may interest you. I would like to be able to see what Rahb saw."

"Stand behind him. Place your hand on his shoulder. I will place my hand on your shoulder. Then I will invoke The Dark Heart of Time again. And we will see what we will see."

With all three situated as Rafmana wished, she began the half-chanted instructions. Then Tarzan saw through the eyes of Rahb's mate. He knew her eyes were the instruments because he could see the chain attached to his—her—neck, part of her body, the black woman, the baby, and the soldiers.

He saw, many miles away, the gigantic peaks of the mountain that he recognized as Kilimanjaro, located in British East Africa near the border of German East Africa. Tarzan knew it well. It was awe inspiring, the largest mountain on the continent, and sacred to many native tribes.

Of its three most prominent peaks, the highest was Kibo, blue Kibo, said to be over 19,000 feet high. Anyone within a hundred miles of it in any direction could see Kibo.

No man had as yet climbed to the top of Kibo or close to its top.

Except for Tarzan.

A few years ago, before the war started, Tarzan had been high up on that mountain near the summit of Kibo. A madman named Idaho Leeper had put him in a cage with a man-eating leopard. But Tarzan and Sheeta had escaped. This was part of the tale which Tarzan thought of as The Adventure of the Very Sick Circus Horse.

This adventure was bizarre even for Tarzan, the man around whom the bizarre seemed to flourish.

Though Kilimanjaro was in the tropics, Tarzan had almost died of the Arctic-like cold while being hunted. But he had survived that and also food poisoning from eating the circus horse and a battle with a pack of twenty of Leeper's specially bred red-and-white garmhounds. And he had disposed of Leeper in a very peculiar way with a weapon he'd used only once in his life.

One result of this adventure was that he deeply detested the taste of horse meat.

The dried and frozen carcass of the leopard must still be far up on the ice and snow of the summit of Kilimanjaro. Some day, some explorer would find it. That person, and then the world, would wonder why a leopard had climbed so high to the very cold and lifeless area.

As of now, only Tarzan knew why.

He stepped away from The Tree. He now knew just about where Rahb's mate and baby were. Westward of the mountain, fifty or so miles from its base and in a direct line from where Sheeta had died, was the hut where the two were prisoners. He and Rahb could someday search that area within sight of the mountain, and they would find her and the infant.

Waganero's turn to consult the The Tree came. He, however, did not spend nearly as much time as the apeman and the bear-man had. Only a minute had passed when, despite the fact that his wrist was being held by two powerful men, Waganero lifted his hand from The Tree.

At the same time, his wailing rose high above the tower and evoked screeches from an eagle circling above it. He was shaking and ashen under his dark pigment. His eyes were wide open and rolling.

Rafmana had been standing behind him, her right hand on his right shoulder. When the harpist tore his hand from The Tree, she stepped back from him. Her voice quavered from behind the mask.

"I saw it, too," she said. "The place of The More than Dead, within the belly of The Ghost Frog. It has been more than a hundred years since last I saw it. I hope I will never see it again!"

Waganero finally managed to get control of himself though his face still showed horror.

He said, "I, too, saw the place where The More than Dead live! And I saw my love, Lutsu! How could I have told myself I would face it, and would summon Lutsu from the belly of The Ghost Frog with my harp and my singing? I did not know how horrible it was! Nor did I really believe that Lutsu was a ghost, that nothing I could do, nothing . . ."

He began sobbing, and he hid his face in his hands.

Tarzan wondered how The Tree worked. How could he see through Jane's eyes and also see Kala through his own eyes? Why through Jane's eyes the first time and through his own eyes the second? Why had Rahb seen through his baby's eyes and why had Tarzan seen through Rahb's mate's eyes?

Perhaps The Tree acted randomly within a limited area? Who had made—or grown—The Tree? Why?

And then there was Rafmana's statement that she had not seen the place of The More than Dead, inside The Ghost Frog's belly, for over a hundred years. Did she mean that literally?

Tarzan did not believe that there was another world in that creature's belly, no matter how big it was. Nor did he believe that the belly held The More than Dead. But he had witnessed that which seemed to be true. Or was it, perhaps, partly subjective? Were he and his companions seeing what was real, or what they wanted to see?

Rafmana had much explaining to do. However, he had no way of forcing her to enlighten him.

Nor did he, Tarzan, have time for loitering. Having seen Jane, he knew she was alive.

Or do I? he wondered.

If she were alive, how long would she stay alive? Where were she and the man he assumed was Obergatz? Whatever the true situation was, he must get away from this area as soon as possible and go northward. When he did, he would have to travel swiftly.

He looked around him, and his heart went into eclipse. He was surrounded by fierce warriors. He was in a place where the only escape seemed to be to jump from the top of the peak to the water, many hundreds of feet below him.

He looked across the lake surrounding the peak. Where the water ended, a solid wall of stone rose to at least three hundred feet. The land beyond it seemed to dip down. Then, at a distance of several miles, it started to slope gently upward. He could see the brownish and greenish squares of farmlands and dark clusters of villages. Beyond them, the sheer-sided mountains rose for several thousands of feet.

From what Waganero had said, the lake became a narrow river a few miles southward beyond the tower. Then the river, after speeding for many miles, hurled itself into an underground cave.

He looked back at The Tree. The hand-sized and fluttering-edged shapes were circulating through the trunk and the branches. The Dark Heart of Time was still pulsing.

Rafmana had ordered more beer for herself and the captives. The harpist drained his gourd, but the ape-man and the bear-man waved theirs away. Rafmana, having emptied her mug, spoke to Tarzan. She was so close to him that, despite her mask, her breath came to him. It smelled of honey fermented with some kind of cloves.

"Despite what I just said, you must see through The Tree for a third time. I had a sudden feeling . . . almost a voice . . . that told me you must look through The Tree again."

Tarzan detected a very faint fluttering in her otherwise firm voice. He interpreted it as alarm.

But what could alarm her?

31

RAFMANA EXPLAINED FURTHER, and told Tarzan that he would get the answers to some of his questions.

Rafmana herself, she said, though very ancient and very wise, did not know everything. Nor did she want to know all. According to the traditions of her people, the person who knew everything would die from the burden. That person's liver would swell and split open, or so the legend stated.

"Of course," Rafmana said, "my people don't know that the brain is the seat of intelligence and self-awareness. But why should I enlighten them? If I did tell them the truth, they might come to doubt me. That, as they say, might be the crack in the shell that killed the turtle.

"But I'll explain what I can. I can see somewhat into the future. I have seen some of yours, though the images were very hazy and did not last long. For instance, I know that you will become a god. If what I have seen comes true, you will be a god very soon, as Time flows."

"A god? Me?" Tarzan said. "Are you telling me I will die soon?"

"All human beings die soon," Rahmana said. "But you . . . I have not seen your death, soon or late."

"I do not believe that the future is fixed," Tarzan said. "That would mean that all events are already determined. It would mean that we behave mechanically, without true will, act and think as some outside force determines."

"I will tell you one thing," the voice behind the mask said. "What I see as the time to come may not necessarily be what will be. I see what is the most highly probable. But that does not always happen. However . . ."

Her voice trailed off.

Tarzan waited for her to resume, but instead she ordered him and his companions to exercise, to run around the circle of the inside of the tower. Tarzan was glad about that. He sorely needed to run, and so did his fellow captives.

Nevertheless, while jogging, he watched, and wondered what Rafmana was doing with The Tree. She stood facing it, the flat of her right hand against the trunk. Her head was cocked far to one side as if she were listening to something. Yet, The Tree made no sounds. At least, as far as Tarzan could tell, it did not.

He had the feeling that she had a goal which she had not so far revealed. But, in good time or bad time, like it or not, he would find out what it was.

Tarzan began running faster. Soon, he was racing at full speed on the stone path that circled inside the waist-high walls. His companions and the small contingent of soldiers keeping pace with them dropped far behind.

Now! he thought. He could leap over the wall now and fall outside the tower to the lake. Or jump off this path the other way and fall down into the inside of the hollow tower and the hollow peak, into the lake there. But that would be a final desperate try. His chances for surviving that fall would be very small.

No. Wait.

When his run was finished, some slaves poured water over him from buckets. Rafmana stood for a long time, as if she were as much crystal as The Tree. Finally, she stepped back from it. Tarzan wondered what she had seen. She went into the house. After a while, the captives were summoned into the building to eat with her counselors and priestesses.

She sat on a tall stool. The others squatted on the floor. After about thirty minutes of silence except for the smacking of lips and heavy chewing noises, Rafmana spoke.

"You asked me certain questions, Tarzan. I will answer those to which I know the answers. But, while I talk, do not interrupt me. You may ask questions when I am done."

She began with long long ago, when the tribe of Ataka had just moved into this land from the north. Rafmana was leading them. She did not remember how old she was then. Perhaps fifty or so.

The Ataka had slain all the aboriginal inhabitants or had chased them into the forest far away. These were a small, yellowish people. *Bushmen or Hottentots,* Tarzan thought.

At this point in the tale, she rose to her feet and lifted her right hand, the index finger extended. The voice behind her mask deepened and became louder.

"But when we got here, we also found The Twins, the divine pair, Arinu and Watanu, brother and sister. They said that they had been here long long ago and had come here in a boat from another world. It was very long ago that it happened! Then, the mountains were taller than they now are! But wind and rain and even the light of the stars, yes, the starlight, too, had worn away the mountains since their arrival."

Tarzan was startled. Of all he would have expected to hear, he had not thought of this.

"They came to us Ataka from vast distances and through space as cold as the heart of Dwak, She Who Existed Before Time and Space Began!"

Rafmana revealed that The Twins looked much like humans. "They were black skinned, and their hair was woolly. But their noses were large and long, and their lips were thin. Their eyes, however, were slitted and pale, the eyes of a snake. And their god, Swika, was human looking from the waist above but below that had the body of an enormous python.

"Arinu and Watanu had great magic, the powers of gods. Indeed, they were the children of the Creator, of Swika herself. Or so they said. They gave me the power of becoming young again, and of staying young for as long as this world lasts.

"They also showed the Ataka how to make materials for The City Made by God, the stone that grows, and how to build The City. Then, after this tower was built—a tower just like this one, for the first tower has been rebuilt many times—then they planted the seed of The Glittering Tree on top of the wall of the tower. The Tree you see shining in the sun, its Dark Heart beating with the pulse of Time herself.

"Finally, when the work of growing The Glittering Tree was done, The Twins said that they were going to return to the star where they were hatched from the divine egg of Swika. But, after many generations had passed, they would come again to us. With them would be many of their kind. And, amidst the great sorrow of my people, The Twins did depart in their boat to the star, the great white one that is the jewel in the mind of the world.

"Many more generations passed. The Saweetoo tribe came into this valley. I allowed them to live in The City Made by God because that fulfilled an ancient prophecy.

"Then, two beings from the stars, looking just like Arinu and Watanu, arrived in a boat. They said that they were twins, too, though born from the good eggs of Swika. Arinu and Watanu had lied to us—the newcomers said—about their genuine intentions. On the star they came from, Arinu and Watanu were known as The Evil Twins. But they had been defeated, and were now imprisoned inside a star. The newcomers, Tsapa and Ekweni, were The Good Twins, they claimed. They had come to undo the wicked work of the first two."

Rafmana took a drink of water. Using one hand she held up her mask, but not so far that anyone could see her face.

"Some of us believed the newcomers. Some thought they were liars, that they, not Arinu and Watanu, were The Evil Twins. There was war among us, and during this, the twins were slain. The killers then said that Tsapa and Ekweni were indeed lying. If they had been divine, we could not have harmed them. That is what I believed.

"No one knows what the truth is. Nor do we know what will happen when the star beings come again. Will we be rewarded for having slain The Evil Twins? Or will we be punished for having slain The Good Twins?"

After a pause, Rafmana revealed that the first Star Twins had explained to her why The City Made by God and why The Tree of Time had been grown from a seed planted in the rock of the tower. The network of crystal roots would enable The Twins to communicate with the home star world and with other worlds where their kind had established colonies. The network would also allow them to travel from star world to star world without using a star boat.

And the complex of roots throughout the earth enabled people everywhere on earth to see and talk to people everywhere and anywhere on other parts of this world.

But when the first pair of twins had left this world, The Tree had ceased growing its roots. Thus, through them, those using the network could see only to the ends of the roots. Rafmana did not know how far the roots had grown. But they extended to points far far away.

She, The Great Mother of Snakes, the Rafmana, had learned how to use some of the other powers of The Tree. So—here she indicated with a finger the three captives—through the Rafmana others could see people in the past or the present. Only she could see into the future.

She saw dimly and blurred into the things to come. Sometimes, she was not sure how to interpret what she saw. That showed that she still did not know how to use all The Tree's powers. But, someday, she would know all of them.

She pointed at Tarzan.

"You, Ape-man, I sense that you are a great doubter. You have to be shown a thing to believe that it does exist. But I will remove your doubts. You will be given the great gift of seeing through the eyes of your ancestors back to the beast who ceased to be a beast and became human.

"The ability to use The Tree, so The Twins said, comes from the circular flow of Time itself. What that term means is a secret only known to The Great Mother of Snakes, that is, to myself."

Tarzan felt cold, and he shivered. He was in the presence of something vast and impersonal, yet, at the same time, *very* personal. His mind could not yet grasp the concept nor its implications.

Then the sense of immeasurable depths vanished. But he realized that this tree and what it could do was the greatest treasure of all. Gold and jewels and the greatest fortune in the world were nothing to it. It opened Time itself. Also, Place itself.

He would have liked to stay here for a very long time and explore at least part of what The Tree offered. But he could not.

Rafmana said, "It has been prophesied by The Evil Twins, who may be The Good Twins, that the Ataka and Rafmana must beware of one man! He was only called The One to Avoid; the name his mother gave him was not uttered."

She stopped speaking for a moment. She stared hard at Tarzan with wild eyes, and pointed a shaking finger at him. Then she spoke.

"The ancient prophecy is that The One to Avoid will come unannounced and without claims to any greatness or any word of the disasters he brings. Indeed, he does not know that he is The One to Avoid. He does not know that he is the nexus of those forces that bring death and destruction to this land. He brings these just by his presence. He brings these without any ill will or malice toward the land which he will destroy. Storms, floods, death-dealing lightning, fire from the bowels of the earth, earth shakings—these follow his scent as if they were hyenas!

"Yet, he is innocent!"

The room seemed to crackle.

Rafmana had lowered her hand. Now, her finger again pointed at Tarzan.

To Tarzan, a shiver seemed to run through the air. It was like that not-quite-seen ripple, that shiver, he felt when he was next to Tantor as she talked to elephants miles away from her and those elephants were answering her. Human beings, even Tarzan, could not hear those messages. They were beneath the level of those sounds which humans could detect by ear alone.

But this Tree-caused atmospheric disturbance was not quite like what Tarzan was accustomed to. Yet, it did shiver the air.

"*You!*" Rafmana shouted. "The Tree told me through its eyes who you are! I was wrong! I thought that it might be this beast-man! But it is you! You are not *just* Tarzan the Ape-man, Lord of the Trees!"

She paused once more.

Tarzan knew what she would say. The revelation had come as if the sky had rolled up and a great light had blazed through his brain.

"You are he whose coming The Twins prophesied! You are The Uncaused Causer! He who is also known as The One to Avoid, The Unwilling Giver of the Unwanted! I can feel them now! The dark forces, the unholy ghosts whirling around you!"

32

FITZPAGEL DID NOT move, but his gaze swiveled from side to side. Finally, he fastened it on Helmson. He seemed to have made a decision.

He said, "I am a colonel in the Imperial German Intelligence. I specialize in Irish affairs, and my identity as an Irishman goes far back, long before this war started. I've been busy making trouble in Ireland for the English and running guns via U-boats into Ireland. These are for the Irish Republican Army. I also established my reputation as a wild-game hunter and explorer. The Fatherland wanted me to operate in East Africa and to encourage native unrest. I have two missions to perform for the Kaiser, if need be.

"But I am not officially here to spy on you. I have a different mission, a third one, my own mission, though I will admit that my superiors would be pleased if I fulfilled my personal mission. I don't know if you'll believe what else I'm going to tell you. But here goes."

Helmson noted that Fitzpagel—or whatever his real name was—spoke in standard English, that of London.

Helmson said, "Continue. Convince me."

Now the man spoke in standard American English, midwestern.

"What do you know about Greystoke's exploits fighting the German East African forces?"

"Some of them," the American said. "But not really

much. My superior didn't think that a detailed history of Tarzan's war activities was necessary."

"Did you know that a German officer led his unit into British East Africa before the news of the war between the United Kingdom and Germany had even reached certain settlers? Did you know that this officer burned down Tarzan's ranch while Tarzan was absent. Did you know that?"

"Yes," Helmson said.

"Did you know that the officer killed a native girl and then left her badly burned, almost completely charred body in the ruins? Or that the officer placed Lady Greystoke's wedding ring on the finger of the Waziri girl before burning her? Or that that ring convinced the ape-man that the badly burned body was his wife's?"

"I heard that," Helmson said. "I also heard that Greystoke had been taking revenge for the supposed death of his wife. He'd been creating havoc, confusion, and chaos among the German forces ever since. Meanwhile, a Lieutenant Obergatz of the enemy forces had taken Lady Jane Greystoke into the Belgian Congo. Tarzan, I heard, was getting ready to go into the Ituri forest after Obergatz and Lady Jane."

"Did you know the name of the officer who had burned down the ranch and taken the Englishwoman away?"

"No," Helmson admitted.

"Did you know that Tarzan tracked down the man he thought had murdered Lady Jane? And Tarzan killed the man in a most hideous way, fed him to a starving lion? But Tarzan had mistaken the dead man for his brother. When Tarzan discovered his mistake, he tracked down the real officer and killed him, stabbed his heart with the knife you took away from him, his father's hunting knife. Did you know that?"

Helmson said, "No." Then he added, "I'm getting tired

holding this gun. I may just shoot you unless you get to the point very soon."

"The man whom Tarzan mistakenly thought had burned down his ranch and crucified a Waziri tribesman and killed and burned Tarzan's wife, the man whom the ape-man fed alive to a hungry lion, that man was Major Bolko Schneider. And the man who had really done all these deeds, the man whom Tarzan killed with the knife, that man was Captain Fritz Schneider.

"Their father was General Bolko Schneider!"

Helmson was silent for a moment. Then he said, "And your full name is . . . ?" But he had already guessed part of it.

"Colonel Sigurd Schneider!

"The two men the ape-man murdered were my brothers! General Bolko Schneider is my father! He made the arrangements for me to come to Africa and to track down and kill the ape-man! But I would do this after the ape-man had paid in full for what he did! Paid with as much pain as he can tolerate before dying! I would never permit the ape-man to be delivered to the American billionaire, Stonecraft, who so desperately wants the ape-man alive for some reason or other. Not if I have anything to do with it!

"I will cut off the ape-man's head with his own father's knife, and I will find some way to preserve it. And I will take it to my father and throw the head onto his desk in our ancestral home in Prussia. And I will say, 'Father! I, Sigurd, your only surviving son, have avenged your sons, my brothers!' "

Helmson spoke slowly. "Now I begin to understand."

He thought for a minute, then said, "But why shouldn't I just shoot you now? You're a German spy. You've come with me so you can kill Tarzan and thus deprive me of the reward for bringing him in alive. Why shouldn't I kill you? Right now!"

"My father is very rich—except in sons," Schneider said. "Still, he could not pay you as much as Stonecraft now offers you. But what if we captured Tarzan and made Stonecraft pay twice, maybe four or five times, what he now offers? He can afford it. When Stonecraft has paid us, we kill the ape-man, and I take his head to my father? There are many places you can live under an assumed identity, and live like a millionaire, some neutral South American country, for instance.

"We can say that you did capture Tarzan but that someone else, some unknown person, stole him from you. That person is the one demanding the ransom. The one who takes the money but does not deliver Tarzan."

Helmson considered this offer. He also wondered how Schneider had found out that Stonecraft was the man behind the whole scheme. He would ask him about that later. Of course, Schneider had access to German Intelligence.

"You have more chance of surviving now if I'm here to help you," Schneider said. "You also have more chance of finding and catching the ape-man."

He paused, then added, "And you'll have much more chance of coming back and getting all this gold, the statues and God knows what else. I'm not really interested in getting the gold, not now. I'll have Greystoke's head and the ransom Stonecraft'll pay. That's enough for me."

Helmson stared at the German's long, foxy face, his vulpine smile, his red hair. He certainly looked like the stereotype of an Irishman. No wonder he had done so well as a Hibernian.

But he could never be trusted—except to do what was good for him.

Nevertheless, he would be very useful in this situation. Once he was no longer necessary, he would be put out of the way. The crocodiles could eat him.

"Moreover," Schneider said, "if you kill me, my men

will desert as soon as possible. If you try to stop them, they will kill you."

Helmson looked around. All bestial and sinister Africa seemed to sweep in on him. Suddenly it did not matter that Schneider would undoubtedly kill him when he could do without him. For the time being, he was an ally. Any white man in equatorial Africa badly needed an ally. A lone white man in this particular situation was desperately in need of an ally.

Helmson clicked off the safety of his gun and stuck it into its holster.

He said, "Very well. We'll talk more about this in the morning. Meantime, let's sleep. When dawn comes, we'll go inland, toward the cliffs. We're on the left side of the river. So far, there've been no natives on this side. And the cliffs on this side are close. We can get through the jungle on this side to the cliffs. We'll climb to the top and make our way along.

"At least, until we've passed the swamp. If there is a Ghost Frog, we'll bypass it."

They all slept uneasily that night. Though very tired when they arose, they felt better as soon as they had put a mile between them and the edge of the water. Near noon, the safari was halfway up the cliffs. Helmson and Schneider were the highest. They sat on an outthrust of limestone. Below them, at various altitudes, the other men formed a broken line. They rested on projections of rock or in shallow caves. The climbing was hard, but not as bad as scaling a sheer mountain. And, so far, no one had suffered a serious injury or fallen to his death.

Schneider wiped the sweat from his face with a bandanna, then took a long swig of water from his canteen. He said, "Someday, when we're drinking whiskey high in the cool city of Quito, high in the Andes . . ."

He stopped. His eyes widened. Helmson stared at him,

then tried to get to his feet. Then he thought better of it, and he gripped projections in the rock beneath him.

The side of the cliff shook. The rock seemed to wave like a flag in a stiff breeze.

From somewhere came a dim boom, like a vast cannon firing, though far off.

He cried out, "Earthquake!"

The distant cannon boomed again and again and again. The noise was coming closer. The cliffs were shimmying.

Far below him, where the jungle had been, was now water. Raging, swirling, high-tossing water. It lifted great trees as if they were toothpicks for God.

The roar and the shaking got worse.

Then the main body of the flood came. Helmson could not hear his own screaming.

The boiling sea rose higher and higher. Parts of the cliff began falling off. He saw a ledge with a dozen men on it break up and fall into the water.

Now, the raging surface was only a few feet below him.

Helmson closed his eyes. For the first time since he had left his boyhood behind, he prayed.

It seemed to him, however, that the voice of the water and of the earth was God's. And God was not pleased with him.

33

TARZAN WAS CATAPULTED straight up. The bottom of his feet were at least six inches from the floor before he fell back.

Though he came down straight, landing on his feet, he was immediately slammed onto his back. His breath was knocked from his lungs. He was stunned for several seconds.

When he recovered enough to try to get up on all fours, he was knocked down again. The stone beneath him arched as if it were the back of a frightened cat. Wide zigzags shot across the floor. Many of the square stone tiles were tilted upwards or sank down.

Another shock wave ran through the tower. From far below, outside the tower and inside it, rose the loud sound of splashes. These were things that had fallen at the first shock, blocks of stone, tiles, and perhaps humans. This noise rode over the screams of terrified men and women.

Massive shocks—one, two, three, four, five, and on and on—thrust the floor upward again and again. Tarzan quit struggling to get to his feet. He was in the grip of a force even he could not deal with. Now on his face, he tried to dig his fingers into the stone beneath him. He was not consciously willing his fingers to hang on to the tiles. They were obeying some deep impulse to keep from falling when the tower fell.

So far, though the tower swayed as powerful tremor after tremor seemed to make the stone floor turn into a half liquid, its walls had not collapsed. But parts of the floor had broken off. They hurtled down, some bearing shrieking men and women with them.

Then, the shocks quit, though the structure still quivered for a time. A silence blanketed the top of the tower. It was as if the building itself and all on it or in it were holding their breath, while waiting for the next shock.

Tarzan became aware that the leaves of The Glittering Tree were tinkling. Deep deep down, beneath the lake, in the earth and in the stone roots of The Tree, the massive vibrations had not as yet died.

The black shape within The Tree, The Dark Heart of Time, was still pulsing. But its beats were erratic. They slowed, then speeded up, then slowed again. It behaved as a heart under stress behaves.

Tarzan had a strange thought then. If The Heart quit beating, would Time itself die?

He sprang to his feet. Waganero and Rahb were still lying flat on their chests. He spoke quietly but loud enough for them to hear.

"Now! Now! Follow me!"

Some of the natives were getting up. One of them was Rafmana. Seeing the ape-man leading his fellows toward the steps in the interior of the tower, she shrieked.

"Stop them! Do not let them escape!"

Some of the warriors rose and picked up their spears. Others were slower to obey. They, however, would soon be ready to seize the prisoners.

Tarzan growled, and he leapt twice. At the end of the second jump, he reached out to grab Rafmana by her neck. She stepped back. His fingers clutched the sides of her mask. Roaring, he pulled hard. He tore the mask from her face.

He looked into the face of a young black woman with

a long thin nose. She was neither ugly nor beautiful. But her eyes looked very old. They were so ancient, they could have seen the first of the beings from the stars, The Good Twins. They seemed to be as ancient as if she had witnessed the first rays of starlight to begin wearing away the mountain called The Great Mother of Snakes. Whatever had been human in them had turned into something indefinably different. Even Rahb's eyes looked far more human than hers.

She shrieked again, and she grabbed for the mask. He sent it sailing over her head, out over the broken coping of the outer wall and down into the lake. Her cry rose after it. A large eagle soaring high above them echoed the cry with his own scream.

Rafmana dug her nails into her face and pulled down on them. Blood flowed in the furrows.

"Kill them! Kill them!"

Tarzan expected to be transfixed by a dozen spears. But the weapons clattered on the floor. Wondering what had happened, Tarzan looked around.

The warriors, in fact, all the men and women, had turned their backs to her and had covered their eyes.

"Kill them! Kill them!"

They did not obey her. She ran to a fallen spear and bent to pick it up. Both Tarzan and Rahb were on her then. The ape-man tore the shaft from her hands. The bear-man hit her hard on her jaw with his huge fist. She crumpled, but he caught her and lifted her high above him.

"Do not throw her into the lake!" Tarzan cried in Rahb's tongue. "We will take her with us. Her people will not interfere. They have been forbidden to look on her face. If they do, they will die."

Tarzan did not know for sure that that was true. However, from the natives' behavior, he surmised that it was as he had said.

He went down the steps of the well inside the tower.

When the warriors, their backs to him, blocked his path, he shoved them away. They did not turn around to see what was happening. His companions followed him, Rahb just behind him, the slack body of Rafmana over one shoulder. The descent wasn't easy because, here and there, the stones with carved steps had fallen into the water. There they had to hang with their fingers gripping the projecting edges of steps and then let themselves fall onto other projections.

Nevertheless, though bleeding from cuts and scrapes, they got to thirty feet above the surface of the water before being stopped. At this point there were no steps.

Tarzan looked above. He had expected to see tiny faces ringing the open circle at the top, outlined by the light of the day. But still, apparently, no one dared to look.

Superstition was working for him.

He crouched for a moment. A stone tile, narrowly missing him, plunged loudly into the water. He was wondering if he should take Rafmana with them or kill her. But he had no time to decide.

The walls again began shaking violently. More tiles, mixed with some large stone blocks, hurtled into the water. That was heaving and swirling as if a volcano was about to burst from the bottom of the well.

He cried, "Jump!"

Before he could launch himself, he was hurled outward. He hit the water and came up quickly, but he was not able to swim southward through the arching way into the lake outside of the tower. The water rose and rushed forward. He barely escaped knocking his head against the top of the arch. Then he was being swept along in a burst of water so violent he could not fight against it. After that, he was turned over and over and plunged beneath the surface again and again.

Now and then, he banged into something hard. He

supposed that these were logs or snapped-off or up-rooted trees. But he was not hurt badly by any of them.

He kept fighting, trying to rise to the surface of the water—when he could see light above him. But he fully expected to be dashed at any time against the bottom of the river and crushed or scraped to death.

Something struck him on his left side. He reached out as if to ward off the thing. His hand closed around a large round object. He held on to it. A moment later, just as his lungs were about to explode, he saw light. And he sensed, dimly, that the thing he had grabbed was taking him upward. His head burst above the surface. He breathed out deeply and then in deeply. During his second intake of air, he clearly saw the thing that had dragged him along with it.

It was Gimla the crocodile, and a giant among his own kind, themselves giants. The ape-man was hanging on to his leg.

He did not seem aware of Tarzan. Tarzan doubted that he would be until he attained a place of safety. Just now, his entire will was focused on staying above the water. However, immense as his strength was, it was all he could do to keep from being plunged down to the bottom and crushed.

Tarzan hung on even when the fury of the water did ram them far below the surface. Gimla had more control than he could ever muster; Gimla's strength exceeded his.

Finally, the moment he had been hoping for, though not really expecting, arrived. The huge saurian was being swept alongside the cliff to the left. Tarzan, despite the water that was being dashed into his face, could see a wide break in the stone cliff ahead. Some cataclysm long ago had riven the cliff from its top to below the surface of the roaring flood. There was at least room for four men abreast in the gap.

Tarzan was on the crocodile's right side. Quickly, he

pulled himself out of the water by grabbing the ridges on the great reptile's back. And then, despite the violent bobbing of Gimla's body, Tarzan managed to stand up. He hoped that the crocodile would not dive or be dragged underwater just then.

He crouched, estimating the distance between him and the gap in the cliff. It was coming up fast, and he would have to dive and enter the gap at exactly the right time. Otherwise, he would strike the stone side of the cliff very hard. The blow could kill him or badly cripple him.

It was then that Gimla must have seen the gap in the cliff and decided to swim into it. He swerved violently, nearly dislodging the ape-man. But Tarzan seized the back ridges, so much larger than those of the crocodiles he was accustomed to. He hung on while the reptile turned at right angles to the current. Tried to turn, rather. He only half-succeeded.

Tarzan stood up and held out his arms on both sides to steady himself. Then it seemed as if—he could not be sure in the heaving and the tumult—the water suddenly rose. Perhaps the front of the flood encountered a rock projection that was hidden from Tarzan. In any event, the water hurled itself upward.

The edge of the great crack in the cliff struck the crocodile in the middle of his right side. A second before the impact, Tarzan sprang outward, away from the south wall of the chasm. Then he was in the water and being thrust into the left side of the saurian.

The collision with Gimla numbed his right side. Gimla must have been killed or hurt badly. He sank. Tarzan, too, would have been severely injured or killed if the reptile had not been between him and the cliff.

With his unhurt left arm, he grabbed hold of a branch of a tree lodged in a crevice. The water dropped away from him, leaving him dangling. He managed to twist his body and swing his feet up. A moment later, he was in the space between the underside of the wedged tree and the stone shelf. It was a tight squeeze, and he suffered.

Long before night had come and passed and dawn had rushed in, his right side had lost its numbness. Able now to see clearly, he climbed slowly and in some pain to the top of the cliff. It was only forty feet above the tree. He was in a ruined land and far far away from the tower. But he was free to start the long journey back to the place where he had begun to search for Jane.

First, he had to eat. While walking along the edge of the top of the cliff, he saw the bodies of several Manu the monkey. They had been killed when the tree in which they had taken refuge had toppled. He ripped off their skin and dug out their organs with his fingers. And he ate until his belly was full.

Thus, eating raw meat from beasts slain by the earthquake, he survived. He also found berries and nuts and insects to vary his diet. A day later, he came to where the tower had been. It was beneath the still-swollen and raging waters. So was The Glittering Tree.

Perhaps, far down, buried in the mud, The Dark Heart of Time still pulsed. Or, perhaps, the savage force of the flood had torn The Tree loose from its roots, and it had been carried far down the river. Whatever the situation was, Tarzan felt strongly that The Heart was dead. But Time was still flowing. His strange thought that it might die with The Tree was just that, a strange thought.

He regretted having lost the chance to see through The Tree. To miss going backward through Time, seeing through the eyes of his ancestors, back to . . . when? . . . the first humans to have language? . . . to miss that was a great loss. It was also a loss to science. He could think of many uses it would have in the hands of a skilled toucher. Too bad.

He turned away and resumed walking northward. The

Tree, Rafmana, Rahb, Waganero, and Helmson were behind him. He corrected himself then. He did not know what had happened to Helmson and the men with him.

He growled.

If, somehow, Helmson had escaped the fury of the earthquake and the flood it had caused, he would not escape Tarzan.

At the end of that day, the ape-man came to the place where once had been The City Made by God, the false city, the shining pillar from which the king had been hurled. There was no sign of the city. If any of it still existed, its twisted arches and tall pillar were at the bottom of the flood. He doubted that, though. The water was boiling, bubbling, hissing, and steaming. Its source was a redness at the bottom of what had been the lake. Tarzan studied it for some time, then decided that lava was making the red glow and the heat.

The flowing hot rock far below had broken loose from the deeps of the earth. It was beginning to form a volcanic cone on the bottom of what had been a lake but was still a part of the great river. Whatever the nature of the material that had formed The City Made by God, that hard shiny substance was probably melted by now.

He resumed his swift travel northward. Soon, he broke into what the North American Indians had called the wolf's walk. For fifty strides, he ran, then he walked another fifty, then ran again. He ate up the distance.

By late afternoon, he observed that the flood waters had seemingly taken a dive. Somewhere downstream, he thought, the great hole in the earth that he had imagined, the hole that might or might not exist in reality, had swallowed much of the flood. The water had come out of the earth, and it was now going back into the earth.

Whatever the explanation, the river level was now far below the tops of the cliffs. That it had risen above the cliffs before subsiding was shown by the devastation it had worked on the top edges. All the trees had been swept off. All the soil was gone, stripped off by the raging waters. Everywhere he looked was a wasteland.

But the surface of the river still carried many trees from upstream. They, along with corpses and carcasses, floated swiftly toward whatever destination awaited them. There were no hippopotamuses or crocodiles or any of the water creatures that once had thronged the banks. Nor were there any birds. The trees that had been along the river were gone. Only glistening mud was left.

After trotting for several miles, Tarzan heard a far off and thin trumpeting. He picked up his pace. It seemed to him that the sound was made by Tantor the elephant. But, as he came closer to the source of the sound, he also heard another noise. It was a thunderous croaking, mingled with many voices.

The trumpeting puzzled him. What was Tantor doing? Tantor sounded infuriated and, at the same time, fearful.

But the croaking and the human voices did not make him wonder. He knew what made that sound.

Presently, he stopped. He leaned over the edge of the cliff and looked downward. The cliffs here formed a semicircle, a sort of natural amphitheater. Perhaps seventy feet below the base of the precipice was a cove with a mud beach.

34

THE COVE FORMED a stage for a very strange drama.

The side to the right of Tarzan, the downriver corner, was jumbled with many uprooted trees that had been caught by the edge of the cliff. They had piled up into a high tangle of rain forest trees. Some were titans. Most were smaller but still large.

Sticking from the bottom of this logjam was a gigantic creature. Its shiny and bumpy skin was a pale green. Its gargantuan and goggle-eyed head and its forelegs were free of the tangle, but the main part of the body was held down firmly. The weight of the mass surely must be crushing the back half of its body and its back legs.

Its forelegs, however, were moving, and its padded paws were trying to grasp the creature that was attacking it.

That was Tantor, the captive elephant who had spoken to Tarzan in her rumbling language. How she had gotten here without being drowned or badly injured, Tarzan could not guess. But here she was.

Her front legs were still manacled, and she was dragging chains that were still attached to the great stakes. Even now, as, trumpeting, she charged The Ghost Frog again, the stakes bounced along at the ends of the shackles. These, and the depth of the mud into which she sank for six inches or so with every step, slowed her running. But she charged swiftly enough to evade the brobdingnagian paws reaching out for her. She rammed the ends of her tusks into The Frog just below its mouth.

That mouth was open, and its lower jaw revealed rows of long, sharp, and sharkish teeth.

Frogs did not have teeth. Therefore, this beast, no matter how much it looked like a frog, was not a frog.

That is, thought Tarzan, it is certainly not a terrestrial frog. Surely, it must have been created by some entities from a planet revolving around a far-off star. Perhaps, those entities were The Good Twins Rafmana had spoken about. Or The Evil Twins.

The Frog may have been a natural denizen of that planet, and it or its ancestors had been brought here by The Twins. In any event, Earth, when shaping its creatures, had not shaped this one.

The Frog's croak roared up to Tarzan. Its very magnitude startled the ape-man, though it did not make him cower. However, the two men in their torn and filthy clothes below him did cower.

They were on a ledge of rock twenty-five feet up from the mud. The ledge was fifty feet from the mouth of the cove and the edge of the river.

The ape-man could not see their faces. But he saw the knife in Helmson's right hand, his only weapon. It was the blade Tarzan had inherited from his father and had used to slay Bolgani, the gorilla that had gone amuck when Tarzan was but a stripling. It was the knife that had enabled him to kill Tublat, his hated foster father. It was the weapon that had raised him above the much more powerful Mangani, and had allowed him to conquer many a Numa and Sheeta. And its keen point had been driven into the putrid hearts of many a human enemy.

Seeing it, Tarzan growled.

However, his attention shifted away from the white men when he heard Tantor begin screaming with terror. The Ghost Frog had grabbed one of the elephant's tusks in its mighty paw. Though Tantor tried to back away, out of its grip, she could not. She kept slipping in the mud.

There was a very loud cracking noise.

The Ghost Frog had twisted the elephant's left tusk, then had pulled it out of its socket. Tantor shrilled her pain, and the sound, filtered by blood, bounced off the side of the cliffs.

Tantor crumpled to her knees. The Frog seized her other tusk with its left paw and dragged the still-struggling elephant to its gaping mouth. The Frog's jaws closed on Tantor's trunk. Then The Frog pushed Tantor away from it. She slid backwards in the mud while still kneeling. Blood jetted from the hole where her proboscis had been, and it seemed to be propelling her.

Then the batrachian opened its mouth. Its long, slender—relatively slender—tongue flicked out, then back into the cavern of its mouth.

From his angle of sight up on the cliff, Tarzan could not see the beast swallow. But the trunk was gone down its gullet.

Tantor died.

By now, Tarzan was more than halfway down the face of the precipice.

His foot dislodged a small stone. It bounced off from several projections on the way down. Startled, Helmson and his companion looked upwards. Their mouths formed lopsided and dark O's in their dirty brown faces.

Tarzan bellowed a challenge at them. Their response was to start climbing at a reckless pace down the cliff. By the time the ape-man had reached the mud of the cove beach, they were slogging along close to the left side of the cliff. Their path was taking them as far from the amphibian as they could get. Helmson still had the knife in his right hand.

It was evident that they hoped to get to the river before Tarzan caught up with them. This would bring them to a point thirty-five feet or so from The Ghost Frog.

They were gambling that they were out of range of the long tongue.

Helmson lost.

As he got to the end of the cliff, just before he could leap into the river, he was caught. The tongue flicked out like the shadow of a shadow, an imperfection in the air. Its end lashed around the man's chest, and it jerked him upwards. Then it coiled, holding Helmson in the air as it shot back into the wide-open mouth. Helmson screamed.

The other white man kept on running. But the mud slowed him down. Then he slipped and sprawled forward. For a moment, he was face down in the muck.

Tarzan yelled. This time, his voice was full of fury and of desperation.

He would lose his father's knife unless Helmson dropped it before being swallowed.

But Helmson had not let loose of it. In fact, even as he was taken into the mouth, he began slashing. The upper part of his arms were bound to his body, but he could swing the lower part of his right arm and thus bring the knife edge against the bottom of the tongue.

The Ghost Frog bellowed, though whether from pain it was impossible to tell. However, he did not release the tongue from its coil around Helmson's body.

Tarzan did not think of the possible consequences of his action as he leapt up and out. Though he could not attain the speed he would normally have had if the mud had not impeded him, he leapt onto the dead elephant's back. He ran two steps, slipping somewhat because of the mud on his feet, then bounded outwards. He yelled again as he flew into the wide-gaping mouth, the tooth-portcullised gate. Then the lower jaw snapped shut. Light disappeared. The ape-man was in darkness, hanging on to the slimy, slippery tongue and Helmson's legs.

Though the jaws were closed, he could hear a sound as of many men, women, and children talking. It seemed to come from the amphibian's flesh itself. It traveled up through the muscles from the vast belly toward which he was being slid.

Flesh pressed down around him. He thought he should still be in the gullet, though he could not be sure. His arms were bound down, squeezed by the monstrous throat.

But, with one of the greatest efforts he had ever made in his life, he elbowed the greasy throat-muscles aside, just enough to reach up and grope along Helmson's side.

The American's arm was also clamped down against his thigh by the throat muscles. But Tarzan found the hand, and he felt the blade, still in Helmson's grasp.

Jerking it away, Tarzan had to act very swiftly now. He could not breathe. In a minute or so, he would be out of air. Usually, he could hold his breath for more than five minutes. But his exertions had tired him out and left him with little wind to draw on.

The Frog's gullet muscles, moving like snakes, were pushing Tarzan's body along toward the house-sized belly. He forced his arm down and against his chest, then he made some space between him and the muscles that were gripping his body by sawing with the knife. He felt a gush of blood, then ribbons of slashed and sawed flesh. Though the swallowing motion stopped, he was still trapped. He could do nothing but keep on cutting and hoping he could last a minute or two longer.

Suddenly, he was jerked along again. He did not know where he was going now, toward the stomach or back up the throat. But something had happened, and he was being slid along much faster than before.

Then, there was light. There was also air and a sense of freedom, of flying without wings.

He opened his eyes, but blood still was veiling all his vision.

He began turning over. He bent his knees to bring them up against his chest. Before he could complete that movement, he struck something hard. He landed on his back. His lungs, which had seemed on the edge of bursting, whooshed out air he had thought he did not have.

Dazed, blind, sucking in air, he lay in mud. For a moment, he did not know where he was. He also did not know where he had just been.

But his senses rallied. He wiped the blood and mucus from his eyes with the back of his hand. And, suddenly remembering that he might be open to attack, he tried to get to his feet.

Now, he could see dimly. He wiped the mud again. Near him lay a body. It was Helmson's. He, too, had been expelled.

The Ghost Frog was not yet dead. Its forelegs waved. Its paws became fists, then its fingers opened, then closed. Blood ran from its open mouth. But its tongue shot out toward Tarzan, then flicked back into its mouth, then lashed, quicker than an arrow, out again.

Its tip fell into the mud a foot away from Tarzan. He was safe from it. But that tongue was what kept the other man, Helmson's companion, from sneaking up and braining Tarzan with the thick stick in his hand. He had to circle around, hoping to attack Tarzan from the rear.

The ape-man had just time to scoop up water from a nearby shallow pool. His knife held between his teeth, he splashed the water over his face. Though it was dirty, it was clean enough to wash off the blood and mud from his eyes. He shifted his knife to his hand.

The man stopped. His face twisted with hate, he spoke in German. But he rattled off the words so swiftly that he garbled them. Then he was silent for a few seconds. He seemed to be trying to get hold of himself.

That the man had used German revealed to Tarzan that the man was not English or American. A man in the throes of a high emotion reverts automatically to his native tongue.

This man, Tarzan thought, *must be a German spy.*

The man waved the club, and he took one step toward the ape-man. Tarzan growled, and advanced two steps toward his opponent, then he stopped. He crouched, his knife ready for stabbing.

The enemy's eyes were a madman's.

He spoke again, this time in English. "You do not know me."

It was a statement, not a question. Tarzan did not reply.

"Does the name Schneider mean anything to you?" the man said.

The ape-man studied the man's face for a few seconds. It was smeared with mud, but the long, lean, and vulpine features reminded him of . . . whom? The name he was very familiar with. But the men he pictured in his mind had been taller and much more fleshy. Yet . . . there was a certain family resemblance.

"The only Schneiders I know were two brothers," Tarzan said. "One was Captain Fritz Schneider. The other was Major Schneider. I do not know his Christian name. They were both members of the German East African forces. The captain arrived with his men at my ranch and was welcomed by my wife. She did not know that war had been declared. Then the captain treacherously burned down the ranch buildings, killed my Waziri servants and warriors, put my wife's wedding ring on the finger of a dead Waziri woman, then burned her.

"I thought her charred corpse was my mate. But my mate still lived. The Germans took her away. Not until recently did I discover that the burned corpse was not my wife's. Long before that, however, I killed Major Schneider by mistake. I had thought that he was Fritz Schneider. But I then killed the captain and so I finally avenged the dead Waziri, none of whom deserved to die."

"I am Sigurd Schneider!" the man cried. "They were my brothers! My father grieves for them, and so do I! I am here to avenge their deaths! And I will kill you and bring your head to my father!"

"Brave talk," Tarzan said. "How do you plan to do that?"

He slid his right foot forward, then his left.

Schneider, instead of backing away, screamed and tried to run at the ape-man. He slipped, fell on his face, and slid forward until his head touched Tarzan's foot.

The ape-man tore the club from the man's grasp and threw it away. He then put his knife back between his teeth and picked the screaming, gesticulating, and kicking Schneider up with both hands and held him high above his head. He intended to shake him to death.

But Schneider quit screaming. Now he sobbed, but between sobs he cried, "Wait! Wait! . . . I have something . . . don't kill me . . . yet. Wait! I have something to trade . . . for my life!"

The ape-man did not put the man down to the ground. But, through the knife in his teeth, he said, "What is that?"

Schneider spoke above Tarzan's head. "I know who is behind this conspiracy to capture you and deliver you to him. I am the only one who knows, except the man's secretary and certain people in the Imperial German Intelligence. If you will spare my life, I will tell you who he is. And I will tell you why he is doing this to you."

Tarzan lowered Schneider feet first to the mud. Then he gripped the man's neck with one hand and held the knife to his throat. Schneider, gasping, said, "Will you promise not to kill me if I tell you?"

Tarzan considered. After twenty or so seconds, he said, "I give my word. If you know anything about me, you know my word is my life's blood. But . . . keep this in mind . . . I will spare you *this* time. The next time our paths cross, I will put you down in the earth with your brothers. You have my word on that, too."

"Very well," Schneider said. "Though how I can stay alive in this ruined and lifeless land before I get to a place where . . ."

"That is not my concern!" Tarzan said savagely. "Tell me, who is this man, this unknown enemy of mine?' "

Schneider told him the name. Tarzan had heard and read of Stonecraft several times while in London or at his estate in Cumberland County in northern England.

"This man may be the richest one in the world," the ape-man said. "He is reputed to be a great philanthropist and patron of the arts. He is also said to be very religious. Why would such a man take any interest in me? I have nothing he could possibly want."

"Stonecraft is all you say he is," Schneider said. "But he is also a ruthless old man, a hypocrite, a scoundrel who should have been hanged for his many crimes, even murder by proxy, while gaining his early wealth. He is very shrewd. But he is also a fool! A fool!' "

Tarzan said, "The reason he wants me! Do not put off telling me that."

"He wants to live forever! Or, at least, to slow down his aging, perhaps even regain his youthful body. He has launched these expeditions and gone to enormous expense to have you delivered, alive, to a secret place in New York. Why? Because he thinks that you may be immortal. Or, at least, you may have in your blood something which makes you age very slowly. He thinks you know the secret formula or recipe or whatever for living long past your natural span of life! He's always been very interested in that subject . . . physical immortality, I mean . . . and lately he's been having heart trouble.

"He thinks that he can get chemists to take specimens

of your blood and analyze it and then re-create the formula needed to live a long long time, perhaps forever."

"Why would he think that?" Tarzan asked.

"Have you forgotten that witch doctor in Uganda whom you saved from a lion?"

Tarzan said, softly, "Ah!"

Now he knew why Stonecraft had been so desperate to capture him.

Some years ago, that grateful witch doctor had claimed that he could bestow on Tarzan an artificial longevity, that he could keep the ape-man young for a much longer time than anyone had a right to expect.

Tarzan, curious though doubtful, had let the old man put him through a month-long series of treatments. Some of these had involved chemical formulas unknown to any but the witch doctor. Or so he had claimed.

Tarzan had questioned local natives who had known the witch doctor when they were very little children. They had verified that he had known Tippoo Tib's grandfather. Tippoo Tib was a well-known Arab trader who had been a friend of the journalist Stanley, of Stanley and Doctor Livingstone fame. Tib had been born in the 1840s or 1830s. Thus, Tib's grandfather had lived as early as 1790 or even earlier.

The ninety-year-old villagers who had known the witch doctor since they were children swore that he had not aged since they had known him. And their great-grandfathers had said the same.

Tarzan said, "The witch doctor and the villagers could have been hoaxing me. Anyway, I am now only thirty. Stonecraft would be stupid to abduct me now. He should wait until I'm forty to make sure that I haven't aged."

Schneider said. "He is grasping at anything that promises him a healthy and longer life. He is also, I believe, half mad, though only those very close to him would know that. He is very self-controlled . . ."

"Enough!" the ape-man said. "I know what I must do. You may go. But keep out of my way. If I see you again, I will kill you."

He paused, then said, "Just as I will kill Stonecraft."

He watched Schneider start climbing wearily back up the cliff. When he was sure that the man would soon reach its top, he turned back to The Ghost Frog. By now, he was dead, though Tarzan knew he might have the same galvanic reaction that smaller frogs exhibited after death. He climbed up the pile of logs to the back of the amphibian's head.

Schneider had just reached the top of the cliff when he heard a sound that raised the hairs on the back of his head. His skin turned cold in the tropical heat.

It was the victory cry of the bull ape.

Later, after Tarzan had eaten a raw steak cut out of the great frog, he started once more northward. Someday, after he had rescued Jane, he would rescue Rahb's mate and her cub—if they still lived. He would take them to their native jungle. Perhaps, there was another male of her kind. Rahb might not have been the last one of his species.

That was the least he could do for the Ben-go-utor.

35

I TOOK MORE than a year before Tarzan could finish with certain adventures and then try to find and rescue Rahb's mate and child. But he was too late. When he did locate where she had been, she was long gone. She had freed herself and fled into the jungle with her child.

The ape-man hoped that he would someday encounter her. Then he could tell her what had happened to Rahb.

Tarzan was staying in a prominent Manhattan hotel when he telephoned. But he called from the lobby of a cheap hotel, and he did not take long.

Bevan answered the telephone. He asked for identification. The ape-man said, "Project Soma."

Bevan said, "What?" though he had heard clearly.

"Tell Stonecraft it's about Project Soma."

A moment later, the secretary burst into his boss's office without knocking. He was pale and round eyed. He said, loudly, "I've just talked to a man who wishes to speak to you! He'd only say that it's about . . . ah . . . the African project! He has an English accent!"

The magnate also turned pale. His voice was firm, but Bevan, who knew well the very slight undercurrents of alarm in his employer's voice, understood that he was shaken.

"I'll take it, Bevan. You listen in on your line."

Seconds later, Stonecraft picked up his telephone. He said, "Hello! Who is this?"

A deep voice said, "No one lives forever."

Stonecraft gasped. Then he said, "Who is this?"

"Africa. Immortality. Revenge," the voice said.

Stonecraft shouted, "For God's sake, man! Who is this? Tell me who you are or I'll hang up on you! I warn you . . ."

"Tarzan! Tarzan of the Apes!"

The receiver clattered on the desk. There was silence. The listener in the hotel lobby heard a door bang. Then he heard, "Oh, God! He's dead! He's dead!"

Tarzan hung up. His smile was grim. He had slain many with his bare hands, his powerful arms, his teeth, a thrown rock, a knife, a spear, an arrow. But this was the first time that he had felled an enemy with a few spoken words.

Perhaps, he was becoming civilized.